LADD
FORTUNE

Dianne Venetta

LADD FORTUNE
Book #2

Ladd Springs Series:

LADD SPRINGS ~ #1
LADD FORTUNE ~ #2
HOTEL LADD ~ #3
LADD HAVEN ~ #4
LOSING LADD ~ #5

Other novels by Dianne Venetta

Romantic Women's Fiction
The Gables Trilogy:
JENNIFER'S GARDEN
LUST ON THE ROCKS
WHISPER PRIVILEGES

Women's Fiction
CONDEMN ME NOT

Copyright 2013 by Dianne Venetta
All rights reserved
ISBN 9780988487130

Ladd Fortune
Copyright 2013 by Dianne Venetta
ISBN: 978-0-9884871-3-0
Publisher: BloominThyme Press
Editor: Best Foot Forward
Cover Design: Jaxadora Design

Acknowledgements

As anyone who's ever visited Tennessee can attest, it's some beautiful countryside. From the hills and streams to the trails and sky, Ladd Springs represents one of my favorite summer destinations. But more than a beautiful setting, Ladd Springs represents family and friends and good times.

While we can't choose our family, we are fortunate for the role they play in our lives. Family sticks to you, whether you like it or not. They're made from the same stuff, see life much the same way...

Family is a part of you like nothing else in this world. Family is more than blood. Family is love, and Lacy and Annie are proof-positive that love can conquer all.

Dedication

This book is dedicated to the Good family,
my friends, my family, a bond strong enough to withstand the
test of trials, tribulations and time.

Meet the cast of characters of Ladd Fortune...

Ernie Ladd ~ Owner of Ladd Springs

Albert Ladd ~ Ernie's brother

Susannah Ladd Wilkins~ Ernie's sister (deceased)

Jeremiah Ladd ~ Ernie's forsaken son

Loretta Flynn ~ Jeremiah's girlfriend from Atlanta

Lacy Owens ~ Sister to Annie Owens

Malcolm Ward ~ Hotel developer and partner to Nick Harris

Annie and Casey Owens ~ Jeremiah's ex-girlfriend & her daughter

Candi Sweeney ~ Annie's best friend

Delaney Wilkins ~ Ernie's niece

Felicity Wilkins ~ Delaney's daughter

Nick Harris ~ Founder, Harris Hotels

Travis and Troy Parker ~ Neighbors and friends of Felicity

Fran Jones ~ Owner of Fran's Diner, aunt to Annie and Lacy

Ashley and Booker Fulmer ~ Susannah's best friend & her husband

Clem and Willie ~ Criminal cohorts

Chapter One

Lacy Owens tamped down the flutter of pulse skirting through her chest. Parked across the street from the salon, she stared at the day spa, the mirrored glass display window splashed with fancy lettering. Trendz. Inserted between a sandwich shop and an insurance office, it was painted glossy black and stood out like a bald eagle in a blue sky. The hoagie shop to the right had been there for as long as Lacy could remember, its exterior faded to drab beige. The insurance agency was new and remarkably boring, its window marked by white block letters spelling out the company name and agent. Beyond the building, the green hills of Tennessee rose into the sky, a batch of patchy white clouds floating lazily in the distance.

Would Annie be happy to see her? Would she be angry? Lacy's breathing grew shallow. The temperature in the car was rising, heat pressing in on her. Their reunion could go either way. Knowing Annie, she'd try and toss her baby sister out on the sidewalk with a kick to the rump—which would hurt, in more ways than one.

While Annie might throw her out on sight, Lacy had to try. It was meant to be. She knew it the minute Jeremiah Ladd walked into the lounge, announcing to his girlfriend, Loretta Flynn, they were headed for Ladd Springs. Ladd Springs. Tennessee. *Home.*

It was her opportunity. The stars were in alignment. That very day her horoscope said it was time for a return to the fold. Lacy nibbled at her lip, fiddled with the steering wheel. Atlanta had never been home. Atlanta had been her escape.

A woman pushed out through the front door of Trendz, her brown hair straight and shiny in the midday sun, her clothes fitted and chic. Lacy wondered if the woman had had her nails done. Was Annie in there? Lacy glanced at the clock on her dashboard. Three o'clock. She slid her gaze back to the salon. Annie would have to be, wouldn't she? She still worked full-time, didn't she?

Nerves sputtered and popped. Grabbing a slim leather purse from the passenger seat, Lacy pushed opened her car door and headed in. It was now or never. Hopefully, Annie would understand. Hopefully, she'd forgive her. Hope was all she had. As Lacy crossed the street, her legs felt boneless, like she'd dissolve into a mess on the street, this instant. It was a wonder she could even walk! But walk she would. She'd walk straight into that salon and face her sister, once and for all. It was time. This mess between them had gone on too long and it had to stop.

Lacy opened the salon door and was immediately sucked in by the strong scent of hair products, nail polish and perfume. Her heart thudded as she scanned the salon's interior. A line of mirrored stations manned by a bevy of women dressed in black created a corridor down the center. Each stood by their chairs wielding blow dryers, flat irons and scissors over their clients. From above, drips of blue hung down in the form of ceramic lighting. Lacy thought the subtle hues very modern, very sophisticated. Venturing in a few steps, she noticed the nail station was empty. Her spirits fell. No Annie. She heaved a sigh, eyeing the receptionist who sat smiling behind her check-in desk. She was a perky young blonde who didn't look a day over fifteen.

"May I help you?" the girl asked.

"Um..." Lacy hesitated. She looped short curls of hair behind an ear. Should she ask about Annie? Should she leave her name, thus warning her sister of her arrival?

Absolutely not. A surprise visit was best, sort of a spontaneous reunion where she could gauge her sister's reaction on the spot and respond accordingly. "Well..." Lacy paused, suddenly second-guessing her entire scheme. "I was wondering about having my nails done."

"Great! We have a nail tech who's the best in the business."

Lacy didn't doubt it. When she and Annie were kids, her older sister forever practiced on her nails, creating stripes, polka dots—the works. Lacy had always been amazed by her sister's uncanny ability to "stay within the lines" as she painted and wished she could have done as well, but she never could. Polish forever smudged and dripped. Annie was good with hair, too. Lacy could apply makeup, but hair and nails were Annie's area of expertise. "Hm," she hedged, "do you happen to know her name?"

The receptionist looked at her queerly.

Dingbat—of course she did! She worked here, didn't she? Flummoxed, Lacy clarified, "I mean, I want to make sure it's the same woman my friend recommended."

"Annie Owens. Is that who you were looking for?"

Lacy's heart raced at the confirmation. She nodded.

Flipping through pages in her appointment book, the receptionist said, "She has availability Friday afternoon, and then next week." She dragged her pencil lightly down the page and said, "Tuesday morning and Wednesday afternoon." Checking with Lacy, she asked, "Will any of those work for you?"

But Lacy didn't answer. In the back of the salon, Annie had emerged and currently stood immobile in the center aisle. Dryers whirred, conversation chattered, but Annie only had eyes for Lacy.

Lacy gulped. Without looking at the young woman, stammered, "Um, let me think about it, okay?"

"Sure thing," the receptionist replied.

Annie came to life and approached Lacy with a hard line in her gaze, a chop to her step. Familiar blue eyes bore into her. Annie's wrath arrived ten steps ahead of her, followed by a sharp whoosh of displeasure, which strummed in the air around them as the women stood face-to-face. "What are you doing here?"

Despite her sister's animosity, Lacy thought Annie looked good. Her hair was shorter now, cut into a cute pageboy, her black-clad figure trim. Her makeup was flattering in shades of pink and other than the vile look in her eyes, Lacy discovered her sister had grown into an attractive woman. "Hi, Annie." Lacy gave a short wave, flushing with an uncomfortable awkwardness.

Apparently catching onto the underpinnings of anger between Lacy and Annie, the receptionist closed her book and busied herself with something on her desk.

"I asked you a question," Annie repeated flatly.

Lacy shuddered beneath the caustic tone. People could hear her! "I wanted to let you know that I'm back in town," she ventured softly.

"Why?"

"Um..." She bit her lip, averting the gaze of the receptionist, the inquisitive glances from hairstylists. "Because we're family, why else?"

"Is Jeremiah with you?"

Without thinking, Lacy nodded.

Loathing poured into Annie's expression. "So you two are still together."

"No!" Lacy exclaimed, pressing a hand to her chest. "Oh, no, we're not together at all!"

Annie's eyes narrowed to slits. "Then why would he be here same time as you? Coincidence?"

"No. He's with my friend Loretta. Loretta Flynn."

"Your friend?" Annie asked, disbelief crawling through her eyes.

"Yes, yes—we work together at a lounge in Atlanta." Or did. She'd quit on her way out the door as she headed home for Tennessee. "That's how I know he's here. He told Loretta he was coming home and I...I..." Lacy didn't know exactly how to say it. *I needed an escape*? *I wanted to come back home*? By the icy nature of Annie's reception, it didn't seem like her sister much cared why Lacy had returned. Only that she had—and it wasn't good news.

"What do you want?"

Lacy glanced about the immediate vicinity. Was the middle of the salon's entrance really the place to be having this discussion?

As though taking her cue, Annie stalked off toward a white leather nail chair. Beside it sat a square black ottoman, a pristine white towel draped over one side. A myriad polish bottles lined the work table, shades ranging from the sheerest of pinks to the darkest of plums. Files and clippers were lined neatly to one side, the workspace made all the brighter by a petite but powerful black lamp. Lacy thought her sister had come a long way from the rinky-dink salon in which she started her career as a teenager. From what Lacy could tell, Trendz was top of the line, as nice as any in Atlanta and a surprise find in this backwoods town. When Lacy lived here, the fanciest store they had going was the flower shop, and they only stayed afloat because of weddings and funerals.

Struggling to continue the conversation with something harmless, Lacy decided on a compliment. "This is a nice place you work in."

"This isn't a social call."

"Isn't it?"

Annie glowered, crossing arms over her chest. "What do you want, Lacy?"

"I'm here to say hello."

"Goodbye."

Lacy reached out for her sister but quickly rethought the gesture. Annie looked as if she might bite her arm off. "Annie," she pleaded, "what about all the letters I wrote you? Why didn't you write back?"

"Because I had nothing to say to you. Still don't."

Crestfallen, Lacy couldn't believe her ears. This wasn't how she'd envisioned their reunion. Rocky, maybe. Thorny, possibly. But absolute rejection? Her sister didn't even want to try? Sliding a hand up her narrow purse strap, Lacy asked, "Can't we catch up on old times? Get back in touch?"

"The old times I remember are you running off with my boyfriend. Sorry, but it's not something I care to catch up on."

"But Jeremiah wasn't really your—" Lacy scrambled for reason. She'd never thought that Annie and Jeremiah were a serious couple. Jeremiah had been with so many others. Could Annie really be that upset she'd moved to Atlanta with him?

"He was my boyfriend," Annie declared, "the one you decided to chase to Atlanta. The fact that he wasn't faithful doesn't change the truth."

Lacy breathed easier. *So she did know.* Then why so mad? "I'm sorry, Annie. I just thought—"

"Thought what? That because he was playing around behind my back, it might as well be you he was playing with?" Disgust rolled through Annie's expression. "You're dead to me."

"Annie Grace!" Lacy cried, punctured by the hateful remark.

"What?" A glimmer of pleasure crept into her sister's gaze. "You don't like hearing the truth?"

Lacy smoothed the ruffled layers of her blouse and searched for onlookers. Eavesdroppers in these parts were as common as oxygen and sure as she was breathing, Lacy knew word would get out about her arrival and this dreadful showdown. But Lacy would not be deterred. "Annie, the truth has more sides than one. I'm sorry you're upset with me about going to Atlanta with Jeremiah, but I thought you two had broken up."

Annie laughed, the sound biting to Lacy's ears. "And I'm supposed to stand here for a lecture on the truth from someone who wouldn't know the truth if it jumped up and smacked her on the head?"

"*Annie.*"

"Don't *Annie*, me. You fibbed as a child and you fibbed as a teenager. I don't expect it to change."

Tears pushed behind her eyes, but Lacy held them in check. She didn't want to break down in front of her sister, the entire salon. It was bad enough people were staring at her from clear across the room. They didn't have to witness her losing it completely.

Lacy pushed back her shoulders and said plainly, "I'm sorry, Annie."

"You're darn right, you are."

Staring into Annie's blue eyes, the black pupils punctuated by white from an overhead drip light, Lacy's heart fell. "This was a mistake," she said quietly. She had hoped to make amends. She had hoped to forgive and forget and move forward with the only family she had left. Daddy was dead, Momma was gone. Annie was it.

Lacy turned to go but stopped. Lifting her chin, she said, "I'm truly sorry about Jeremiah. If I had known you believed he was still your boyfriend, I wouldn't have run off with him. I thought you two were over."

"Save it for the choir boys, will you? Your pouts don't impress me."

Lacy nodded and a heavy tear burst free. "See you around," she said, and plodded toward the door.

"Why don't you go back to Atlanta where you belong," Annie flung at her back.

Because Atlanta isn't home. Lacy pushed out through the front door, the sun bright, the air a blanket of warmth enveloping her body. She breathed in deeply, but expelled the breath in a rush of despair. Annie hated her. Pure and simple. She hated her sister, her own flesh and blood, and would never forgive her. Tears flowed, but Lacy wiped them away. She wouldn't give her sister the satisfaction of hurting her. She wouldn't let Annie know how desperately she had wanted back into her life.

Plodding to a stop, she looked both ways and waited for a slow moving truck to pass. Lacy had been lonely in Atlanta. Not alone, but lonely. Men were always ready and available, but none were interested in her for who she was, what she had to offer as a person. They only wanted what she could do for them, her manager a case in point. He'd chased her, hired her, but the minute she gave in to his advances, he became expectant. Demanding. She had to play by his rules and his rules only. Lacy crossed the street, her calves contracting tightly as she ran across the pavement in heels.

Well, Lacy Owens played by her own rules. She was the boss of her destiny and no man, no how, was going to dictate to her what she was and was not allowed to do—especially when it came to the attention from other men. *How would she ever find Mr. Right if she didn't entertain their flirtations?*

She wouldn't. Besides, she loved men! Men were bold and daring. They were big and strong. Joy sizzled through her veins. Men were smart. Men would help guide her to her destiny, slide over the rainbow with her and share in the treasure of gold waiting at the other end. Pressing the key fob to unlock her car door, she heaved a sigh. Some man would, anyway. Jeremiah had turned out to be a fool, but that didn't mean all men were. Where Annie didn't know he was a two-timing cheat, Lacy did, but she hadn't cared. The day he asked her to join him on his way out of Ladd Springs was the day she'd believed her life would take a turn for the better. They were going to the big city, the land of opportunity.

Unfortunately, opportunity didn't always look the way a girl wanted it to look. Lacy dried her eyes, got into her car and drove to her Aunt Frannie's diner. Time to break the news that her "girls" weren't getting back together.

Annie hurried out of Trendz, headed down the street to a competing salon, Bangs. She had to talk to her best friend, Candi Sweeney. She would freak when she heard about Lacy, though Annie herself could hardly believe she'd come back. What was she thinking, sashaying her way into the salon where Annie worked, trying to play the role of sweet innocent sister in search of reunion? Was she nuts? Desperate?

And Jeremiah. Nerves shimmied through her limbs. She'd only been bluffing when she told Delaney she was going to call him. Those were words spoken in the heat of anger. Was it possible he'd arrived in town at the same time as Lacy by coincidence? A shudder ran through her. Annie didn't know, but she was going to find out. Swinging open the entrance door to Bangs, she hurried past the hairdressers, most personal friends of hers, in a bee line for the back. Set up similar to Trendz, the stations lined the walls, the shampoo chairs in the back situated right next to Candi's chair. But there was no Candi, only a woman sitting in her chair. Was she mixing up color?

"Hey, Annie." Comb in hand, Ida Shore waved to her. She was a good friend of her Aunt Fran's and part-owner of the Bangs salon. "How you doing?"

"Good," Annie replied absently, more concerned with Candi's whereabouts at the moment.

"She's in the color closet," Ida confirmed. "You can go on back."

Annie nodded thanks and hurried past. Hairdressers were like family. They worked at different salons, but no one held it as a sticking point. Each had their own client list, loyal as hound dogs, and gossip was gossip. Ida would expect her dose of information after Annie's visit with Candi and wouldn't mind for a minute that it came second-hand.

Turning the corner, Annie found Candi wearing gloves, plastic bottle in hand, her torso length apron tied securely around her petite waist. As expected, she was mixing up hair color for her client. "Hey, girl! What are you doing here?"

"Lacy's in town," she said breathlessly.

Candi's hands stilled. Chocolate brown eyes became saucers, her face framed by her straight brown hair streaked by wide blonde chunks. "She is?"

"Stopped by the salon less than an hour ago."

"Oh my..." Candi sliced the room with a conspiratorial gaze and whispered, "What's she doing here?"

"Don't know." Heartbeats scampered across her breast. "Said she's here for a visit."

She gaped. "A visit?"

Of course Candi was horrified. She knew their history. "But get this—" Annie hushed her voice. "She says Jeremiah is in town, too."

Where Annie expected Candi to fall over dead from shock, instead, she glimpsed a glimmer of awareness dart behind her eyes. It caught Annie on the chin. "Did you know he was here?" she demanded abruptly.

"No," she blurted. "Er—I mean, not exactly."

Annie's insides caught on fire. "Not exactly?"

"Well..." Candi smacked her color bottle down to the counter, then whisked a flat brush through the goopy contents in her bowl. Mixing briskly, she confessed, "I called him, Annie. I called him and told him about Delaney and Felicity and how they were trying to steal Ladd Springs from him."

Annie took a step backward, as though hit by an unseen force of intense magnitude. "*You what*?"

"I had to, Annie! They were stealing the property clear out from under your feet and I had to stop them! You said so yourself, didn't you? You threatened to call Jeremiah. You told Delaney you'd let him know what she was doing."

"I told Delaney that I'd call him to scare her, Candi. I never intended to go through with it!

Candi's eyes rounded—froze—like a deer caught by a flash of headlights. "*You didn't*?"

Annie fell against the counter. "I didn't."

"Oh, no... I'm sorry, Annie. I was just trying to help and now I've made a mess of things! I only wanted you to have a chance to work with Jeremiah, to get the property for Casey. She deserves her part of it and well, you do too, and I..." Candi's hand fell from the bowl, dropping her explanation like an overheated flat iron. "I thought it would help you and Casey."

Staring at her friend, Annie thought "mess" was only the beginning of how she'd describe Jeremiah Ladd's presence in town. He was here. Because Candi called him. Bringing a hand to her forehead, Annie groaned. What must he think?

Would he assume that she put Candi up to it? Would he think she did it to force him to claim Casey as his own?

Annie sharpened her focus and latched onto Candi. "Tell me everything you said. Everything, Candi—don't leave a single word out."

Chapter Two

Delaney Wilkin's hands trembled as she sat huddled around her kitchen island with Nick Harris and Malcolm Ward, Nick's partner in Harris Hotels. The piece of paper was one document out of hundreds she'd collected, but it was perhaps the most important one. It was a copy of the title to Ladd Springs—the very same Ladd Springs that she feared might now be in jeopardy. "What am I going to do if Jeremiah comes back and contests Ernie's life estate deed? What recourse will I have?" She homed in on Nick, hotel developer and the man instrumental in helping her secure title to Ladd Springs for her and her daughter, Felicity. This land was their home, their legacy, but now she and Felicity stood to lose it all.

Because of Jeremiah Ladd. Because of Annie Owens.

Nick smiled, the confidence in his dark brown eyes quieting her angst, much like his dimples. They reminded her of more friendly times, times when her future didn't hang in the balance. Nick was a man of calm, a man of strength under pressure. From his formidable six-foot-four stature to his determined, steady gaze, he'd know how to make this right. "When there's a lawyer involved," he said, "you always have recourse."

"But what? Jeremiah's as entitled to Ladd Springs as I am. His father, my mother..." Delaney didn't want to think about the repercussions of her cousin's presence, but she had to—she might have to go up against him in court. And while she hadn't seen Jeremiah since they were teenagers, she remembered one thing about him. One very important thing. Jeremiah Ladd was a man who cared little about the consequences of his actions.

Nick reached over and took the paper from her. Securing her hands within his, he was her rock. Strong. Steady. Fearless. Everything she didn't feel at the moment. "Don't *worry*, Delaney. Jeremiah doesn't have a stake in this claim. Your uncle was sole owner and he signed this property over to Felicity. I intend to see that it stays that way."

Delaney wanted to believe him, wanted to believe it would happen, that she would keep Ladd Springs, but... She dropped her gaze to the papers strewn about the butcher block surface, a miscellany of warranty deeds, tax bills, any shred of paper bearing the Ladd name that she could get her hands on. She'd collected as much information as she possibly could on the property, dating back to the turn of the century, searching for clues as to how Jeremiah might possibly take it from her. Like a Swiss watch, the hands of time ticked through the line of ownership, recording generation by generation, each and every name a Ladd. But Jeremiah's name was nowhere to be found.

"I agree with Nick," Malcolm said. "You're in good shape."

Peering at him, Delaney thought his sky blue eyes cradled a gentle intelligence. Wisdom. Malcolm's appeal was softer than Nick's rugged, swarthy looks. Malcolm was elegance in the male form, sophistication, grace and aplomb. His tanned complexion was smooth and refined, his body lean, like a runner's. Add the shock of white-gray hair on his head and you had the yin and yang in men. Black and white. Lion and lamb.

"Challenging a life estate deed is tough," Malcolm said. "Your cousin would have to contest the validity of the deed, prove that your uncle did not have authority to sign over the property, or that he was coerced in some way."

Delaney rustled through the papers, as though the answer lay buried within them. "But Annie said it was in the fine print. I've read through every document—twice. I don't see anything written by Grandpa Ladd that says Jeremiah has rights to the property."

Nick cocked a brow. "It's not a wonder, the way you Ladds write contracts."

Delaney assumed he was referring to the deathbed promise Ernie had penned for his sister, Susannah, the one swearing he would give Delaney rights to Ladd Springs. Fear zipped through her stomach. "But Annie said it was here. I'd lose the title because I overlooked the fine print." She pushed at the papers and said, "I don't see it!"

"Have you considered the possibility that Annie was bluffing?" Nick asked.

"Bluffing?" Delaney scoffed. Annie Owens was a lot of things, but a poker player was not among them. "She's not that smart."

"You don't care for her much," Nick observed, a question lingering in his voice. Malcolm seemed interested in her answer as well.

Delaney sat back on a wooden saddle stool, one of four placed around her kitchen island. Pulling a bare-footed heel up to the curved seat, she wrapped her arms around her leg and rested chin to knee. "I don't," she said. "Though it's funny...when we were young, we used to be good friends."

"What happened?"

Delaney's mind ripped through the past, their cat fights with regard to boys, the petty jealousy... Jeremiah had been a good-looking, scrappy kinda boy when they were growing up which drew the eye of the girls. Delaney took him for granted. He was her cousin, her constant playmate and the last boy on earth she'd ever be interested in. Jeremiah had been hardened by his father, and the shell he'd built around himself was impenetrable. He'd take risks that would take her breath away, like the time he jumped off a rocky ledge into the river below, not knowing how deep the waters ran before taking the plunge. He could have been killed, but instead broke through the surface with a whip of blond hair and a raging smile. "Your turn!" he'd hollered.

"Not on your life!" she'd told him—on more than one occasion. She'd stick to horse-back riding and mountain hikes and leave the cliff-diving to him.

"Annie had a thing for Jeremiah," Delaney said. "For as long as anyone could remember, she pined away but he didn't know she was alive. And if he did, he could of cared less. Until she threw herself at him in high school, that is."

"And I'm assuming he did what every hot-blooded teenage boy would do," Nick said.

Delaney nodded. "She gave herself to him and he took full advantage. She claims that Casey is Jeremiah's."

"Is she?" Malcolm asked, as if alerted to a new wrinkle in their plans.

With a shrug, Delaney replied, "Who knows? There were rumors she was sleeping with Clem at the time, too."

"Clem Sweeney?" Nick asked, his demeanor jolted by the revelation.

She looked at him. "Why so shocked?"

"Annie's a good-looking woman," he replied, shooting a hand up between them to fend off the distasteful look Delaney fired his way. "Don't get me wrong, she's not my type, but Clem?" Nick glanced between her and Malcolm. "The guy is a loser."

Delaney glared while Malcolm chuckled.

"Annie is average, *maybe*," Delaney gave him. "But good taste is not one of her strong points."

Nick reached for Delaney, but she unfolded her body and rolled off the barstool, ignoring his attempt at appeasement. Annie Owens was the enemy. She was the one responsible for bringing Jeremiah back into the picture, and if Nick wanted to use this property for his hotel, he'd better get his alliances straight. She turned, unsettled by the two men staring at her. Two very handsome men, neither of whom bothered to mask his masculine appreciation. Dressed in tank top and jean cut-offs, Delaney suddenly felt exposed in her minimalist attire. "It's Annie's fault Jeremiah is involved," she declared with a cross of her arms. "I want him stopped."

"Understood." Nick gathered her in his sights.

"As I see it, he has two ways to go," Malcolm said, holding his fingers up. "Jeremiah can challenge the validity of the deed based on procedural error or duress."

"What does that mean?" Delaney asked.

"Procedural error is just that—something done wrong in the procedure of filing and recording the deed," Nick explained. "Undue duress or coercion means that Ernie signed the deed over to you against his will."

"But Ernie signed it over willingly."

"You and I know that, but the judge doesn't."

"Jeremiah will have to challenge you in court—or the validity of the deed, that is—and prove that you forced Ernie to sign," Malcolm said. "But I'll tell you, reversing a deed is not easy."

"That's good, right?" Delaney asked.

"It's good," Nick confirmed. "But it doesn't mean we're out of the woods yet."

"I checked with the clerk of the court," Malcolm continued. "The deed was filed and recorded per the state's requirements. So challenging you on procedure won't work."

"So he'll have to prove Ernie signed it over under force?"

"Yes. And seeing as how he's of sound mind, I think it will be tough argument." Delaney and Nick shared a glance that unsettled Malcolm.

When Nick called Malcolm to Tennessee, he never mentioned the possibility they would be embroiled in a firestorm of family dysfunction. Nick said the land deal was done, solid, they were moving forward with construction of the hotel. That's where Malcolm came in. He was here to walk the land, incorporate his vision for a secluded mountain retreat into the hills and forests of Ladd Springs and get the bulldozers rolling. Legal disputes had not been on the agenda. Emotionally-charged family feuds had not been on the agenda. "He is of sound mind, right?" Malcolm looked from one to the other, a trickle of foreboding raising the fine hairs on his neck. "Ornery, but sound?"

"Well," Delaney hedged. She nibbled her lower lip.

"Well what?" Malcolm asked sharply.

"Ernie is ill," Nick said. "He has terminal cancer."

"Great."

At Malcolm's groan, Delaney glanced to Nick. "What? Could they use that against him somehow?"

"If the man is dying of cancer, Jeremiah could most certainly allege that he was coerced, that he was pressured until his defenses gave way and he signed."

Delaney cupped a hand to her forehead. "Oh no..."

"But you said no one would tell Jeremiah about his father's illness." Nick searched her gaze and Malcolm didn't like where this was going. "That everyone knew the two couldn't stand each other, that Jeremiah wouldn't care if Ernie died."

"That was before money entered the picture," Malcolm declared. "You know the smell of green changes everything.

"Or gold." Delaney rushed to Nick. Placing a hand to his thigh, she implored, "We can't let him find out about the gold."

"Delaney." Nick took her hand in his. "He won't find out about it. And he won't find out about Ernie's illness. None of *us* are going to tell him. Ashley certainly isn't going to tell him. She was the one prepared to help you get title to begin with."

"What about your daughter?" Malcolm asked. He'd only met the girl a few days ago, but seemed to have a good head on her shoulders. "Does she know?"

"I don't want her caught up in this mess," Delaney stated bluntly.

"She knows," Nick answered for Delaney. "She was there when we received the news from Ashley."

"Will she tell anyone?" Malcolm asked.

"No," Delaney snapped. "She won't tell anyone."

Nick peered into Delaney's eyes. "What about the boys?"

"She wouldn't tell them. She has no reason to tell them," Delaney said, as if willing it to be true.

Malcolm made a mental note of her reaction, then asked, "So we know, and Ashley knows, right?"

"Ida knows," Delaney reminded. "If Ida knows, the whole town could know!" Delaney paused. "And Candi works with Ida."

"So?" Nick asked, as though it were irrelevant.

"Candi is Annie's best friend."

"Wonderful," Malcolm said and slapped his knees.

"But you can't be sure," Nick said.

"I can't be sure of anything at the moment!" Delaney cried. "She may very well know as we speak!"

"There, there, Delaney."

Nick pulled her to him, but she resisted, putting several feet between her and them. She paced the living room. "This is horrible—now Jeremiah *and* Annie will find out about the gold and the fact that Ernie is sick. They'll gang up on us in court and we'll lose for sure!"

Nick stood. "Let's not get upset about something we don't know to be a problem, yet."

"Exactly how are we going to determine if this is a problem?" Malcolm asked Nick. "Get our hair done and listen to the latest gossip?"

Nick looked to Delaney for the answers—but she returned a blank look.

"Are you close with Candi at all?" Nick asked. She shook her head. "Do you know anyone who is? Anyone that will talk to us?" Nick walked toward her but seemed to think better of it and stopped. "What about Ashley? She must be able to ask Ida."

"She wasn't supposed to tell anyone in the first place, remember?"

"There has to be someone we can ask, probe to see if the news of gold has been leaked."

Malcolm looked to Nick who looked to Delaney. The room felt like a ticking time bomb. They didn't have time to waste fighting in court. He and Nick had already drawn up the rough sketches for the new hotel. If this Jeremiah character challenged them in court, he could tie their hands for weeks, months—months they couldn't afford. Not with Jillian Devane breathing down their backs from a mountain range over. According to their attorney, Malcolm understood Jillian had closed on her deal and was ready to submit permits. Once she squared those away it was a race to the finish line—opening day. Tension rippled across his neck and shoulders. Malcolm had only been in town for a week and already the time was stacking up against them. It was not a position he preferred to be in.

Unable to sit idle another minute, Malcolm stood. "I say we force his hand. We consult with a local attorney. Odds are we have nothing to worry about." Unless there was something Delaney and Nick weren't telling him. By the looks of them, he realized it was a distinct possibility.

Chapter Three

When Jeremiah pulled into his old homestead with his girlfriend Loretta Flynn seated by his side, a slew of emotion washed through him. It had been almost twenty years since he'd last set foot on this property. Twenty long years since he'd ditched this place for Atlanta in search of new horizons, a new life. Slowing his truck, he settled his gaze on the house he grew up in. The roof was falling off, the porch was battered, worn to the point of near collapse. Windows were cloudy from years of dust and grime, the front patch of grass nothing but weeds creeping over a gravel driveway.

But neglect was the way Ernie Ladd rolled. Throughout his childhood, Jeremiah recalled his life as endless days fending for himself, nights huddling beneath the covers in the darkness, scared of who or what may walk through his door. Alone with his father, there had been no comfort for a young boy's fears. There was nothing but bitterness. His mother had left them. She dropped him at grade school one morning and never looked back. Not a call, not a visit. Not so much as a card.

Jeremiah couldn't blame her. Living with Ernie Ladd was hell. He drank, he bickered, he grumbled and he beat. He was miserable, and made sure everyone around him was the same. The only bright spot in Jeremiah's life had been his Aunt Susannah. When she dropped by the house, his old man turned quiet. Sober, brooding, and he kept his mouth shut.

Unfortunately, Aunt Susannah's visits were too far and few between.

Tossing the truck into park, Jeremiah's stare glazed over. Actually, he was surprised he'd stayed as long as he had. But in the beginning it had been tolerable. Almost normal. Then the old lady took off and the remaining years amounted to a prison term. Twenty years, Jeremiah mused. Twenty long years and now it was time to collect. He'd done his time, paid his dues. It was time the old man paid his. Pulling the keys from the ignition, Jeremiah deposited them in the center console and slid free of the vehicle. His gut tensed as he looked to Loretta. "I'll be back in a sec."

Loretta waved him off with a wriggle of her fingers and a pop from her chewing gum.

Jeremiah shook his head. Loretta was a bleach-blonde babe, an ex-stripper he met in the city but one with the mannerisms of a child. Of course with her body she could act any damn way she pleased. Not like he was dating her for her quirks.

Albert Ladd spotted Jeremiah immediately and even from this distance, Jeremiah detected the shade being drawn over his eyes. He wasn't welcome. Even the oaf understood. *The prodigal son's return meant trouble.* Jeremiah swallowed old resentments and strode over to the porch. Uncle Al had been as bad as Ernie when it came to the beatings, though his belt had been swung across Billy and Robby's hides, the sting was felt by all three. Jeremiah and his cousins were six months and two years apart in age. They swapped stories, swapped joints—they also plotted an end to the abuse. It was an end that never happened. Billy was sent to juvie for robbing the local gas station and Robby took off running. Jeremiah wasn't far behind, ditching Tennessee at seventeen, headed for Atlanta.

Taking the steps two at a time, Jeremiah landed on the top with a decisive thud. "Hello, Uncle Al," he said, a notch more cheerfully than warranted. "It's been a long time."

Albert visibly cowered, all trace of ease erased from his dope of a face. He was still enormous in size, still wore the same dingy denim coveralls Jeremiah remembered from his youth. His stringy brown hair was thinner, the scraggly ends hanging down to his shoulders. Didn't look as if old Albert had changed a bit. "What's a matter?" Jeremiah taunted. "No words to welcome back the prodigal son?"

His uncle evaded him with a sideways glance.

Jeremiah laughed. "Oh, c'mon Uncle Al. Be glad it's not your own son showing up on your doorstep. Now in that case I'd say you had something to worry about!"

"What are you doin' here?"

At the familiar voice, Jeremiah turned. There in the doorway stood his father. Through the filmy screen of dust, Ernie Ladd was a stick with his tan shorts pulled nearly up to his chest. Jeremiah could clearly see the dark eyes boring into him, magnified by black framed glasses. The old man certainly hadn't lost his vigor for hate. Jeremiah could feel it from six feet away. Squaring his shoulders, he took his father head on. "I'm here to collect what's mine."

"What are you talkin' about?" Ernie snarled.

"I'm talking about Ladd Springs." The old man stiffened. "I understand you're trying to steal it right out from under me."

"I ain't done no such thing!" his father exclaimed.

"That's not what I heard."

"Well, you heard wrong," Ernie countered, but didn't move a muscle. Which meant he was worried about his son's next move. "This property ain't yours, it's mine."

Jeremiah savored a private smile. It gave him great pleasure to watch his father squirm. So much, he hated to see it end. "Either way, I intend to find out." Glancing up the mountain, toward his Aunt Susannah's cabin, he asked casually, "Is Delaney home?" Lacy Owens had told Loretta that his cousin had moved into her mother's hillside hideaway. She'd also mentioned that Delaney had a daughter.

Ernie followed his line of sight and muttered, "I ain't the woman's keeper."

"Only her benefactor," Jeremiah said, pinning him down with a scowl.

If looks could kill, Ernie would have obliterated his son. Gladly watched as his son crumbled to nothing before his very eyes. Jeremiah laughed again, but this time, threw his head back to make a grand show of his disdain. Drawing his head forward, Jeremiah leveled, "You haven't changed a bit. You're still the pathetic little man I remembered you to be."

"You go on from here," his father growled, as though chasing off a pesky raccoon. "Go on!" he hollered, retreating into the dark confines of his cave.

Coward. The man didn't even have the courage to step clear of the threshold and face his son man-to-man. With a fleeting glance to Albert, unease nakedly exposed in his expression, Jeremiah turned and hammered down the steps half-wishing one would break. That would make it easy. He'd sue and take the old man for everything he was worth. It'd prove a lot cleaner than sparring with Delaney. Was she still as hot and hellacious as he remembered?

He chuckled. Time to find out up close and personal.

Jeremiah navigated the steep, narrow trail, carefully climbing over jagged rocks and exposed roots. He slipped on a wet patch of clay and cursed under his breath. Grabbing a gnarled root for an assist, Jeremiah hauled himself up another few feet higher. At this rate, his new ostrich boots would be destroyed by the time he reached Delaney's cabin.

Make that her mother's cabin, the one *his* father built so she could evade the wrong end of a belt. Her father's. Grandpa Ladd had been a hard-drinking man with a temper to match. He'd whip off his belt for as little as a cross word, smacking his boys as easily as he swatted flies. It's no wonder Ernie and Albert never amounted to much. Their father set the bar out of their reach, then stomped them into the mud when they failed to achieve. But that didn't give them the right to take it out on their own boys. It wasn't *their* fault life stunk like rot on a carcass for Ernie and Albert. They could have left, same as he did. But they didn't. Neither one. They stayed, then took out their miserable hate on him, Billy and Robby.

Reaching the top, Jeremiah paused, more winded than he expected to be. Glancing at the tiny wooden structure, the basic four walls and porch that had been etched in his memory, he inhaled deeply. The scent of evergreen and laurel and oak permeated his being, transported him back to days spent running through the forest, sneaking behind the cabin, crouching in the brush to evade detection by Delaney. Visions of Aunt Susannah flooded him. Smiling, sweeping her porch, she waved. Jeremiah almost raised a hand in return. Delaney and he had run circles around this place. They played hide and seek, cops and robbers, war—whatever they wanted, Aunt Susannah let them play. *Kids were meant to be kids*, she'd tell them. Spare the rod and love the child had been her motto. He had longed to live with her, hide out, like she had, and live without fear of ever being beaten again.

But life didn't work that way. Life sought you out and found you without fail. Like Jeremiah's games of hide and seek in the woods with Delaney, one could only stay hidden for so long. Then the night critters came to call and the fun ended. That was how life worked.

Jeremiah breathed in, filling his lungs with fresh air, his mind and spirit with hope. Sometimes you caught a break. The possibility of gaining title to Ladd Springs had come at a perfect time for him. He owed money and a lot of it, but once he owned this property, the money he could gain from selling it would pay his debt, plus a truckload extra. He smiled inwardly. And he and Loretta could surely burn through money.

Jeremiah pulled his body erect and stood tall. Catching glimpse of movement inside the cabin, he swelled with pleasure. Delaney was home. *Knock, knock, guess who? None other than your old pal, Jeremiah.* With a renewed sense of purpose, he approached the cabin.

The sharp knock on the door stopped Delaney's heart. She flashed to it, then to Nick and Malcolm. Overwhelmed by the thwacking in her chest, she couldn't move. Couldn't breathe. The tall figure visible through the etched glass was too familiar. Apprehension iced her blood.

Jeremiah.

Nick strode over to the door, checking with Malcolm as he did so, as though silently coordinating their battle plan. Delaney was struck by their communication. Constantly conferring, it felt like the two men shared brain cells, spoke in terms of ESP.

But she was grateful. At the moment, two defenders felt better than one.

Nick opened the door and her nerves caught. Taking up nearly the entire space stood Jeremiah Ladd. Taller than she remembered, his blond hair had turned sandy-brown. Cut in layers, it was cropped short around his face. While his jaw was set in the firm line of confrontation, his light brown eyes held a mischievous gleam. He was the same old Jeremiah she knew in an instant—the one who, given the chance, would taunt relentlessly.

Jeremiah glanced indoors and wrapped his gaze around her, meeting her eyes after a lustful once over. "Hello, Delaney. Long time, no see."

His pleasure slid down to his mouth, opening it into a smile of comfort and ease. Delaney steadied her voice. "Hello, Jeremiah."

"It's Jerry, now."

"Jeremiah," she returned bluntly. "What brings you by?"

He chuckled. "I see some things don't change." Addressing Nick, currently blocking his entrance, Jeremiah asked, "May I come in?"

Nick opened the door and stepped aside, allowing him to pass. Without closing the door, he shadowed Jeremiah's movements inside the cabin as her cousin surveyed the interior. Wood floors polished to a subtle shine, log walls and ceiling marked by exposed beams, a lone painting by the fireplace—a scene straight from the river banks. Her home was rustic, simple, and all she needed.

"I like what you've done to the place," Jeremiah commented. "Especially the floors."

Delaney didn't thank him. This wasn't a social visit. Flipping her gaze to Nick and Malcolm, she registered their silence. This was *her* deal and they were allowing her to take the lead. "What do you want, Jeremiah?"

Bringing hands to his hips, he slid his fingers into the front pockets of his jeans. Still opting for cowboy boots—his current ostrich more fashion than function—Jeremiah wore a purple and navy shirt with a floral pattern woven into the background. Seems the Tennessee hillbilly had gone metro. Dressed in red plaid and jeans, Nick looked more country than Jeremiah.

"I think we both know why I'm here," Jeremiah said smoothly.

Remaining by the kitchen island, she replied, "Maybe you should spell it out for me."

"I understand you're the new owner of Ladd Springs."

"I am."

"Actually..." He paused, tapping a knowing gaze to both Nick and Malcolm. "Your daughter is."

At the mention of her daughter, Delaney tensed, thankful Felicity was with the Parker boys today. Delaney didn't like the idea that her child was mixed up in this mess at all, but like Jeremiah said, it was *her* name officially listed on the deed.

"Is she here?" He rolled his eyes to the bedroom, the loft. "I'd like to discuss some business matters with her, if possible."

"You leave my daughter out of this," Delaney snapped.

"What?" He feigned shock. "She's the owner, isn't she?"

"You have any business with Ladd Springs, you deal with me." Despite herself, she stole a peek at Nick.

"I see." Jeremiah nodded, crossed his arms over his chest. "So what is Felicity, about sixteen, seventeen?" He glanced at the men and grinned. "I bet she's a looker. Does she take after you, Delaney?" he asked, and seemed to purposefully plant his gaze on her breasts. "You're still as hot as ever."

Anger spit through her veins. "I'm warning you, Jeremiah. Back off."

"You're here about the property," Nick intervened. "We know." Jeremiah shot a smug smile toward Delaney as Nick continued, "But the title has been transferred and recorded. There's nothing you can do."

Jeremiah sighed, a tad more exaggerated than warranted. "Yes, you have a vested interest, don't you? Building a hotel, right?"

Where Jeremiah received his information, Delaney had no idea, but he was dead on. Smooth as silk, too, Delaney marveled, and wholly different from the brash boy she remembered. The old Jeremiah would have come in half-cocked and punched Nick in the face by now. But not this one. He was cold and calculating.

"Too bad you wasted your time. Unfortunately for you, my father saw fit to transfer title without first consulting with me."

"He doesn't need to," Nick informed. "It's his property to do with as he sees fit. Apparently, that judgment didn't include you."

"I'm not sure if you know my father, but he's not exactly of right mind," Jeremiah said, tapping Malcolm with a glance as though putting him on notice, too.

"His mind is right enough to know a losing proposition when he sees one."

Jeremiah stilled. His features remain pasted with ease, but his eyes grew cold. "I guess banging my cousin makes you feel entitled to insult me, but I'd advise against it. I'm not a man to contend with lightly."

Delaney gripped the edge of butcher block, taken aback. Jeremiah had nerve, she'd give him that. Near the same height as Nick, his build was nowhere near the mass. One strike from Nick and Jeremiah would go down. In a flicker of wishful thinking, Delaney almost hoped he would.

"Nothing less than I'd expect from a guy like you, resorting to trash talk when you have no facts on your side. Pathetic, but predictable."

Malcolm stood silent. Vigilant.

Jeremiah's façade showed the first signs of cracking. "Take your shots now, funny man, because soon there will only be one us laughing and I'll take great pleasure in watching you run out of town with your tail between your legs."

Nick stepped toward him and Delaney braced for impact.

"Gentlemen," Malcolm interceded, placing a hand to Nick's forearm. "I think these matters are better discussed in a court of law."

Malcolm knew his partner well, Delaney thought, heartened by his presence. No sense in giving Jeremiah an assault charge to add to his list of grievances. Lawyers lapped that stuff up like butter on a biscuit. Privately she doubted Malcolm was physically capable of putting a stop to a fight should one break out. Loafers, linen slacks and silk shirt suggested a man unaccustomed to the bull ring.

"Believe me, we will." Jeremiah squared his shoulders to the men before him. "Take this as your notice. You will be served."

Nick chuckled derisively. "Fancy words for a country boy."

Malcolm turned to Nick, but said nothing.

"Expectations have a way of surprising," Jeremiah said, as though his confidence had never escaped him. He looked to Delaney and winked. "See you later."

The three of them watched him go, Malcolm tossing the door closed behind him. "What the hell were you doing?" he said to Nick. "Are you trying to stoke him into attack?"

Nick glowered. "He's a cocky bastard who deserves a firm one across the jaw."

"Whether he does or doesn't is not relevant. You hit him and you're adding to the problem." Anger rippled through Malcolm's calm. He lobbed a glance between Nick and Delaney and said, "The man may have a case."

"Do you think he does?" Delaney asked.

Malcolm nodded. "I think it's a possibility. And a head-ache we don't need."

Chapter Four

"Aw, sugar, you haven't touched your coke," Aunt Frannie said as she rubbed Lacy's back in the quiet of the diner. Fran's Diner was *the* place to go for breakfast, lunch and dinner, but at the moment, the main lunch crowd had cleared. Cooks prepared for dinner, the air drenched with the sumptuous smell of Lacy's favorite fried chicken and fried okra. Mixed with the scent of her aunt's Shalimar perfume, it reminded Lacy of her momma. It was the perfume of choice for both women, one that held fond memories. Every time she'd caught a drift of the fragrance in Atlanta, Lacy had been transported back home, to the wonderful world of family, friends and fun.

None of which her hometown resembled at the moment. Hitched up to the eat-in bar, her elbows propped on the counter, she dropped her chin to her palms. Home wasn't as sweet as she remembered. It was downright bitter.

"Annie will come around," Frannie added quietly, her loving blue eyes filled with compassion. Red hair tucked up in her hair net, her uniform the same white-collared dress she'd always worn, the red apron a match to her checkered curtains, Aunt Frannie and her diner hadn't changed a bit. Red, red, red—booths red, chairs red. Red was Frannie's favorite color.

"I don't think so," Lacy replied glumly. "You didn't see her face. She *hates* me."

"You stop that nonsense, right now. Annie Grace doesn't have a hateful bone in her body."

Lacy turned and shrieked, "She does for me and uses her hateful bones like bats, I tell you!"

"C'mon, child," Frannie hushed her. Seizing her neck, she massaged with a strong hand. "You've got to pull yourself together. She needs time, that's all. She's been dealing with that wicked Jeremiah since the day he left town. You need to see it from her point of view."

"Jeremiah's been in Atlanta. How's she had to worry about him?"

Frannie loosened her hold, slid her hand down Lacy's back. "She has a daughter, Lacy. That changes things."

Lacy shrugged. She didn't have any kids, though she wanted some. Bad. And she was getting old. At thirty-five, her clock was ringing like crazy. Alarm bells were clanging so loud, the roosters were envious. Lacy needed to find the right man and quick! But she wanted a good man, a nice man. Atlanta had been full of slick men who wanted nothing but sex and she was high tired of it. Every last one of them claimed to want her forever, but none wanted to commit. None saw the beauty in who she was. Then she read her horoscope. The stars said she had to return to her roots to find love. Next thing you know, Jeremiah walked into the lounge and she knew what she had to do. Without a second thought, Lacy packed her bags and followed him and Loretta Flynn back home to Tennessee.

Only her plan for a family reunion wasn't working out like the stars had promised. Her first day back and already her sister was trying to kick her out of town.

Frannie leaned onto the counter and scooted close, her brown eyes assumed a sudden heaviness. "You've got to understand. Annie has had a rough time of it, especially since the overdose."

Lacy whirled. "Overdose? Annie?"

Frannie shook her head, saddened. "Her daughter, Casey."

Lacy covered her mouth with a hand as the news trickled through her heart. How dreadful! "Is she okay?"

"Physically, yes, but the girl's going through a difficult time and Annie's real sensitive about it."

"Why? Because of Jeremiah?"

Frannie nodded. "Him and this whole mess about the property. Annie has it stuck in her craw that Casey deserves half of Ladd Springs and she won't let it go. She's like a pit bull, I tell you, and it's causing her a heap of turmoil. Part of me wishes she'd just give it up and move on, though I understand why she won't." Frannie shook her head. "It's a plum shame she and Delaney don't get along anymore."

Lacy absorbed the information, calculating its significance. Annie was trying to get her hands on Ladd Springs? Lacy had always loved the place and it would make a great place to live, to raise a family. She looked into her aunt's eyes and asked, "Do you think she has a chance?"

"Aw, sugar, I don't know. Jeremiah is the one with any possible claim to the property and even he's gonna have a hard time. Ernie Ladd has already signed it over to Felicity."

"Felicity?"

"Delaney's daughter. She's about Casey's age and stands to inherit the entire property upon Ernie's death."

Lacy blew out her breath. "Wow." Thoughts zipped to and fro through her mind, bounced off the walls of her skull. Delaney's daughter gets everything? "But if Jeremiah is Casey's father like Annie's been claiming, wouldn't that make his daughter entitled to half? I mean, Delaney and Jeremiah are cousins. The daughters are cousins...that makes them equally entitled, doesn't it?"

Frannie's blinked. "Child, what are you thinking?"

Lacy pressed her lips together. Did Aunt Frannie know that Jeremiah was back in town?

"C'mon, now. Fess up." Frannie cupped her chin firmly. "I know you and I can see those wheels spinning a thousand miles an hour."

"Well..." Lacy's gaze darted toward the kitchen but returned to the sharp brown eyes of her Aunt Frannie. Thickly brushed with mascara, her lids were colored in shimmery blue. Same as they had been for thirty years. "Well, if Casey did get part of the property," Lacy proposed, "maybe Annie would let me live on Ladd Springs—for a while—just until I get settled, you know."

Frannie furrowed her brow and demanded, "Where are you staying right now, child?"

Lacy's shoulders sagged. "At a motel."

"Lord a'mercy!" Frannie exclaimed. "You better go pack your things this minute! Why, I *never*." She slanted her gaze toward the front door. "No niece of mine is staying in a motel when I have plenty of empty rooms in my very own house."

Lacy's heart caught and she ventured a smile. "You do?"

Smacking the countertop she cried, "Course I do! You know that. Ever since my sweet old Deacon died, my footsteps have been echoing through the halls of that big old house. You are moving in this afternoon and I won't hear another word about it."

Lacy knew Aunt Frannie wasn't kidding when she said big and old. Her house was one of the original homes in the area, three-stories in height, complete with wide interior halls, beautiful wood floors, and a wraparound veranda the whole town envied. The third floor of Aunt Frannie's home used to be one of Lacy's favorite hideouts. When she was little, she'd sneak up there and read and sing, play with her stuffed animal moose. Aunt Frannie never cared that she was up there. Said it made it easy to find her when her momma called looking for her. "You sure you wouldn't mind?"

"Mind? What I'll *mind* is if you stay another second in that motel, young lady."

Lacy hugged her with all her might. "Thanks, Aunt Frannie! I'll pack my bags this afternoon."

Bells clanged at the front door. Aunt Frannie looked over Lacy's shoulder and called out, "Hey, sugar!"

Lacy turned to see Delaney Wilkins walk in, accompanied by two men. Two very handsome, tall men. Lacy perked up on her soft cushioned stool. Things were continuing to look up! Fussing with the frilly layers of her blouse, she slapped on her biggest smile and called out merrily, "Hey, Delaney!" Lacy waved happily.

Delaney scowled, but the men with her smiled. One was tall, dark and handsome, reminding Lacy of a lumberjack in his plaid shirt and jeans while the other was sleek and sophisticated with a shock of white hair against tanned skin and blue eyes. The first wore Levis and a denim button-down, the second boasted a silky navy polo and fancy tan linen pants that looked expensive. Shame on Delaney for being so unfriendly, Lacy thought. Annie may have shunned her but what did Delaney have against her?

Delaney and her men neared but didn't take seats. "Long time no see!" Lacy greeted cheerfully.

Giving Lacy the once-over, Delaney crossed her arms over her chest. "So you're back in town, too, I see."

"I am."

"Ain't it great?" Frannie piped in, patting Lacy's arm. "She's back for a spell."

"For a spell?" Delaney eyed her. "What's the occasion?"

"Well," Lacy began, conscious of the men staring at her. "Jeremiah told me he was coming back and I thought, you know..." She twirled the short hair at her ear. "I haven't been back home in while and maybe it was time for a visit."

"Jeremiah's back in town?" Aunt Frannie asked.

"Yes," Delaney replied, eyeing Lacy like a bird on a worm. "Didn't Lacy tell you?"

"Now we haven't had *near* enough visiting time to get to *that* silly fool," Lacy defended, evading Frannie's direct gaze as guilt seeped into her heart. Would Frannie be mad?

The white-haired man reached a hand between the squabbling women. "The name's Malcolm Ward."

"Lacy Owens," she replied, placing her hand in his palm. He bowed slightly, lifting her hand to his lips where he placed a gentle kiss. Excitement flitted across her breast.

"It's nice to meet you," he said smoothly, branding her with a heated gaze.

"Nice to meet you," she quipped, admiring his silken white hair shaped by an expensive layered cut—striking for a younger man like him. Add his remarkably blue eyes, pale blue, yet penetrating within his browned complexion and she found it a fascinating combination. The shirt he wore hung straight as a board past his pants, suggesting a lean build, and the unmasked desire in his eyes warned Lacy he was a man accustomed to having his way with the ladies.

She could see why. He was intoxicating to look at.

"Nick Harris," the other man said, drawing her attention from the first. Much darker than Mr. Ward, this one kept close to Delaney's side. Territorial, Lacy mused. He must belong to Delaney. She returned her focus to Malcolm. Did that mean this one was available?

"Y'all hungry?" Aunt Frannie asked them.

"Starving," Nick replied. Lowering to a stool on the opposite side of Aunt Frannie, he ordered, "Cheeseburger and fries, please."

Aunt Frannie turned to Malcolm. "And for you, young man?"

"I'll have what she's having," he said, indicating Lacy with a flirtatious grin. Lacy giggled.

"Then you're going to go hungry," her aunt remarked. "That girl plum don't eat."

"Oh, Aunt Frannie!" Lacy set a hand to her breast, spreading her fingers wide, showing off her fiery red nails she had manicured before leaving Atlanta. "Don't be silly, of course I eat." Lacy batted her eyelashes at Malcolm. "Your fried chicken and okra are out of this world."

Malcolm sniffed the air. "Smells like it." He turned to her Aunt Frannie and said, "I'll have the chicken and okra."

"Coming right up!" She pushed up from the bar stool, headed for the kitchen.

Lacy trailed her aunt's figure until Delaney lassoed her attention, demanding, "So what are you really doing here, Lacy?"

"I told you. I decided it was time for a visit. Haven't seen the kinfolk in ages."

"Last I remember, you couldn't wait to get out of Dodge," Delaney said, taking a seat next to her man. "You high-tailed it out here with Jeremiah faster than a wild hare. What happened?"

To Lacy's delight, Malcolm Ward settled in on the stool vacated by her aunt, bringing him up close and personal. She suppressed a rush of nerves. Why did Delaney have to bring up the past and ruin her afternoon?

"Well?" Delaney persisted. "What happened to bring you home?"

Life happened. The city happened. Disappointment happened. Must she be chained to one decision? "I was bored with Atlanta," Lacy replied as casually as she could, maintaining a sharp eye on Mr. Ward. Seemed he too was interested in her answer.

"Bored?"

Lacy nodded and tapped the tip of her straw. "Bored. Plain B-O-R-E-D," she spelled out.

Delaney cocked her head and retorted, "I don't believe you."

Malcolm smiled. "I've been to Atlanta and I have to agree. Once you've seen the magnolias and peaches, you've seen it all." He winked. "I like Tennessee much better."

"Are you from here?" Lacy asked sweetly, grateful for the distraction.

Malcolm laughed. "No, darlin', I'm not," he drawled, mimicking a southern accent. "But I sure do like what I see."

Desire was something Lacy had become accustomed to seeing in a man's eyes and she never tired of it. She liked to play the game of cat and mouse and she liked to get caught—once a man proved he was worthy of catching her. Though admittedly, these days she wanted more. Lacy reached for her coke and politely inquired, "Where are you from, then?"

"Everywhere," he replied evenly.

"Everywhere?"

"What he means," Nick pitched in, "is that he travels a lot. We own a hotel chain and Malcolm here travels the world."

Astonishment poured into her. "You travel the *world*?"

"I do. But the best places I've found are the small towns." He leaned toward her ever so slightly and lowered his voice, "That's where the best people can be found."

Lacy grinned broadly. Things were definitely looking up!

Delaney led the way out of Fran's Diner and stopped mid-sidewalk to wait for Nick and Malcolm. Pulling up the rear, warmed by the sunshine and thoughts of Lacy, Malcolm loitered a moment. Damn, but she was fine. A pixie of fresh-faced beauty and flirtatious attitude, he'd been particularly drawn to her mouth. With a heart-shaped face and short-cropped black hair, round cheekbones and blue eyes that could draw men from across a crowded room, it was her mouth that had garnered Malcolm's attention. Naturally pink, her lips were full, but not overly so, and when she ate, all he could think of was kissing her. Not that her body didn't have curves in all the right places, it did. Forget breast men and butt men, he'd take a sexy mouth and a woman who knew how to use it any night of the week.

Swells of pleasure rippled through him. Lacy Owens was a surprise find for a small town, a find that would make his stay all the more tolerable. Delaney was attractive, he'd give her that, but hers was a country appeal and he, a city man. While he appreciated a cowgirl in jeans and on horse-back, Malcolm preferred the savvy smile of a city girl, a girl who'd been around the block, enjoyed the late night scene and filled her gaze with a knowing tease. Had he not been dining with Nick and Delaney, Malcolm would have scooped that woman up and taken her for the ride of her lifetime.

But he was here on business, and business had to come first—though it shouldn't preclude him from seeking her out in his spare time. Heading back to the car, Nick and Delaney flanking his side, Malcolm asked, "So who is that Lacy, anyway?"

"Trouble," Delaney quipped.

"Trouble?" Now she had his attention. "What kind of trouble are we talking about?"

"The kind you want to steer clear of."

"Lacy Owens is sister to one Annie Owens," Nick clarified.

Malcolm let out a low whistle. The same Annie Owens responsible for inviting one Jeremiah Ladd back to town. "Talk about complicating matters." Glancing at Nick over Delaney's blonde head, he said, "No cavorting with the enemy, right?"

Nick grinned and Delaney snapped, "Exactly."

Malcolm chuckled. "And just when I thought this town was getting interesting."

"If it helps to cool your engines," Delaney pitched out, "Lacy ran off with Jeremiah as a teenager."

"Ah...and the plot thickens," he said, intrigued by the connection.

"Thickens, hardens, turns into dried spit gum, if you ask me. Annie wants nothing to do with Lacy, which is why I'm surprised she's here."

"Doesn't she have other family in the area?" Malcolm asked.

"Only Fran," Delaney replied. "Fran is her aunt and the only blood relative she and Annie have left around here. Her father died of a heart attack when they were little and her mom moved to Chattanooga. Just up and left after Lacy took off for Atlanta."

Malcolm turned the information over in his mind. "The mother left, leaving Annie alone?"

Nick frowned. "I didn't know that."

"She was of age," Delaney told him. "No reason Annie couldn't take care of herself."

"And all she has left is her daughter Casey?" Malcolm asked.

"That's right. And *trust* me," Delaney said, slowing with Nick as they reached his parked car, "Casey will take to her Aunt Lacy about as warmly as a hawk on a squirrel."

Surprised by the venom in her voice, Malcolm commented, "That friendly, huh?"

"There's no love lost between the Owens girls. Annie wasn't real fond of Lacy growing up, but at least they were on speaking terms back then."

"And now?"

Delaney squinted against the late afternoon sun and explained, "Annie is the jealous type. She's jealous of me, jealous of Lacy. Pretty much any female, except Candi Sweeney, and Annie never took kindly to the fact that her younger sister Lacy was prettier than her, or the fact that she stole her boyfriend."

Malcolm exchanged a knowing glance with Nick. Annie was not an ugly woman, by any definition of the word. She may not have the knockout figure of her sister Lacy, with her slim hips and busty cleavage, but Annie was attractive in her own right.

"Annie is going to become an old maid," Delaney predicted, "because she can't see past her own envy."

Point noted. *Don't bring up Lacy around Delaney.*

Nick pressed the key fob and with a double beep, the car doors unlocked. Nick opened the passenger door and Delaney lowered down to the seat. Nick closed the door and turned to Malcolm. "It's not a good subject."

"I see that." Dropping a fleeting gaze toward the seated Delaney, he asked, "Will I be disowned if I cross enemy lines?"

Nick smiled. "You might be." Placing a hand to Malcolm's shoulder, he said, "But you're a gambling man, so I'd suggest you proceed at your own risk."

"Any idea where I might bump into Lacy on a Friday night?"

Nick grinned and shook him lightly. "The only place in town anyone goes. Whiskey Joe's."

Malcolm winked. "Sounds like my kind of place."

Chapter Five

Candi homed in on the man walking through the salon. Her pulse quickened, her eyes sharpening in alarm. *Jeremiah Ladd.* While he had changed, matured, there was no mistaking it was him. Here—in her salon. Dressed in indigo blue jeans, ostrich boots and fancy purple-blue shirt, Jeremiah popped like a firecracker as he marched toward her. She gulped, clutched her station's chair back, noting that several hairstylists were glued to his every move.

Slowing, he drawled, "Candi Sweeney."

She tightened her grip and said, "Jeremiah." Candi tried to smile, but standing rigid, the attempt failed. Darting a glance around the neighboring styling stations, she wondered what the women were thinking. Most of the stylists were too young to know Jeremiah, but Ida did. Would she recognize him?

Easy and familiar, he ignored the other women and their clients, seemingly focused only on her as he asked, "How the heck are you?"

"Good."

"You look great," he said smoothly, eyes freely roaming her face, her body, over the black dress and apron she wore, clear down to her glossy black toenails.

Nerves fluttered across her breast. Candi remembered Jeremiah and his smooth talking ways only too well. Back in the day, he'd been smoother than a Tom cat on the prowl, a bad boy magnet for the girls. For as long as she could remember, Jeremiah had been the one the girls talked about, flocked to—herself included. She tamped the memory back. But that was then, this was now. "Oh, Jeremiah..." Candi batted the compliment away. "How you do go on. I'm just a hillbilly, you know that."

"You don't look like a hillbilly to me," he observed. "In fact, you put the women of Atlanta to shame."

Candi nudged her way farther behind her chair, wondering why Jeremiah was here. She'd told him everything he needed to know. There was no reason to stop by and speak to her in person. She whittled a glance around the salon and thought if word got back to Annie that he was here making nice, it would not sit well. Her friend was already unhappy over the fact that Candi had called him. The last thing Candi needed was for Annie to suspect something was going on between them. She shuddered. "Jeremiah, what are you doing in a women's salon, anyway?" she tried to tease. "I'm sure you have better things to do."

"Now, Candi. You know I have the hots for you." He leaned closer and she caught of drift of his cologne. "Always have. And you called *me*, remember?"

Was he seriously here to make a pass at her?

"Well," Candi stammered, "you know I did and you know very well *why,*" she whispered, willing him to understand that this was a private matter.

Jeremiah winked. "I'd like to think it was more than helping out an old friend."

Candi didn't like the lust gathering in his eyes. Feeling the heat from shifty glances, she wanted Jeremiah out of her salon and quick. Ida would send word through town faster than a swat on a fly putting Ashley first on that list, followed by Delaney, Annie, Fran—the whole town would know by supper time!

Candi struggled to stay calm. "What can I say?" she began carefully. "When I heard about Ernie signing the property over to Delaney and Felicity I had to call you. It ain't right!" she cried righteously, hoping it would sway him from making further advances.

Jeremiah smiled, as though he understood perfectly. "Doesn't mean you and me can't have a little fun while I'm in town."

"Jeremiah," she said tightly, checking for witnesses to their encounter.

"What? It could be just like the old days..."

Candi shook her head vehemently. *Please don't say any more.*

When she didn't respond, Jeremiah pulled back, apparently taking her refusal in stride. "Your loss." He surveyed the salon in short order and said, "About the property deal. What exactly do you know about it?"

"Nothing," she replied abruptly, relief streaming through her. "Other than Delaney is trying to get it all for herself and Felicity—like I told you."

"Those two men with her are the hotel guys, right?"

Candi balked. "Two men?"

He nodded. "Two."

She smoothed the hair down on either side of her face, knowing the ears of her gossipy coworkers were burning red hot over their conversation. But at this point, all she could do was get Jeremiah out and the only way to do that was to answer him. "Well, Annie told me about the one, man. His name is Nick Harris. According to her, he's the one who wants to build a hotel on the property."

Jeremiah's brow rose. "Must be his partner."

"Maybe." Candi nodded, flicking an annoyed glance at Ida, openly staring at her now. "He was trying to buy the property from Ernie before Delaney got her hands on it."

"Any idea why the old man wouldn't sell?" Jeremiah asked, searching her gaze. "Seems to me a hotel man could offer a pretty penny for the place."

"I don't. But you know Ernie—he's as hard-headed as they come! The only one he seems sweet on is Felicity." Jeremiah perked at the mention of Delaney's daughter. "Felicity plays her flute for him. That's what Casey says, anyway." At

Jeremiah's blank look, Candi added pointedly, "Casey is Annie's daughter."

Something he already knew.

"Casey and Felicity are friends?" Jeremiah asked, as though surprised by the revelation.

"Kinda. The Parker boys are the common tie between them."

"Parker boys? As in Morton Parker?"

"Yes. He has a passel of kids and the youngest two are twins, Travis and Troy. Well, they hang out with Felicity and Casey, and Casey gets most of her scoop from the boys."

"I see." He swung a conspiratorial gaze around the salon and asked, "Where do I find these boys?"

"The twins? Why they're everywhere, but usually you can find them at Fran's."

Jeremiah's expression closed and Candi realized he would be persona-non-grata there.

"What about Casey?" he asked. "She around somewhere?"

Candi blinked. "Have you not spoken to Annie?"

"Why would I?" he questioned, in what Candi found to be a wholly contemptuous tone.

"Because she's—" Candi gasped, and cried under her breath, "Annie!"

Annie stood like a stone in the Bangs reception area, her eyes fastened on Jeremiah. She held her breath as she stared, shock swirling through disbelief and curiosity, mixed with an emotion that bordered on hate, which oddly included a murky longing.

Jeremiah turned from Candi, the instant recognition transforming his expression from lazy pleasure to a steely interest. Candi jerked her hands away from her styling chair, the look in her eyes one of sheer desperation. Annie's brain felt muddled. Fuzzy.

Racing around Jeremiah, Candi hurried down the center aisle toward Annie. "Annie!" she exclaimed and quickly saddled up on her friends' side.

But Annie only had eyes for Jeremiah. It was the first time she had seen him since he and Lacy took off for Atlanta. Eighteen long years since she'd held the man in her gaze, in the flesh. She'd have to give him his looks. He still looked good, his body lean, seemingly in shape. As he approached, she noted the lines in his face, but rather than old, they added depth, maturity. Jeremiah Ladd looked the same as he had when he left, only older, wiser.

Better. Annie swallowed the lump in her throat and said, "Hello, Jeremiah."

"Hello, Annie." He stopped front and center, his glance lingering on Candi's as though the two shared a secret.

Annie looked to Candi who blurted, "Jeremiah just stopped by—like five minutes ago—wanting to know how to find you." She dodged his gaze and added, "And here you are."

Candi fussed with the blonde hair around her eyes, ran her hands down her apron, then slipped them into her front pockets. Wondering why Candi was rambling, Annie turned back to Jeremiah. And why had he come to Candi to find her? Her name hadn't changed. She was in the phone book.

"How ya been?" Jeremiah asked her. "You work here, too?" Setting hands to hips, he hurled a presumptive glance around the salon, as though he owned one just like it.

"No," she replied automatically. "I work at Trendz."

Jeremiah nodded, but didn't delve deeper. "So listen, Candi," he said. "We'll be in touch, okay?"

Like a wet cat with her tail ensnared in an electrical outlet, Candi look horrified.

Smiling syrup and slime, Jeremiah tossed to her, "See you around, baby."

Annie watched him walk out of the salon, sunlight setting fire to the gold in his hair. The door swooshed closed and he was gone. Suspended in a haze, she stood dumbstruck within the confines of the busy salon. Had that really happened? Her gaze drifting from the front door to Candi, Annie noted the fear squeezing out through the brown eyes of her friend. Questions plagued her. Why had Jeremiah stopped by? Why check with her first? The image of Candi and Jeremiah standing together by her chair crystallized in Annie's mind. Epiphany pinched. "Is something going on between you two?" she asked.

"No! Why would you ask?"

"Well, when I walked in here, you two seemed awfully cozy..."

"What? No way! There is nothing going on between me and Jeremiah."

At Candi's fidgety scan of the salon, Annie swept around to see what she was looking at. All eyes were on them, yet no one spoke a word. Humiliation welled deep in her heart. With great effort, Annie turned faced Candi directly. "Candi Sweeney, don't you lie to me. What was Jeremiah doing here?"

"*Nothing*, Annie. He stopped by looking for *you*."

At the crack in her voice, Annie's trust shriveled. "I don't believe you."

Candi's demeanor began to unravel. "Annie, it's true! You have to believe me. There is nothing going on between me and Jeremiah, you know that."

"What was 'see you around, baby' about?"

"Guy talk—*loser* talk. You know Jeremiah, he's always tried to have his way with girls." Annie stiffened. When Candi appeared to realize her mistake, she cried, "*Please*, Annie, let's not talk about this here." Candi grasped Annie's elbow but she yanked free. Annie didn't want to go anywhere with her at the moment. "Annie, *stop*. C'mon, this isn't like you."

"This isn't like you, either," Annie derided.

"We need to talk about this," Candi said firmly. "In the lounge."

The women glared at one another.

"We need to talk," Candi pleaded.

Reluctantly, Annie followed her friend through the salon, past the hushed glances and into the privacy of the employee lounge. A sole table was littered with cookie packaging, its gray Formica top covered in black crumbs. Four empty chairs sat at haphazard angles around it. Suspicion clawed at Annie, but she was willing to hear Candi out. This was her best friend. Maybe there was a good explanation to why Jeremiah was here, calling her "baby" and not out looking for *her*. Fleeing, in fact, when he found her. "Well?"

Candi eyed the door, as if someone would burst in any minute and intrude on their privacy. "Annie, I swear I don't know why Jeremiah was here."

"You said he was here looking for me."

"He was—but we never made it that far. He was only here for two minutes before you walked in, seriously."

"And?"

"And..." Candi dropped to a seat and buried her face in her hands. "Oh, Annie."

Fear clambered through her. "Oh, Annie what?" she asked, dreading what came next.

Candi lifted her face, tears catching in her mascara, the black smudging across her cheeks. "Jeremiah and I had a one night stand."

Annie felt the swift kick to her stomach, clutched at a chair to steady herself. "What?"

Candi nodded, shame oozing like sewage from her eyes. "Before he left—after you two were together. I was drunk, it was one time. I'm so sorry..."

Annie stared at Candi. Limbs liquid nothing, her insides were a vacuum. "I can't believe it," she uttered, the breath trapped within her lungs.

"It didn't mean anything. I wish it never happened."

"But it did." Hate trickled into Annie's heart. "You slept with my boyfriend behind my back."

"It was one time. It never happened again."

"And you never told me," she hammered. "You, Lacy, and how many others?" Disgust roiled through her, infusing her limbs with steel. "You slept with my boyfriend behind my back—you two-timing *bitch*."

"Annie!"

"I don't ever want to talk to you again."

Candi shot up from her chair. "You don't mean that!"

Annie glowered, anger turning the hate into a molten mess of loathing. "I've never meant anything more in my life."

Lacy checked out of the motel and returned to the diner. Aunt Frannie was having a set of keys to the house made, as well as packing up Lacy's favorite food for dinner. Didn't want her to starve, she claimed, explaining there wouldn't be much in the way of food at her house. Which made sense considering her aunt spent all her time at the diner. Thoughts of a home-cooked meal simmered in Lacy's mind. It may be diner food, but Aunt Frannie's recipes were second to none and she an amazing cook, personally supervising the process.

Lacy loved Aunt Frannie. She was generous, fun, and glad to see her. Unlike Annie. Her sister had been downright mean to her this morning and all she'd done was stop by and say hello.

Why don't you go back to Atlanta where you belong?

It the meanest thing anyone had ever said to her, and coming from her own flesh and blood made it all the meaner. As Lacy entered the diner, bells announced her arrival. Hovering by the hostess stand, she inhaled the scent of greasy cheeseburgers mixed with fried chicken, the sweet aroma of baking biscuits mingling in between. She closed her eyes and expelled a sigh.

The smell was heavenly.

Opening her eyes, she took in the interior. Good gracious, but she had missed this place. The red and white curtains were still cut halfway across the front windows, the black and white checkered floors were spotless. Red booths, round counter stools—it was as if she hadn't missed a single day, the picture of her youth snapped in time, frozen for eternity. Back in high school she'd come by after class for French fries and root beer floats, eggs and biscuits every Sunday after church. Her daddy's favorite had been the chicken fried steak and gravy, with a side of fried okra and collards, while her momma preferred the chicken and dumplings.

Lacy languished in the memories. She loved it all. Fried chicken, fried okra, plump, gooey dumplings and warm flaky biscuits. She breathed in the scent, reminiscing purely by her senses. Her mood dipped. She should have stayed in Tennessee. Life would have been easier here. Simpler, more pleasant. People here were honest. The air was fresh, the rivers and streams were clean and clear. But she was itchy back in the day and needed a change in scenery. Or thought she did. Catching a glimpse of a familiar face at the bar counter, Lacy caught her breath. *Was that Loretta?*

Lacy hurried over. Nearing the blonde seated at the food counter, she realized she'd been right. Surprise and delight streamed through her. "Hey, Loretta!"

Loretta turned and beamed, her glossed red lips setting off her perfectly white teeth. Her eyes were a blend of blue and green, favoring one or the other depending on the shade of clothes she wore. Today's cobalt-colored shirt made them the bluest of blues. "Hey, Lacy-lou. Fancy meeting you here!" Loretta hugged her friend. "I was wondering if I'd see you around town."

"You've come to the right place," Lacy returned proudly. "This here's my Aunt Frannie's diner."

Loretta's eyes widened. "You don't say?"

"I do." Lacy slid onto the red-cushioned stool next to her friend and asked, "Have you eaten, yet?"

Loretta looked beyond Lacy and then replied quietly, "I have."

Lacy looked behind her to see what Loretta was interested in and, not surprisingly, there were two handsome young men seated farther down the counter. She turned back and gave her a wry smile. "What are you up to, Loretta Flynn?"

She lowered her eyes, her lashes thick with black mascara, her lids a shimmery aquamarine. "Oh, you know me, Lacy," she replied bashfully and reached for her coke. "I can't help but admire handsome young men."

Lacy laughed. "And you're not fibbing! Other than Jeremiah, I've never seen you so much as peep at a man more than twenty-five-years old."

Aunt Frannie breezed out of the kitchen toting a large white bag in her arms. "Hey, sugar!" she called out to Lacy.

"Hi, Aunt Frannie!" Lacy waved eagerly.

Frannie made her way around a waitress, currently wiping the counter near the boys, and deposited her bag on the counter before Lacy. "Fried chicken and mashed potatoes, complete with a side of fried okra and black-eyed peas."

Lacy squealed. "You always knew my favorites!" Frannie eyed Loretta and Lacy promptly introduced her. "Aunt Frannie, this is my friend, Loretta. She's from Atlanta. Loretta, this is my aunt," she finished, feeling a swell of pride that filled her entire chest.

Loretta stuck out a slender hand, her nails long and glossy red. "Pleased to meet you."

Frannie shook hands and said, "Likewise."

"She's Jeremiah's girlfriend," Lacy informed her, surprised by the abrupt cooling to her aunt's demeanor. Then it dawned on her. Annie was angry about the Jeremiah thing and so was Aunt Frannie. Lacy frowned. How could she be so thick-headed and forget?

"Jeremiah's girlfriend?" Frannie asked.

"Yes."

Loretta exchanged a glance with Lacy, as though realizing this was not good news.

Frannie glanced down the counter to the young boys sitting at the other end, then back to Loretta. To Lacy, she said, "Your food's gonna get cold, honey. You best be gettin' it home."

"Oh, I don't mind cold fried chicken," Lacy replied. "I actually prefer it."

"Yes, well..." Her aunt's gaze lingered on Loretta, as though contemplating something important. But if she had something to say, she kept it to herself. "Lacy, sugar, if you want any pie, help yourself to one in the case. I don't have any at home."

"Thank you. I might do that!"

As Frannie excused herself and returned to the kitchen, Loretta muttered, "She don't like me none, does she?"

"Aw, it's not you, Loretta. It's Jeremiah they don't like."

"On account of he left town?"

Lacy shook her head. "No. He had a thing with my sister back in high school and she got pregnant."

"Jerry has a child?" Her eyes rounded. "He never told me that."

"He doesn't think it's his."

"Do you?" Loretta asked.

"Oh, I don't know." She dismissed the question as easily as if Loretta had asked her the time of day. "It's none of my business. My sister Annie wouldn't tell me the truth one way or another, anyhow. She hates me."

"Why?"

"She thinks I ran off with her boyfriend."

"You mean Jerry?"

Lacy nodded. "But I swear I didn't think they were still together. I never really thought they were boyfriend and girl-friend to begin with." She peeked into the bag of food, the warm moist aroma saturating her nostrils. Her stomach rumbled.

Loretta sipped from her coke, appearing to absorb the information. She cast another glance toward the boys, a small smile forming on her lips.

Lacy turned and this time studied the boys more fully. She had to hand it to Loretta. She had good taste. And twins! While they didn't look a day over eighteen, and barely legal, they certainly were handsome with sexy brown eyes and brown hair, strong builds, though the farther one was more natural. The closer boy was bigger, his muscles obviously developed from lifting weights. Lacy's gaze tickled around his biceps, dropping to the hard line of his thigh in close-fitted jeans. Definitely cute. But much too young for her liking. She preferred older men, always had. Lacy turned back to Loretta. "You're not trying to pick them up, are you?"

Loretta quickly shook her head. "Course not."

Through the server's window, Lacy saw that her aunt was keeping an eye on her and Loretta. Something told her it was because Loretta was flirting with those two boys and Lacy would bet her Aunt Frannie knew them. Probably watching them like a hawk, ready to report back to their parents. Whatever, Lacy mused. It wasn't her problem.

Pushing up from the seat, she grabbed her bag of food. "It's good to see you, Loretta, but I need to get going."

Loretta nodded. "You too, Lacy."

"Maybe I'll see you later?" she asked, hoping she would. Loretta was one of the few friendly faces around, and it would be nice to visit with someone who cared enough to be with her. "There's a night spot called Whiskey Joe's that might be fun."

"Really?"

"It's not like anything we have in Atlanta, but it's been around forever. Used to have great live music for dancing."

Loretta perked at the mention as Lacy knew she would. Between the two of them, they'd often cut a line dance or two after working the lounge, and Whiskey Joe's was the only place in town for dancing. "That would be nice," Loretta replied, "though I'm not sure what my schedule will be." She ventured another peek at the boys and Lacy wondered again at her friend's intentions. "But who knows?" She smiled broadly. "Anything's possible."

Lacy nodded, the bag growing warm within her arms. "Okay. Well, have fun, whatever you do." She waved good-bye to her aunt back in the kitchen and headed out. Fun was something Lacy wanted to have too—and would—right after she moved into her aunt's home and devoured this delicious food.

Chapter Six

Malcolm's instincts were humming as he pulled into the parking lot for Whiskey Joe's. A small establishment, it was far from his normal swank—LA clubs with modern interiors, artsy lighting and filled with beautiful people—but it would do, especially if the woman in question could be found inside. According to Nick, this was the place to be. From what he saw around town, it was the *only* place to be.

Which made his quest simple. One lady, one bar, that's what he called easy pickings.

Parking his rental truck, Malcolm strolled inside. Struck by the stale smoky smell, he realized the non-smoking trend had not reached this part of Tennessee. Scanning the interior for sight of the black-headed beauty, he browsed a wooden dance floor surrounded by a deep maroon carpet flecked with beige. Wooden high-top tables lined the perimeter, their surfaces sleek and pleasing to the eye. A group of young ladies crowded around one set nearest the floor. Dressed in skirts and boots, they had styled their hair to salon perfection, applied cosmetics like a work of artistry. He raised a brow. A few looked barely legal but totally gorgeous.

Malcolm chuckled to himself. Far be it from him to alert the authorities. He'd rather enjoy the view, although he was disappointed that view didn't include Lacy. Granted the half dozen females in house were attractive, but they weren't the one he was looking for. A few older men sat hunched over the bar as he ambled up, flagging the bartender. The bar back was mirrored in good old-fashioned saloon-style, the selection of alcohol fairly adequate from what he could discern. A clean-cut cowboy hurried over to him and smiled. "What'll it be, mister?"

"Scotch." He surveyed the bottles lining the wall behind the bar, searching for his preferred brand. "You have Macallan?"

The man shook his head. "Johnny Walker."

Malcolm nodded. It would have to do. "On the rocks with a splash of water, please."

"Yes sir, coming right up."

Leaning a hip against the bar, Malcolm turned and settled his gaze on the women clustered around the table. He hitched a heel up behind him and wondered how many of the girls were interested in companionship, or were they out for a girls' night of gossip. With few men to speak of, he didn't see a lot of hooking up to be had, but perhaps that kicked in later. He heard the plunk a glass behind him.

"Thanks," Malcolm said with a tip of his head. Lifting the drink to his lips, he treated his senses to the blended Scotch whiskey, detecting a hint of spice. One eye securely wrapped around the table of women, he enjoyed the liquid gliding across his tongue, fanning through his veins. The brand wasn't as mellow as he was accustomed to and had none of the oak flavor, but it hit the spot all the same. In the two weeks since Nick had dragged him halfway across the continent, Malcolm lacked the comfort of his usual amenities, the luxury lifestyle and the company of his current squeeze, an auburn siren of the utmost beauty and skill. Nick had insisted he was needed on site. Yet instead of designing, brainstorming and completing the project at hand, he was chasing down possible court challenges and side-stepping family feuds. He shook his head and sipped. He should be on the streets of LA tonight entertaining the ladies of Southern California or carousing among the corridors of his favorite casino in Vegas, not stalking a table of fresh-faced innocents in the hills of Tennessee.

Malcolm turned from the ladies. Staring at girls so young made him feel like a bit of a lech. Course it was still early. It was possible Lacy would still show. Tossing back another sip of whiskey, he pondered what he'd learned so far.

Nick was right on the money with Ladd Springs. After a guided tour from Delaney, he was sold. The place was amazing. Acres and acres of pristine beauty filled with natural wonder and quiet—it was exactly what Harris Hotel guests were seeking. Rivers and streams were clean and clear, the trails wooded and private, but the springs were the clincher. Nick was right. They could definitely develop those to increase the hotel's allure. Where Nick had talked about the wishing well, a sort of fountain of youth, Malcolm envisioned spring water showers and tubs, steam baths that permeated the senses with the finest water Mother Nature had to offer. He'd already decided on how he wanted to incorporate the hotel into the land, creating walls of river rock, recessed lighting that would make guests feel as if they were hidden away within the mountain. Floor to ceiling windows would bring the outdoors in, and of course, a palette of earthy tones that paralleled nature would adorn the interior. He smiled inwardly. The place would scream seclusion, clandestine romance.

Intuition clicked. Malcolm turned his head slow and easy and, to his delight, found one Lacy Owens sliding onto a stool at a high-top in the corner. *Well, look who's here...*

Pleasure danced low in his midsection. Spying the half-empty low ball on the table before her, he sharpened his focus on the brown liquid inside. Bourbon drinker? Desire drummed. Taking another sip of scotch, he watched Lacy settle in and waited for her to recognize him.

When she caught his eye, surprise flickered in her expression. A smile pulled at the corner of her mouth, but she glanced away. Did she have mixed feelings about him? After all, he was a friend of Delaney Wilkins and Delaney was no friend of hers. But certainly she had grasped the signs of his interest this afternoon at the diner. Was she playing hard to get?

He savored a private grin. *Game on*, my dear.

Malcolm raised his glass to Lacy and she acknowledged him but didn't return the gesture. Instead, she pulled out a cigar and lighter. Curiosity flared hot inside him as he watched her bite off the cap, dip the end into her mouth and light up. She gave a few quick puffs and the tobacco blazed orange-red. Sitting back in her chair, she crossed her legs, inhaled deeply and blew the smoke free in one, steady stream.

Dropping his gaze to her legs, Malcolm noted the shapely calves, her arch in the black high heels, the very black, very high heels. Wandering up, he noted her skirt was straight, simple and short—just the way he preferred—and black as night, same as her low cut, sleeveless blouse. He imagined her underclothing to be just as black and entirely lacy. The pun struck him with added appeal. Lacy in lace. Malcolm brought glass to lips, allowing his gaze to ingest the sight of her. Most definitely an appealing combination.

Apparently pleased by his undivided attention, Lacy brought the cigar to her lips, methodically enclosing them over the tip as she stared at him. Lingering, she didn't inhale, only nibbled, toyed with it, her gaze locked onto his. She withdrew the cigar from her mouth, but not too far, and smiled fully at him, fingerlings of smoke swirling around her head.

It required little effort for him to return the favor. *Yes, Ms. Owens. You have my attention.* The nearby table of women erupted in laughter. Lacy inhaled again, rolling an eye toward them as if thoroughly bored by their presence. Malcolm chuckled. It was probably true. The women sitting at the table all looked the same. From their long straight hair to their skirts and boots, it looked to him as if they coordinated their outfits for the evening. There didn't seem to be an individual among them. Lacy, on the other hand, was pure distinction. Her short-cropped black hair shone in the dim lighting, the blue of her eyes punctuated her fair skin even from a distance. Her shapely body competed for his attention, and Malcolm imagined what she would look like on the sheets beneath him. The image stirred deep within his loins.

Lacy held the cigar away from her face and took a prim sip from her drink. Neat, tidy, her movements were those of a dancer. The connection struck him. *Was Lacy a dancer?*

He'd wondered how she made it in a big city like Atlanta. According to Delaney, Lacy had only been seventeen when she left, and it wasn't as if Jeremiah had pockets full of money. How did she survive? Did she dance for a living? She had to have done something to pay the bills.

Lacy returned her attention to him and Malcolm pushed off from the bar and headed over. Time to find out. Rewarded by the bump in her gaze, he was heartened to realize she was interested in his approach. But how interested was the more important question. Malcolm neared and delivered smoothly, "Ms. Owens...so nice to see you again."

"Mr. Ward."

As she reached for her hand, she obliged, lifting it from the table for his taking. Lacy cocked her head to one side and watched him bow slightly, placing his lips to her skin for a kiss. Her scent reminded Malcolm of jasmine and spice. Intoxicating. Gliding his lips back and forth, he treated himself to the sensation of silken skin and luscious perfume before she pulled free. She encircled her hand around her glass as though curtailing any further ideas on his part.

Which amused him. Standing fully, he asked, "What's a beautiful woman like you sitting alone in a bar on a Friday night?"

Lacy's smile dipped, but quickly recovered. "I'm enjoying a little quiet time."

"Quiet time?" He glanced around the lounge, purposefully touching upon the dance floor. Two couples entered the bar, the women chatting busily while the men brought up the rear in silence. "From the looks of this place, quiet is the last thing I'd expect."

"Yes," she agreed, "but the real carrying on doesn't start until much later."

"Ah." He nodded, fascinated by the spark in her eye. It had the mark of intelligence, yet the zeal of youth. Lined in a soft navy, her eyes were sultry, enticing. "You don't dance?" Malcolm asked, coating his tone with disappointment.

She giggled. "I love to dance!" Then, as if she realized her breach, walked the comment back a notch. She dropped her gaze back to the cigar in hand, tapping the ashes into an ashtray. "But I'm not in the mood," she said, then cast her gaze downward.

"Not in the mood? With legs like yours, that seems like a crime."

Lacy flipped up her line of thick lashes and replied, "It's my first day back in town and I haven't received the warmest of welcomes."

"From Delaney?" he asked.

"Yes..." she murmured, as though Delaney was only a secondary concern.

"Your sister?"

Curiosity transformed her caution. "You know Annie?"

"Not personally, but I've heard about her."

"Of course," Lacy said, turning away from him, focusing on the cigar in hand. "You were with Delaney today."

"Is that a problem?"

"No, not really," she said, continuing to reflect on her cigar. She brought it to her mouth for another drag. This time, she closed her eyes as she inhaled.

Studying her soft features, her flawless ivory skin, her artfully applied makeup, Malcolm wondered if she was willfully shutting him out. Had he overstayed his welcome? Was it guilt by association?

Delaney was clearly not fond of Lacy. Was the feeling mutual? "Actually, I don't know Delaney all that well. She's a friend of my friend, Nick."

Lacy acknowledged that she heard but continued to stare past him.

"Are you on shaky ground with your sister?"

She flashed a glance to him, the first sign of displeasure licking at her fiery blue eyes. "Shaky isn't the word. More like icy."

At least he had her talking. "I hear you," Malcolm commiserated. "I have a brother and it's the same thing."

Sitting straighter, Lacy swiveled on her seat to face him fully. "You do?"

"Nothing I do seems good enough for him. Success, money, none of it matters."

She knit black brows together. "What do you do that he doesn't approve of?"

"I'm in the hotel business with Nick. Remember?"

She perked to life. "Do you have one here?"

"We hope to."

Several young men pushed through the front door, a ring of rowdy banter following them as they entered. They immediately scouted for a place to sit. No surprise they chose the table next to the high-top full of women. Malcolm watched the men make their way over, eyes roving over the females as they approached.

Lacy appeared confused. "Hope to?"

Malcolm brought scotch to mouth as he pondered her sudden interest. "That's why I'm here. Nick and are I looking at the Ladd Springs property to build our next hotel."

The revelation crushed her spurt of enthusiasm. "Oh."

"You don't like hotels?"

"No, but I don't' think you know what you're getting yourself into."

"Care to enlighten me?"

"Jeremiah Ladd is back in town. He's after Ladd Springs."

"You know Jeremiah?" he asked innocently, knowing full well she ran off with the man.

"Yes. We both live in Atlanta."

"And now you two are back home for a visit?"

It took her a minute to decipher the insinuation. "Oh—we're not together!" she cried.

"Coincidental visit?"

"Er—no, not exactly." Lacy picked up her drink and seemed to seek refuge in her glass, sipping slowly. It was a dodge if he'd ever seen one.

"I understand he had a relationship with your sister," Malcolm said quietly.

Big blue eyes blinked up at him. Skeptical eyes. Wary eyes. "You could call it that."

Malcolm laughed. Part of him enjoyed seeing her squirm, but the other part of him wanted the sexy, sultry Ms. Owens to return.

"Listen." She hushed her voice. Checking the bar for onlookers, she said, "If you're trying to build a hotel on that property, I'll warn you right now that Jeremiah is here to cause trouble."

Malcolm leaned toward her, enjoying a sudden drift of her perfume, her invitation to inside information. "What kind of trouble?"

Lacy looked at him, her gaze darting up and down as though suddenly realizing exactly how close he was standing, then leaned back into her chair. "Well, he wants the property for himself, though I don't see how that's going to happen. Not going up against Delaney, anyway. But Jeremiah is underhanded, especially when there's money involved. And I hear Annie wants it, too, so all I'm saying is you might have to get in line."

For a woman in town for all of twenty-four hours, Lacy was well-informed. "You have personal knowledge of this?"

"I know Jeremiah. My Aunt Frannie told me about Annie."

"Hmm."

"And Loretta."

"Loretta?" Malcolm echoed, intrigued by the growing cast of characters.

Lacy set her cigar into the ashtray. "She's his girlfriend and she's with him."

"I see." The man he met at Delaney's cabin certainly carried an edge to him. How far would he go to get his hands on Ladd Springs?

"I'm telling you, watch your back with Jeremiah."

"Will do," he said.

Lacy's gaze leaped to the door. Her features changed from those of a willing conspirator to intrigued spectator.

He turned to see Felicity's friend, Troy Parker, enter the bar with a bombshell of a woman on his arm. Malcolm cocked a brow. From what he understood, those two boys only had eyes for Delaney's daughter. Malcolm asked Lacy, "You know them?"

"That's Loretta."

"*Jeremiah's girlfriend*?"

"One and the same." Lacy reached for the cigar and inhaled quickly, blowing the smoke out equally as fast, her gaze fixated on the couple. "I saw her with that boy earlier today."

"You did? Where?"

"Aunt Frannie's."

"At the diner?" She nodded. Malcolm didn't believe in coincidences. "Were they talking to one another, or just in the same restaurant, same time?" he probed.

"They weren't exactly talking, more like making eyes at one another."

The blonde spotted Lacy and waved gaily. Lacy summoned a quick smile and waved back.

Troy Parker took note of Lacy first, Malcolm second, his expression coiling around Malcolm with deadly precision. The boy was clearly not pleased to see he had company. Steering the woman toward a high-top on the opposite side of the bar, Troy treated Malcolm and Lacy to nothing but profile.

The kid was a bull, Malcolm thought. You could feel it in his posture, the hard line of his jaw. His twin brother Travis had the look of a Ralph Lauren model. This one had the look of a boxer. He was trying to play to the woman running her hand up and down his arm—the very attractive woman wearing a low cut blouse, skintight skirt, heels as high as skyscrapers—but Malcolm sensed his attention was on him and Lacy at the moment and *not* his date.

Lacy sipped from her drink, continuing her gawk.

"Does she normally step out on Jeremiah like this?" Malcolm asked.

Lacy shrugged. "Loretta likes the boys and definitely likes them young." Soft lines creased across her forehead. "But chasing them in Jeremiah's hometown?" She looked to Malcolm. "It seems a bit odd, don't you think?"

"Not when you consider that young man is intimately familiar with Delaney and Ladd Springs."

"He is?"

"He is"

Sharpening her focus on the couple, Lacy nodded. "Jeremiah probably put her up to this, then." Glancing at Malcolm, she added, "I told you he'll do whatever it takes to get his hands on the prize. You need to listen to me."

"Point noted." Malcolm encircled his gaze around the two across the room like a noose. He bet she was right. Troy crossing enemy lines was a complication he didn't need.

Chapter Seven

Troy turned onto the driveway of his home and pulled off onto the grass near a mess of trees. Trunks and branches were like a wall of blackness, the underbrush thick and impenetrable. He cut his headlights and stared out through the darkness, contemplating his next move. "Why are you stopping, sweetie?" Seated in the center of the bench seat, Loretta Flynn leaned into him, treating Troy to a waft of her flowery perfume and a press from her generous cleavage. She tiptoed her fingers up his chest. "Is there a problem?"

Yeah. No place to take you. But it wasn't gonna stop him. He turned to her and dropped his gaze to her mouth. "I don't think you want to sneak into my bedroom." She giggled. "Can we go to your place?"

Loretta giggled again. "I don't really have a place," she purred, the smell of liquor rising from her breath. "But I don't mind making love in your truck."

"In my truck?"

She pecked his lips. "Sure. Might be more fun."

Troy envisioned them trying to work the angles of his backseat, the discomfort of trying to wedge himself on top of her on the bench cushion and frowned. Not exactly the kind of thrill he wanted for his first time with her, but he wasn't going to miss an opportunity on account of it. Adjusting his eyes to the light, Loretta pulled his hand to her breasts and he hardened. The decision was made. "Once past these trees, we can park off to the side where no one will see us from the house."

"Perfect." Loretta slid her hand over his groin. "Can't wait," she whispered huskily.

Troy switched on his truck lights and jammed his boot to the accelerator. The truck lunged and Loretta cried out as they hit a ditch. "Oh!" Bouncing back against her seat, she grabbed hold of him and laughed. "Four wheeling!" she squealed. He cut to a clearing on the right and extinguished his lights, rolling several yards before cutting the engine.

They wouldn't be discovered here. His parents went to bed early and Travis was home studying for his finals next week—though why he wasted a weekend to do what he could do in one night was beyond Troy. But that was Travis, always the overachiever.

Loretta's fingers unbuttoning his shirt snapped Troy's attention back into the moment. "I've been thinking about this all night," she said, her voice thick with the sluggishness of drink. Shifting his weight, he eased back to give her better access. For once he was glad not to have been drinking right along with her. He'd have the advantage now. "You are one hot specimen of a man, Troy Parker."

He smiled. "You're not too bad yourself."

Continuing down to his waistband, she tugged his shirt free. "You keep flattering me and see where it gets you." Troy smirked as she slid her hands beneath his shirt, roaming the expanse of his chest and stomach. He tightened his muscles as slender fingers meandered over his abs. "You are so strong," she cooed.

Troy lightly grabbed her face and kissed her, plunging his tongue inside, finding her mouth hot and slick. Loretta ran her hands through his hair, gently pulled at his ear lobes, then skimmed her hands down his neck and under his collar. Troy pulled back and commanded, "Back seat."

Without waiting for a response, he shoved his car door open, reached for her hand and pulled her toward him. Loretta scooted across the seat willingly. Troy marveled at how easy she was. He'd never been with a woman he didn't have to work at, to coax with sweet words and promises. The few girls he had slept with demanded he romance them. Which didn't make sense. They hooked up at a party. They were buzzed. Why romance at that point?

Suddenly grateful his dad made him drive the old quad cab, Troy popped open the back door and guided her in. But Loretta stopped, seized his jaw and pulled him down to deliver the deepest, slipperiest kiss he'd ever had. Desire surged. He wanted her naked. Now. Fumbling with her blouse in the dark, he searched for the front buttons.

"Let me help you with that," Loretta said, and worked herself free from his hold. She hopped up into the truck's back seat and a curled finger. "Come here and let me show you."

Didn't have to ask him twice. With the sliver of moonlight they did have, he was going to see everything he could see. Troy moved between her legs and planted another wet kiss on her lips. Loretta returned the kiss a bit sloppily then he watched in awe as her hands reached for the front of her shirt. *She really was going to show him.*

His pulse pounded as he anticipated what she would look like, feel like. He couldn't wait to get his hands on her, his mouth on her, but a flash of light stopped his heart.

Loretta hands stilled at her bra. "What was that?"

Troy whipped his head around to see Travis' truck emerge from behind a cluster of trees. "Crap!"

"Who is it?"

"My brother," he exclaimed and ducked.

"Will he care that we're here?" she asked.

Probably. Troy groaned inwardly. Mr. Goody Two Shoes cared about *everything* his brother did. When the truck stopped then headed their way, Troy dropped his head onto the soft mounds of Loretta's chest. "Crap," he muttered again.

As the truck neared, Travis called out his name. "Troy?"

Troy knew it was game over—for the moment. Lifting from Loretta, he yelled, "Travis, turn the dad gum lights off, will you? You're blinding me!"

Travis parked and walked over to him. "What are you doing, Troy?"

Troy stood, blocking the open back door. Why did his brother have to look so dumbfounded? What did he think he was doing—playing with himself? "I have company, if you don't mind. Now will you get already?"

"Company?" Alarm scored Travis' expression. "Who?"

"None of your dad gum business, *who*." He pulled the unbuttoned shirt up and around his shoulders and squared off with his brother.

But Travis couldn't help himself and had to sneak a peek through the window. He returned a blank look. "Who's she?"

"I done told you," Troy said. "It's none of your business. It isn't Felicity, if that's what you were wondering."

The relief that filled Travis' eyes pissed Troy off, even though his brother claimed, "I never thought it was."

"Don't give me that bull. She's the only one you'd be worried about sitting in a car in the dark with me."

"Troy." Travis slanted his gaze toward the woman in the truck, silently condemning him for talking about another female in this one's presence.

Loretta sat up, pulling her shirt haphazardly into place. "Is everything all right out there?"

"Fine," Troy swiped back. "My brother here was just leaving."

Eyeing Loretta, Travis whispered, "Don't you think she's a bit old?"

"Did you hear that, Loretta? My brother is calling you old."

Scrutinizing her further, her identity registered with Travis. "Isn't she the woman from the diner?"

"One and the same," Troy confirmed proudly.

"What are you doing with her?"

"If I have to explain the finer details of the reproductive system to you, then you're already a lost cause." Troy paused, struck by the sudden urge to hurt his brother. "I guess it *should* be Felicity in there, since you don't seem to know the first thing to do with her."

Travis punched Troy across the jaw. Troy reeled. Loretta screamed. Anger set fire to Travis' gaze. "Don't you ever use Felicity's name like that again."

Troy lunged at him. Grabbing his brother by the shoulders, he plowed him backward to the ground. Running on automatic, Troy whaled fist after fist, making contact wherever and whenever he could.

Loretta was out of the car, shrieking like a crazy woman. "Stop it! Stop it! *Quit!*"

"Get off me," Travis growled. Struggling against the flying fists, he wrapped his legs around Troy's body and tried to roll him.

Troy felt his energy draining. "You're a son of a bitch," he shouted into Travis' face. In a flash, he was slammed onto his back, arms pinned.

Above him, Travis' face was flushed, his eyes bulging in the shadows of his headlights. "I'm the son of a bitch? You're the one who insulted Felicity."

"I didn't insult nobody but you." With a final struggle, Troy went limp. "Get off me," he said, fully expecting his brother to do so.

"Not until you apologize."

"Sorry."

"I should hit you again for that weak response." Travis shoved Troy's arms into the dirt, then lifted from him. He took a step back, but not before giving Troy a swift kick in the legs.

Troy jumped to his feet and went after his brother, but Loretta grabbed his arm. "Stop it, Troy!"

"Now you need to get this woman home," Travis said, "before I tell Mom and Dad."

Loretta stood, mouth agape, as though she'd never seen two men fight.

"What she and I do is my business," Troy said, thumping his chest. "They don't need to know anything about it."

"You don't have any business picking up strangers," Travis replied, then quickly nodded to her. "No offense, ma'am." She closed her mouth with an indignant gawk. Travis drilled Troy with a knowing gaze. "Do it." With that, he climbed back into his truck and continued his drive up to the house.

Troy stood rigid as he trailed the taillights of his brother's truck. Pompous ass.

Loretta was quick to fuss over him. "Are you okay? Did he hurt you?" she asked, touching his chin as she scrutinized his face.

"Nah, he didn't hurt me." Troy pulled her hand away and brushed the dirt from his body. He didn't want sympathy from this woman. He wanted Felicity. He wanted Felicity to want *him* and not Travis. With a last look at Loretta, Troy started buttoning his shirt.

"Is he seriously going to tell your folks?" she asked.

"Doesn't matter. I'm not in the mood anymore."

"What?"

Taking heart at her distress, he said, "Don't worry. We'll do it again." Troy glanced in the direction of his home. "Just not here."

As he watched Loretta put herself back together, he realized they would definitely be back together and soon. If only to piss off his brother.

Chapter Eight

An hour after the posted start time of one o'clock, Malcolm, Nick and Delaney arrived at the Memorial Day party. It was Ashley Fulmer's annual picnic and Delaney claimed it was the event of the season. Ashley was Delaney's mother's best friend, and according to Nick, the woman instrumental in persuading Ernie Ladd to uphold his deathbed promise. Delaney's mother, Susannah Wilkins, died of cancer years ago. The evening of her passing, Ashley claimed Susannah implored her brother Ernie to pass the Ladd Springs property on to the children. He argued against giving anything to his son, Jeremiah Ladd—a sentiment Malcolm fully understood. He hadn't known the man for more than fifteen minutes and could smell the bad blood exuding from his pores. Malcolm knew the type. Jeremiah was out for number one, no one else, and didn't deserve any respect paid with regard to his feelings.

Malcolm didn't know much about Albert's children, but apparently Ernie wasn't concerned with them. And since it was his name on the title, legally he didn't have to be. In the end, it seems Ernie agreed and swore to his dying sister that he'd include Delaney's daughter in any will thus ensuring the property stayed in Ladd hands.

It was a promise witnessed by Ashley Fulmer, one she had been prepared to testify to in a court of law, had matters made it that far. But they didn't. Ernie acquiesced by signing a life estate deed for the sole benefit of Felicity Wilkins. Malcolm suspected she wouldn't be pleased to hear of Jeremiah's challenge to the deed, either. From what he could tell, the woman was firmly entrenched by Delaney's side.

Pulling up to a yard already littered with pickup trucks and the occasional compact and sedan, Malcolm was surprised by the sheer number of vehicles. "This is some shindig, isn't it?" Malcolm said as they found a space some distance from the house.

"Ashley is somewhat of a hub in this town. If she invites you to a party, you come."

Delaney logged those in attendance by their vehicle. The Parkers were here, which meant Felicity was here. Mary Beth and her clan were accounted for, the Fosters, Shores... Malcolm only half-listened as they hiked up the hill to Ashley's home, a ranch-style painted barn red and adorned with flower pots spilling over with color. There was an old wagon wheel propped up on one end of the home and what seemed to Malcolm the mandatory rockers set out across the front porch.

"Makes me wish I brought that pie," Malcolm muttered. He'd purchased a peach pie, but Delaney told him to leave it behind, something about an ongoing feud between Ashley and Fran for title to Best Pie at the county fair.

"Trust me," Delaney told him, easily scaling the steep slope in her jeans and boots, the same slope of land that caused him to be winded from the exertion. "Ashley would have tanned your hide, you walked in with that pie."

Nick chuckled and Malcolm wondered again, was everything a feud in these parts? It was pie. Wouldn't she overlook the flavor? As it stood, he was empty-handed. In his world, showing up to a party without a hostess gift translated to poor manners. But a newbie to these parts, he wasn't about to argue. Nick had been a trusted ally for near twenty years. If his woman said leave the pie, Malcolm would leave the pie.

The trio reached the house, cruising around back to where the action was in full swing. With most of the guests dressed in jeans and boots, Malcolm felt somewhat out of place in white linen shorts and navy silk T-shirt, but he didn't own any jeans and boots. Hiking boots for scouting properties, yes, but not the cowboy variety. Those were Nick's department. As expected, there was a grill in the corner loaded to the brim with burgers and dogs, a steady billow of smoke rising into the blue sky above. Malcolm picked up the scent of a smoker, too, but didn't see one. There was a live band beyond the grill, a group of middle-aged men belting out a lively tune he didn't recognize. But then again, country music wasn't his norm. He preferred jazz, rock, and the occasional hip hop.

Closer to the house was a long table of food, draped with a classic red and white calico print cloth, laden with plates and bowls heaped with food. As he approached, Malcolm recorded the menu to memory: corn on the cob, coleslaw, biscuits, fried chicken, fried something he didn't recognize, mashed potatoes, cornbread, and greens of some sort. They looked like sautéed spinach, but he'd bet they were something else. Southerners weren't known for their penchant for spinach. His stomach growled. It all looked good. But as hungry as he was, there was something more important on his mind. He surveyed the people milling about the grill, the house, the band, searching for sign of Lacy.

Delaney paused. "Hungry?"

"Famished," Nick replied.

"Not yet," Malcolm lied.

"Well, I'm starving," Nick said. "Mind if we leave and grab a bite to eat?"

"You go ahead." Malcolm walked a few steps with them and caught sight of Lacy. His insides warmed. Decked out in fitted red tank and white miniskirt—a very short miniskirt—Lacy kicked up her black booted heels as she moved about the dance floor. He smiled, tapping Nick in passing. "I'll catch up with you kids later."

Nick followed Malcolm's line of vision and grinned. "You do that."

As Nick and Delaney headed for the food table, Malcolm ventured toward the dance floor, more designated section of yard than floor. Off to one side of the band, dozens of men and women danced in rows, except for Lacy. She was one of the coupled dancers being twirled about by some non-descript man.

Of course she was. The band ended the song and immediately picked up with a country tune he did know. *Cotton-Eyed Joe*. The dancers instantly formed several lines. Lacy's dance partner swept her into his arms and spun her around. Even if she'd wanted to line dance, the guy probably couldn't keep his hands off her. That's the way it would be for Malcolm if *he* were out on the dance floor with her.

As the band played, the fiddler took center stage, swinging his body back and forth as his hand whipped bow over strings. Dancers whooped and hollered and all stepped in unison, their movements quick and agile, even the oldest among not missing a beat. *Where did you come from, where did you go. Where did you come from, Cotton-eyed Joe? If it hadn't been...*

Lacy spotted him and smiled mid-twirl. Malcolm wondered at her dance partner. A man of medium build, brown hair, nothing special, he could be someone from her past. Could also be someone new. Lacy was the kind of woman who attracted men like bees to honey. The man led Lacy around with visible skill, his focus completely tied up in her. Malcolm smiled. Sorry to break it to you pal, but that one's taken—though the two were certainly enjoying themselves, Lacy and her partner. But it was hard not to with such a catchy, upbeat tune. Watching the show, Malcolm was struck by the high spirits of the crowd. Was there a way he and Nick could incorporate the music into the hotel? Not their average version of entertainment, that's for sure, but it certainly fit the region. And staying authentic to the region was one of Harris Hotels' trademarks.

His eyes was his tools and his smile was his gun, but all he had come for was having some fun. Dipping and swaying, rocking to the music, Lacy seemed all the more animated now that Malcolm was watching her. A swell of pleasure unfurled inside him. "Enjoy it while you can, darlin'..." he drawled quietly to himself. Malcolm Ward was about to cut in.

Lacy continued to look his way, despite her partner whooping and shouting. A move that told Malcolm there would be no need to cut in—she'd find her way to him eventually. Better to let the bird fly home than chase her around the yard and back.

The song ended and Lacy's partner lifted her from the ground. Admiring the view as she kicked her boots up behind her, Malcolm waited. The band rolled into another twangy tune, this one just as lively as the last but completely unfamiliar to Malcolm. After a moment of chit-chat between Lacy and the man, it appeared she was making her excuses to come see him.

Malcolm chuckled at the crestfallen look on the man's face. Clearly he wasn't ready for the love fest to be over. But Lacy was headed his way and that's all Malcolm cared about.

Trotting over, Lacy landed before him and gaily greeted, "Hi, Malcolm!"

"Hi, Lacy." He slid his gaze up and down her then slung it toward the band. "Looks like you were having fun out there."

"Oh, I *was*. I love to dance!"

"I remember."

A fleeting confusion brushed the sunshine from her features but didn't linger. "Do you like to dance?"

"I do, but I'm afraid I couldn't keep up with this crowd." She giggled. "Your partner looked like he knew a thing or two about the dance floor."

"Who, Calvin?"

Malcolm shrugged. "He and old friend?"

Lacy smiled. "Calvin Foster and I grew up together. He's a year older than me, but our families have known each other forever."

"Ah..." he replied, relieved to know there was one less hurdle to getting next to the pixie standing before him.

"I didn't know you were coming today," she said.

"Wouldn't miss it. From what I hear, this is the only place to be today."

"Oh, it is, it is," she chirped. "Ashley has always thrown the best parties." Lacy glanced around and she frowned. "Did you come with Delaney?"

Not wanting anything to dampen Lacy's mood, he nodded. "But I ditched them right quick," he teased. "I wanted to see you."

She rewarded him with a bashful smile. "Oh, Malcolm, don't be silly." Sliding shiny black curls behind her ear, she scanned the party grounds. "I know Delaney doesn't much want to see me."

Delivered as a casual observation, Malcolm detected something melancholy in her statement. "Oh, I wouldn't say that. I'd attribute it more to her current circumstances. She has a lot on her mind at the moment."

"Jeremiah," Lacy said flatly.

Malcolm arched a brow. "Among other things, yes."

Lacy flashed a hot glance. "Well she doesn't have to worry. He's not here—wouldn't dare set the first foot on Ashley's property."

Malcolm didn't expect him to be. "So how's your friend Loretta?" he asked. "Ever learn what she and the boy were up to?"

"No. We're friends in Atlanta but other than Friday, I haven't seen her."

"Are you having a good time?"

She tipped her chin upward and dished out a small pout. "Not really."

"Why not?"

"I seem to be persona non great around here."

"You mean grata."

A question gathered in her eyes. "Huh?"

He shook his head. "Never mind."

She dismissed him with a wave. "Same thing."

Malcolm noticed her staring across the crowd and he followed her gaze. On the opposite side of the food table, an attractive brunette strolled to a stop. As she skimmed the crowd, she didn't appear happy to be here. More tense, edgy than a Memorial Day picnic warranted. Conservatively dressed in white T-shirt and jeans, a red scarf tied at her waist in lieu of belt, she looked familiar. "Something interesting?"

"No," she snapped, but her stare turned glower.

"If eyes were daggers, someone would be dead right about now." Lacy swung a petulant gaze his way, as if she were about to object. Instead, she smacked her beautiful, glossy red lips closed. Suddenly struck by the resemblance, Malcolm slipped her a knowing gaze. "Your sister, I presume?"

She turned, mouth agape. "How did you know?"

He glanced back in the direction Lacy had been staring and commented, "She's the only other woman here with black hair and memorable blue eyes."

"There's nothing memorable about Annie." She swiped him with a foul look. "She's mean. Pure hate."

From what Malcolm understood, she had good reason. But bringing that up with the beautiful young woman before him was not going to happen. "How about I get you something to eat?" he asked.

"No, thank you," she replied, absorbed by her sister's presence.

Getting nowhere fast, Malcolm decided to switch tactics. After all, he was here for information, and of course, the company of a beautiful woman. "Have you talked to Jeremiah since he's been back in town?"

"No," she snipped. "And I don't intend to, either." Her expression abruptly changed, dulling the point of hate to a blunt, prurient curiosity. Malcolm checked the source and saw Lacy's dance partner stop and embrace her sister.

Suddenly, Lacy kicked into motion. In stunned silence, Malcolm watched her strut across the lawn, smoothly threading her way through clusters of people until she landed front and center between the man and her sister in a swan dive of sorts. Her body language was fluid, easy, resembling none of the tense discomfort he had witnessed only moments ago. Malcolm rubbed his chin. He had to hand it to her, she made an amazing transformation. Which peaked his curiosity. Why did she find this man so interesting? Was it the fact he was talking to her sister? Determined to find out, he made his way closer.

Lacy had become animated, coy. She was standing near the man, touching his arm every so often in what Malcolm recognized as full flirtation mode. Longing stirred. She was laying it on thick, and where the man should be enthralled with the attention, he wasn't. Oddly, he was more interested in her sister at the moment. Intrigued by the turn of events, Malcolm shifted his weight, continuing to stare.

Malcolm would entertain Lacy over her sister all day long. Granted both were attractive, but Lacy's brand of energy was exciting, stimulating. He'd take her for a swing on the dance floor if she wanted, run his hands up and down the low sway of her back, the round of her bottom. He'd hold her close, pressing her soft curves against him. Oh, he'd keep Lacy close and then some. But not this fellow. In what appeared to be a surprise to Lacy, the man and her sister excused themselves and headed for the dance floor. Engrossed by the state of affairs, Malcolm observed Lacy's reaction with amusement. When she realized the man had dumped her for her sister, steam blew out her ears. Malcolm smiled. *There, there, sweetheart. Come cry on my shoulder.*

"Where's your lady friend?"

Nick's voice startled Malcolm. "She's playing a game of cat and mouse," he replied, amused by the affair.

Standing by his side, Nick glanced in her direction. "Did you have a chance to speak with her?"

"I did, but with no measurable results."

Nick smiled, a spark firing in the black of his eyes. "You're losing your touch, Mal."

"I'm just getting started."

"Listen," Nick said, lowering his voice. "It looks like we may have another problem."

"I'm listening," Malcolm said, watching in dismay as Lacy headed indoors. Was she leaving?

"Travis and Troy are on the outs. In fact, Troy is sporting a shiner."

The names snagged Malcolm back to Nick, pulling his gaze from the home's back door where Lacy had entered. "What?"

"They're at odds right now, but I'm not clear on the reason."

"Could it have anything to do with Troy playing footsies with Jeremiah's girlfriend?"

"That's what I'm concerned about."

"Well, you know I don't believe in coincidences."

"Neither do I." Nick glanced around them. No one was paying any attention to Delaney's new invitees, two strangers in a circle of hometown friends and relatives. "Do you think the woman is trying to get information from the kid?"

"I absolutely think she is, and she's going about it the right way."

Nick raked a hand through his hair. "The boy may know about Ernie. And if he does, there's no reason to believe he wouldn't share it with a woman asking the right questions."

"Trust me, Nick. This lady doesn't even have to ask. She'll whisper in his ear and he'll bark like a dog."

Nick nodded with a smirk. "Don't we all?"

At the approach of Delaney and Felicity, the men quieted. Delaney, carrying a plate piled with barbecue pulled pork, handed it to Nick. "This should hold you over for a while."

"God, I love you," he said to her.

The comment marshaled a wry smile to her mouth. "You're easy."

"I know." He winked. "Lucky for you."

"Though one more serving of that and you'll be splayed out on the couch for the duration."

"Not a bad way to spend an afternoon."

Delaney grunted in response. In the few short weeks Malcolm had known her, he had been surprised by her domestic inclinations. To meet her outside of her family, you'd think Delaney couldn't locate the first pot or pan, let alone know what to do with them. But he'd learned otherwise. The woman could cook like nobody's business and seemed to enjoy waiting on Nick and Felicity.

"You don't look like you're having fun, Felicity," Malcolm said, reflecting on the dull look in otherwise bright features. Fair-skinned, freckle-faced, the teen was a pretty girl, reminding him of a waif model he knew in Los Angeles.

"I'm good." She gave a quick nod, brushed fine strands of strawberry blonde hair behind an ear. "I'm worried about Travis and Troy."

"Why?"

"They're mad at each other."

"Is that unusual?" He glanced to Nick and Delaney as he said, "I don't know about them, but my early days with my brother were loaded with fights."

"Oh, they fight, but usually it's no big deal. They've never been to the point where they're not speaking to each other."

"Don't worry, honey," Delaney said and rubbed her daughter's back. "They'll be fine. It's just a rough patch of trouble, but they'll get over it."

Malcolm glanced at Nick and asked for silent permission to broach the subject of Troy and Loretta. Nick cocked his head. *Why not?*

"I wonder if it has anything to do with the woman I saw Troy with the other night," Malcolm offered, "over at Whiskey Joe's?"

"Whiskey Joe's?" Felicity asked, surprised by the mention of the local lounge.

Malcolm nodded. "He was there with an older blonde. They seemed kinda friendly."

Shock would have been a mild description for the girl's reaction. He flicked a glance toward her mother. Did she not know that a teenage boy had desires?

"I don't know who it could be..." Felicity said, absorbed by the revelation.

"I heard it was Jeremiah's girlfriend," Malcolm said and braced himself for the fireworks.

Felicity freaked, spots of freckles reddening against her skin. "What?"

Delaney gawked. "*Jeremiah's* girlfriend?"

Nick stood passive while Malcolm elaborated, "That's what I understand." He looked between the women. "Any reason why those two would know each other?"

"None," Delaney remarked. "Except one." She turned slowly to her daughter and lightly grasped her arm. "Felicity," she said, urging the girl to look into her face. She did so, but it was clear she feared what came next. "Did you tell Travis and Troy about Ernie? About him being sick?"

Felicity's lips began to quiver.

"We need to know. It's important," Delaney said gently but sternly.

The girl went pale. "I did."

At the admission, Malcolm, Nick and Delaney stilled.

"Is that a problem?" she cried, comprehending that somehow she may have thrown the match into the tinder box.

Chapter Nine

Sitting alone on the front porch, Casey Owens could hear the band banging out an old country song, probably packing the dance floor with old people. The songs they played were ancient and definitely not her thing. She pre-ferred contemporary music and not the dancing kind. On the front porch, the smell of smoke didn't coat her clothes and skin. How people stood next to the grill swamped by gray smoke without plugging their noses was beyond her. It was too much—and she *liked* hamburgers! But smoke saturated clothing was not her idea of a good time. She was only here because she had to be.

As she nursed a tall glass of iced tea, Casey's thoughts went to Troy, Travis and Felicity. As usual, Travis and Felici-ty were stuck together like two pigs at a trough. Normally Troy would be right there with them, but for some reason he kept his distance from the pair today—which was weird. He even boasted a black eye, something Casey had the sneaking suspicion Travis might have had something to do with. That part wasn't so weird. Those two scrapped all the time, but mostly for play, usually started by Troy. Had something changed between them?

Pondering the matter, Casey pulled a slow sip from her drink, the liquid cold, but the tea and ice running together in a bland mess of taste. She set the glass on the floor beside her rocker, tucking it out of the way of her chair. Pulling her legs into a fold beneath her, Casey peered out over the heap of cars and wondered how much longer she had to stay. Her mom would have a fit if she left early. Said it would be a per-sonal insult to Miss Ashley if they didn't stay for at least a few hours. Casey didn't see how it would matter one way or the other. Her godmother was so busy running back and forth between the kitchen and the grill, where Mr. Fulmer kept hollering like a chicken with his head cut off. *Ashley, fetch me some more butter*! *Ashley, we need more cheese out here*! *Ashley, where in tarnation is my spatula*?

If Casey had a husband yelling at her like that, she'd tell him to get his own spatula. She wasn't his servant. But not Miss Ashley. She just ran and ran and ran.

"Hey, darlin'."

Casey's heart stopped, then thudded through her chest like a freight train. "Miss Ashley! I didn't hear you come out," she said, her cheeks flushing hot.

Ashley moseyed near and lowered to a white wicker rocker beside Casey, laughing as usual. "Oh, child—I'm like a thief to the cookie jar when I need to be!"

Casey tried to smile, but the effort failed. Good thing Miss Ashley couldn't read minds. "I guess..."

Ashley sighed. "I'm as full as a stuffed pork chop, I couldn't eat another bite."

Dressed in rhinestone-punched red, white and blue, her boots candy apple red and scuffed with mud, Casey suppressed a chuckle. Splattered with barbecue sauce and grease stains, Miss Ashley's sparkly stars and stripes apron looked as if she ate a dozen stuffed pork chops, some hamburgers, and a few greens to go with them! It was a shame to ruin a pretty apron like Miss Ashley always wore, but Casey knew there were ten more just like this one hanging in her pantry. As to her own wardrobe, Casey had decided against anything red, white or blue just to irk her mother.

In no hurry Ashley eased back in her seat, took a cloth from an apron pocket and dabbed her brow. Her heavy makeup was beginning to slip from the heat, leaving a shine of perspiration in its place. "I swear Mother Nature must be having hot flashes—it's so hot you could pull a baked potato right out of the ground!" She grinned at Casey. When Ashley's smile didn't catch a response, it withered to a frown.

Blue eyes burrowed in. "Child, you know the party's out back. What are you doing out here by your lonesome?"

Casey turned from her. Taking a deep calming breath, she pulled knees to her chest and replied, "I know. Guess I'm not much in the mood for a party."

"What's the matter?"

"Nothing."

"Nothing?" Ashley waved her off and tucked the hand-kerchief back in her pocket. "Nothing doesn't come hide out on the front porch like a bandit." With a slanted gaze she asked, "Who you running from—your momma?'

Casey shook her head and plopped her chin onto her knees.

"Now don't you go fibbin' to your Great-Godmother. It's my job to keep you on the straight and narrow and I intend to see that you do."

Casey smiled. "I'm straight, Miss Ashley."

"Are you?" Ashley leaned forward and placed a hand to Casey's back. She stroked her hair. Tender and caring as she probed, "Are you really?"

"I am." Though at times, Casey wished she weren't. Life was easier when she didn't have to think about everything— her mother's disappointment, the family feud over Ladd Springs, the identity of her father. Most days she'd rather up and forget about it all.

"You know I worry about you, Casey Melody."

"I know."

"You have a beautiful life ahead of you. All you need to do is step up and claim it. Grab a good strong hold of it and say, 'Ready or not—here I come!'"

Casey grinned. She'd always liked Miss Ashley. Positive and outgoing should be her middle name. Unlike her mother, Ashley believed in Casey, believed she could do anything and everything and helped encourage her to chase her dreams. Her mother? Casey could see the disappointment in her mom's eyes as clearly as if it were branded across her blue eyes. Clear as a mountain stream, her mom looked at her own flesh and blood and thought, *You'll never be anything. You're going nowhere and on the fast train to get there.*

"Hey, Miss Ashley."

Casey's nerves zipped through her stomach at the sound of Troy's voice. She gulped, lifting her head from her knees as Troy sauntered over.

"Well hey, good-looking," Ashley said easily, her smile large and welcoming.

Casey privately agreed. Longish brown hair swept over his brow to one side drawing attention to his dark brown eyes. Like her, Troy skipped the red, white and blue and chose a snug black T-shirt instead, tucked neatly into his blue jeans. His cowboy boots were the same dusty brown he always wore, and Casey had to admit there was something strong and manly about Troy Parker. Something that always made her skin tingle.

Troy peered down at her and said, "I've been looking everywhere for you, Casey."

His expression was friendly, sincere, as though he really meant it. Heartbeats fluttered in her breast. "You have?"

He nodded. "Your mom said you'd be out here."

"I'm here," she confirmed, hating that she sounded so stupid. Lowering her legs, she leaned back in her rocking chair and tried to sit like a normal person.

Ashley lifted from her seat, the wood creaking beneath the change in weight. "I think I hear Booker calling my name," she said with a wink. "You know I can't keep the grill sergeant waiting too long, it jerks a knot in his tail." Ashley ambled toward the front door and muttered, "Bless his heart, when God handed out patience, Booker was standing behind the door."

Troy smirked.

Ashley smacked his arm and said, "Don't you go repeating what I said either, young man. I'll have your hide, you mention the first word to Mr. Fulmer."

Troy laughed and held his hands up in surrender. "Dad gum, Miss Ashley—I wouldn't think of it!"

She grinned. "Good."

He shook his head slowly and watched her with a wary eye, almost as if he was anticipating another whack. "My momma didn't raise no fool."

"No she didn't," Ashley agreed, "despite that foolish bruise on your face." Troy touched the lump beneath his eye as she added, "In fact, I think I'll go tell her what a fine young man you are, this minute."

Casey noticed Troy's cheeks tinge ever so slightly.

"Yes ma'am," he replied. When Ashley disappeared into the house, he turned to Casey. "You want some company, or should I leave you alone?"

She shrugged. Casey didn't want him to think she was interested. It'd only make her feel dumb when he turned her down. "If you want."

Troy took Ashley's chair and settled in, as though he planned to stay awhile. As he gazed out over the sloped lawn, his expression quieted. Casey looked over the front lawn, too, but watched him from the corner of her eye, waiting for him to make the next move. She surely wasn't going to make it!

"How ya doing?" he asked finally, concern rippling through his features in what Casey found to be a total letdown. He was just being nice. On account of her overdose.

"Good." She didn't want to talk about it. Not with Troy and not with anyone. It only served to remind her what a failure she was—even when trying to kill herself.

"I'm glad." Troy leaned forward. Elbows to knees he took her in, his eyes searching hers as though the truth lay within them and she was withholding. "I'd hate it if anything happened to you, Casey."

Desire scattered in her chest. "You would?"

He nodded. "Of course. We've been friends since we were two, haven't we?"

Friends. Casey nodded glumly. "Yeah. We have."

"Other than Travis and Felicity, there ain't nobody that knows me better than you."

She inclined her head, considering the statement. Probably true. While the Parker boys didn't hang out with her like they did Felicity, they still saw each other in school, after school, around town, parties like this one. Their families were friends.

"And when friends have problems, they talk, don't they?"

"They do," she said, suddenly aware he might be going somewhere with this line of conversation—somewhere halfway important.

"I've been thinking..."

Casey waited, but when he didn't continue, she prodded, "Thinking about what?"

"I might not go to college," Troy said, holding her firmly in his gaze as though purposely trapping her so she couldn't avoid him.

But she had no interest in avoiding him. "Not go to college?" she asked, astounded by the revelation.

Troy nodded. "I mean, what's the point? I want to work with horses, not books or computers. Why do I need to go to college for that?" He dropped his gaze to the ground and kicked at a stray clump of dirt. "It'll only waste my time."

"But Troy, you're already signed up and accepted. You can't just *quit*."

"Can't I?" He turned, whipping the hair from his eyes. "Why not?"

"Because," she said, grasping for a reason, advice to give him that would dissuade him from dropping out.

But she had none. Troy was the finest horseman she knew. He handled feisty stallions better than anyone she'd ever seen, could calm an angry mare, deliver a foal... Why, Casey didn't think there was anything Troy *couldn't* do with a horse.

"If they had a horse college, I'd go. But they don't."

"They don't?"

"They don't. Not that I ever heard of, anyway." He cast his gaze out over the front, a faraway look taking hold of him.

"What do your parents think?" she asked, genuinely interested in hearing the answer.

"Haven't told them yet."

Casey understood completely. Morton and Betty Ann Parker had high expectations. From grades to behavior, their kids were expected to perform and expected to perform well. Casey always thought it a bit extreme. Not everyone could be perfect. "Are you afraid they'll say no?"

"Dad gum, Casey—I ain't afraid of nothing of the sort," he said heatedly.

Casey believed otherwise, but kept it to herself. Troy was too proud to admit he was scared. No sense in riling him by pressing the point. "When do you plan to tell them?"

He turned his gaze out over the field again. "Soon."

Soon. Did that mean days or weeks? As it stood, the boys were set to leave for college in another two months.

Dark eyes flashed. "What do you think? Do you think it's a good idea?"

Self-doubt was not something she was accustomed to seeing in Troy Parker. He was usually so sure of himself, it was odd to see him hesitate. "What do you care what I think?" she murmured.

"I value your opinion. Do you think I'm ruining my life?"

The statement tugged at her heart. *He valued her opinion.* Troy cared what she thought. Casey shook her head defiantly. "No. I don't think you're ruining your life. I think you're the best dang horseman around."

The compliment rallied a smile to his lips. "You do?"

Sapped by a sudden case of nerves, she pulled her legs up and hugged them close. "I do. I really, really do."

The two sat quietly, the distant sounds of Ashley's party music and rowdy crowd hanging in the background. While Casey wasn't quite sure why Troy was sitting with her instead of Felicity, she wasn't about to complain. She'd always wished he'd give her more than a friendly glance, but he and

Travis were forever fighting over Felicity and it drove Casey nuts. What did Felicity have that was so special?

Casey glanced askance and thought whatever it was, it didn't seem to be having its normal effect. Today was different. Troy had shared his plans about college with her, not Felicity. Better yet, he cared what she thought about it. For Casey, it was a magical combination. Troy pulled out of his trance and from the corner of her eye, she could see him staring at her. Nerves fired in her breast, fluttered against her ribs. What was he thinking? Did he find her attractive? Casey made a steel band of her arms around her knees.

"Do you mind if I ask you a sensitive question?" he asked.

Startled by the tender quality to his voice, she turned. Looking into his eyes, the eyes of a friend, the eyes of a man she desperately liked, Casey hoped Troy wouldn't ask about the drugs. *It was a mistake. It was stupid.* "What?" she replied, preferring he ask her if she liked him, and did she want to go out on a date?

"Do you know your daddy's in town?"

Like a hen's egg dropped to the cement, Casey's hopes crashed.

"Do you know him, Casey?" Troy begged the question, as though it were of vital importance to him. "Have you seen him?"

She hugged her legs hard and shook her head.

"Dad gum, hasn't your momma ever told you?"

"Told me what?" Casey demanded, suddenly angry. "That some man with the last name of Ladd is my father? That he lives in Atlanta and doesn't give a whip about me?"

Thunderclouds entered his gaze, his brown eyes a squall of emotion. The storm eased and he asked calmly, "If your daddy gets Ladd Springs from Delaney, you could get a piece of it, too, right?"

Casey stared at him, barely able to comprehend what he was saying, so torn was she between her mother's greedy ploy at getting title to Ladd Springs and the intensity in

Troy's features. He looked as if he had a horse in the ring, as if it were personal.

"Would you want that?" he asked.

"Want what—to be a part of the Ladd family? To be related to a woman who hates me, a cousin who—" Casey bit the words from her tongue. She didn't even want to say Felicity's name for it might steal Troy's focus from *her*.

Troy looked out over the yard, the cars, and didn't say another word.

Why did he care about her father, about Ladd Springs? What did it matter to Troy one way or the other? Why did her mother have to get pregnant by a man who didn't love her? Sensing Troy was closing down, she wanted to scream, *What do you want, Troy? Why do you care?* Fighting back a wave of tears, Casey thought, *Do you, Troy? Do you care about me?*

Chapter Ten

Annie Owens sat alone at her dining room table. Her lunch was cold, her iced tea warm, her life was falling apart. In the blink of an eye, her best friendship had shattered before her very eyes. Candi had turned from confidant to traitor. How could she have slept with Jeremiah? Had she done so before Lacy? During?

Humiliation slithered into Annie's heart. How could the two women closest to her betray her that way? It was unconscionable. Unacceptable. And to think Candi called Jeremiah back home to fight for Ladd Springs. Why? To help her with her paternity suit Candi had said? Or did she want to see him again for her own gratification... Visions of Jeremiah leaning close to Candi at the salon soured Annie's stomach. She didn't *look* unhappy when Annie walked in. And if she hadn't walked in on them, would Candi have confessed?

Annie dumped her gaze to the plate of leftover barbecued pork. The sandwich that had been half-eaten during the picnic today remained so, because she was in no mood to eat. She was in no mood to plot and plan, to hash out or forgive. Annie was in no mood for anything. Jeremiah Ladd was in town, yet had barely said hello, barely acknowledged her presence. Casey deserved better. Her daughter deserved a man who cared about her, a man who cared enough to at least acknowledge her existence.

But that man wasn't Jeremiah Ladd. Annie's heart ached at the thought. It was her fault. Pushing the plate of food aside, Annie slid her elbows forward and dropped her head to rest in her palms. Casey had a louse for a father because her mother had picked him. Maybe not picked him to be the father of her child, but when you slept with a man, that was a possibility. She knew the facts. She'd played the game. And lost.

How could Annie ever make it up to her daughter? Casey's father was here in the flesh, traipsing through town and the girl had no clue. Casey wouldn't know Jeremiah if she saw him walking down the street. Years ago, when she had asked about him, Annie had told her the truth. *Your father is Jeremiah Ladd.* She had explained his absence with the lie of two adults not getting along, going their separate ways because it wasn't meant to be. She had neglected to tell Casey that Jeremiah went *his* way with her Aunt Lacy. It was a fact that would only serve to add to her pain. And Casey was in pain. Her rebellious spouts stemmed from an attitude that went beyond teenage hormones. Casey blamed her mother for her father's absence and Annie accepted it without recourse. To fight would only reveal the uglier side of the truth. *Your father dumped your mother, ran off with your aunt and to this day refuses to claim you.*

Suddenly, the years felt like a crushing vise-grip around her heart. They squeezed the life from her. Like a boot to the head, they crushed her. Annie rued the day she'd ever taken up with Jeremiah. Why she had wanted him, she couldn't remember anymore. Only that she had. For as long as she could remember, Annie had wanted Jeremiah Ladd but he'd been stuck at the hip to Delaney Wilkins.

And scores of other women.

The man was low, dirtier than a hog wallowing in the mud. But he hadn't heard the last from her. Annie would fight for the property. She would fight him and Delaney, and whoever else got in her way. She might not have been able to give Casey a loving father, but she sure as heck could give her what that father wanted for himself. Ladd Springs. If Jeremiah could fight for his share of the property, then Annie could fight for Casey's. Ernie Ladd would be caught in the middle, no doubt about it, but it was unavoidable. A quick sadness stabbed at her. The man was sick. Terminal. Living out his last days squabbling over land wasn't the way Annie wanted him to go, but Ernie should have listened to her before he thought about signing over the property to Felicity. Casey was equally as entitled to inherit the land, but he wouldn't listen. In fact, Ernie shut her down cold in the most offensive of ways.

Thoughts of Ladd troubles brought to mind Annie's own family woes. Daddy died of a heart attack when he was much too young, and her Momma moved out right after Lacy. Up and moved on without her daughter, Annie. She claimed Annie was a woman of age and it was high time she started taking care of herself. Didn't matter that Annie didn't want her mother to go, that she would have left right along with her had her momma extended the invite. But her mother's intent had been clear. It was time to move on and start fresh. Tears pricked Annie's eyes.

Her mother had gone and not taken her daughter with her.

It was a day Annie would never forget. Not only had Jeremiah left her, but her mother had deserted her, too. Lacy was no different. Visions of her sister prancing into the salon the other day, acting as though they could mend fences with a hug and smile, was insulting. Annie might not be able to count on anyone, but she still had her pride. She could still walk through town with her head held high and her heart and soul free and clear. But it was a road she'd be walking alone. Anger welled. Candi's betrayal rubbed raw. Could no one be trusted anymore? They were cheats and liars—the lot of them—but Casey would be able to count on *her*. Annie would not forsake her daughter, no matter how trying the girl might become. Annie would prove to Casey that not all people left. Not all parents abandoned. Jeremiah might not acknowledge he was her father, but that didn't mean Annie couldn't prove it. With him in town, her lawyer could serve him papers and *force* him to take that paternity test. Then Casey would know for sure. Delaney would know for sure. And no one could deny her child was a Ladd.

For all the good it would do her. Annie pushed back
from the table abruptly. She might not be able to secure a por-
tion of Ladd Springs in her child's name, but the question
would be settled. Once and for all, everyone in this one corner town would know that Casey Melody was a Ladd, not an
Owens—and just as entitled to the wealth of Ladd Springs as
Felicity. Tomorrow. Tomorrow she would pay a visit to her
lawyer and put an end to the doubt.

Annie hurried down the sidewalk, mentally rehearsing
her conversation with the lawyer. *I wanted to inform you that
Jeremiah Ladd, the father of my child, is in town. I'm prepared to press forward immediately with the petition for the
paternity test.* Agitation churned. Heat rose beneath her hair,
the midday sun hot on her skin. Darn it, she had gone over
this! She needed to get it right. She needed to sound calm and
professional. Detached. She was within her rights, the lawyer
had said so. Would it matter to a judge that her daughter was
almost eighteen?

Fear spiraled down her spine. She hoped not. This was
her last chance. This was her last chance to prove once and
for all that Casey was Jeremiah's flesh and blood. His daughter. What if the lawyer told her to forget about it? Annie's
research via the internet last night indicated she could file a
claim until Casey was twenty-one. While Casey was techni-
cally an adult, Annie should still be able to force the paternity
test. Maybe even sue for back child support.

Annie was so tired of playing the "what if" game over
and over and over. What if the information she found online
was wrong? What if Jeremiah refused? Would they spend the
next three years in court? She didn't have that kind of money!

Did he?

Reading the name of her lawyer plastered over a door on
a small, one-story building, Annie's nerves ripped and tore.
Dakota Law and Associates. It was now or never. Casey was
probably too old to expect any financial support from Jeremiah, but at least it would solidify her status as a Ladd.

Annie pulled a tissue from her purse and dabbed at her nose, her cheeks. Crumpling it, she stuffed the paper into a side pocket and froze, paralyzed to move. For the space of several seconds, her heart came to a complete standstill. Not twenty feet away from her, Jeremiah Ladd strode out the front door of her lawyer's office. *Her* lawyer's office. A shudder ran through her. What was he doing there?

Jeremiah's eyes lit up at the sight of her and he sauntered over, the turquoise of his shirt reflecting brightly in the morning sun in a glaring sheet of blue. "Hey, Annie."

Perspiration broke out beneath the silk of her top. Annie's throat closed.

"Fancy meetin' you here." He glanced back at the building. "You have business with Mr. Dakota?"

She clutched her purse to her side. Vocal cords scratched and scraped as she replied, "I do."

Jeremiah drew closer. "What's it about?"

"None of your business," she wanted to shout, and smack the smirk from his face. Visions of him and Candi together congealed in her mind's eye.

"You heard about Ladd Springs?" he asked.

Annie stared at him. The man was clueless. Utterly clueless.

Jeremiah made a click with his mouth and said, "Well, I'm here to get what's mine. Delaney's trying to steal it from me, but I'm not going to let her. That little fox is going to get what's coming to her."

And so will you. A strange band of courage encircled Annie's heart. She pushed her shoulders back and said, "I'm here to establish paternity for my daughter, Jeremiah." She watched for it to register and it did—quickly.

"You still trying to put her on me?"

Good. The statement erased all trace of his previous ease. Jeremiah understood the implications of her statement, clear as the blue sky above. "Casey is your daughter," Annie said flatly. "I intend to prove it once and for all." Unlike Atlanta where he managed to dodge her summons, he could not hide from her around here. These buildings had eyes and ears. Someone would know where to find him at the drop of a gavel. "And when I do, I will see to it that she gets her rightful share of Ladd Springs."

His brow rose at the revelation. "So that's what you're after."

"I'm after doing what's right, Jeremiah. It's been long overdue." A concept he clearly didn't comprehend.

"You're wasting your time, Annie. I know you slept with Clem Sweeney before I left, and I bet your illegitimate brat belongs to him."

Annie slapped him across the face.

Jeremiah shot a hand to his cheek.

Shocked by her response, she curled her fingers into her stinging palm, pressed it to her beating heart. She hit Jeremiah!

He stared at her, rubbing his cheek. A smile twisted his lips. "If it makes you feel any better, I'll tell him when I see him." Without another word, he stalked off.

Annie couldn't believe what she had done. Slapping Jeremiah—was she crazy? Staring after him, she pulled herself together and ran for the lawyer's office. Grabbing the cold metal door handle, she pushed inside, pulse racing. Had she lost her mind?

Jeremiah sat alone in his truck in the parking lot, behind the single-story cement block building. Painted white and lined with black metal doors, it was the strip center that ran down Main Street, the one where Candi's salon was located. Loretta was off trying to get information from the Parker kid after her night at Whiskey Joe's turned up zilch. She got nothing, except a second chance. They were having lunch at Fran's Diner, and this time, she'd better not blow it.

Speaking of blow, Jeremiah needed to blow off some steam. Running into Annie outside the lawyer's office this morning had been a complete surprise, as had her reaction. The bitch actually hit him! If she thought that was the way to get him to acknowledge her bastard child, she had another thought coming. There was no way in hell he would claim that kid as his own, even if she was his, especially since Annie seemed to think the girl was her ticket to *his* inheritance. Did she think all she had to do was prove the kid belonged to him and she had her ticket to his dough?

In her dreams, he fumed inwardly. *In her dreams*. Why Candi hadn't told him that little morsel was something else he needed to find out, but getting the lowdown from her while she was in the salon wasn't gonna to work. Approaching her out back would save him from gawking strangers while he coaxed her into giving him the information he wanted.

So he sat. And waited. Eventually, Candi would have to come out of the salon. Since it was almost the lunch hour, he anticipated that time to be soon. After a few minutes, the salon's rear exit door opened and out pushed an old woman. Jeremiah checked his watch. High noon. As he imagined, the women were flocking to their cars like cows to sweet feed. Two more followed, one's head dumped in her purse as she searched it, most likely for car keys. All three women drove off. The minutes ticked by. With his engine turned off, the sun baked his truck, raising the interior heat to unbearable levels. Jeremiah swiped the moisture from his brow, his upper lip. He'd run his air-conditioner, but who knew how long he was going to have to wait and running gas cost money. Money he didn't have.

The salon door swung open again and Jeremiah's insides shifted. *Bingo*. He pushed out his car door and strode toward Candi. As though she sensed his presence, Candi looked up. He savored the look of fear that swept her features. That's right. *You should be scared. Lying to me about your intentions was a dumb move.*

Candi hurried to her car—as though she would beat him to it—but Jeremiah was faster and pulled the keys from her hand. "Hey, baby, why the rush?"

"Jeremiah!" Candi exclaimed. She fired a glance around the parking lot, heartbeats stampeded through her chest. The other hairstylists were nowhere to be seen. Narrowing in on him, she wondered how she missed his approach in the outrageous blue shirt. "What do you want now?"

"Information."

Candi shuddered. The word slithered out like a snake's tongue. "I told you everything I know."

"Really?"

"Yes, *really*. Now if you don't mind, I'm in a hurry." She tried to grab her keys, but anticipating the move, he whisked them behind his back.

"Actually, I do mind." He smirked. "You see, I ran into Annie at the lawyer's office this morning."

Candi's heart missed a beat. Heat clung to her skin, moist and hot beneath the hair on her neck. "So?"

"Seems she thinks she can file a lawsuit for the property, on account of Casey being my daughter."

"Well." Candi paused. "She is."

Jeremiah chuckled. "Now, now, let's not leap to conclusions. We both know she slept with your brother." He cocked his head in a pompous move, gathering his brow. "For all I know, the kid is his."

"She did not!"

"Did, too."

"She didn't," Candi insisted. "She would have told me."

"Maybe your friend isn't as good a friend as you think she is," he said, pleasure licking at his golden-brown eyes.

"But still, Clem isn't Casey's father. He can't be."

"I don't know that. A woman sleeps with a man, she can get pregnant."

"But Jeremiah, Clem is sterile."

"So what?"

"*So what?*" She gaped at him. Was he that ignorant? "It means he can't possibly be Casey's father."

With a hitch of his chin, he thrust, "Prove it."

"I don't have to prove it—everyone in the family knows!" Why was he being so difficult? Did he really not get it?

"Tell it to the judge, baby. I told Annie the same thing and she shut up pretty quick about it." His tone grew urgent. "Now speaking of your brother, where is he?"

Realizing Jeremiah didn't have any business with her, Candi relaxed, but only slightly. It was best a girl keep her guard up around a man like him. "I don't know."

"My buddies tell me he was pretty tight with my old man and I want to talk to him."

"Did your buddies also tell you that he kidnapped Delaney?"

Jeremiah laughed. "That little hot-head probably deserved it!"

"Jeremiah Ladd, you are a despicable human being. I should never have called you." Her thoughts went quickly to Annie. *She* never planned on calling him. If only Candi hadn't been short-sighted and selfish. God knows, she'd been thinking of herself when she called Jeremiah, thinking how if she could help Annie get a piece of Ladd Springs, Annie would loan her the money to open up her own salon.

It had been a mistake. And now she was paying the price.

"Ah, but you did, sweetheart." He bowed his head toward her. "You did."

She glared. Maybe she could make it up to Annie. If she was worried about Clem being Casey's father, the knowledge of his sterility might be just the tidbit Candi needed to get back in Annie's good graces.

"Now I want to talk to your brother," Jeremiah repeated. "Where is he?"

"Probably in jail, where he belongs."

Jeremiah paused. With a devilish smile, he gazed at her, drew a finger down the length of her bangs. "When did you get so mean, Candi?"

She shook free of his touch. "When I started getting a lick of sense about me."

He chuckled, his eyes mocking. "Make my life easy, will you? Where does he hang out?"

"I don't know and I don't care," she snapped and shoved past him to her car. "Now give me my keys before I start screaming." Oh *yes*, Annie would hear about this. Jeremiah was a no good lowlife and Candi would help her friend put him where he belonged—in court—paying not only child support but half his stake in Ladd Springs.

Chapter Eleven

Parked at a table in her aunt's diner, Lacy poked at her plate of okra, the golden-fried nuggets still too hot to eat. Aunt Frannie had ordered them for her, despite the fact she wasn't very hungry. But that was Frannie's way—eat, eat, eat. It wasn't like she was starving. In fact, she'd eaten enough food at Ashley's picnic yesterday to last her a week! Around her, the lunch crowd was picking up, a steady stream of customers piling in through the front door. She recognized several faces, but many were new, many young, new mothers, new babies. A newborn screamed in her momma's arms.

It made Lacy's heart ache to see life flourishing in the hills of Tennessee while hers sat idle, stale, about as appealing as last week's buttermilk biscuits. She wanted action and excitement. She wanted love and family. As a young mother ushered her toddler ahead, she expertly managed the baby in her arms. Slinging the child onto her hip as she bounced and walked, the red-faced girl grimaced and grew quiet. Lacy longed for a child. She longed for the energy and commotion and the juggling that came along with it. By this time in her life, she'd imagined herself with a passel of kids—boys, girls, twins like on her Daddy's side. As her gaze trailed the trio to their booth, she brooded over the unfairness. It felt like she'd lost decades of her life, wasting away the hours in the bars of Atlanta, the nightclubs and restaurants, with nothing more to show for her time than memories.

Allowing the okra to cool, Lacy took a sip from her coke and pondered her next step. The past was behind her. She was looking forward, moving forward. She needed a job, needed something to do, but what? Work at Whiskey Joe's? Wait tables for Aunt Frannie? Lacy didn't want to do any of it. She wanted an enjoyable job, a job she'd look forward to going to every day. She wanted something fun, inspiring.

Spotting her sister Annie walk by the front window, Lacy's mood perked up. Maybe she could work at the salon. She could learn how to cut hair or maybe answer the phone. Annie swung open the front door, hesitating when she saw Lacy. At least the two of them would be closer. A man bumped in behind Annie, begging her pardon with a sheepish smile. Annie acknowledged him and then marched straight over to Lacy's table. Hope bloomed. Was Annie having second thoughts about tossing her aside?

"Hi, Annie!" Lacy waved.

Annie halted at Lacy's table. She pressed a forefinger to the tabletop and said, "I'm glad I found you."

Lacy brightened. "Would you like to have lunch with me?"

"No, I don't want to have lunch with you. I want to speak to you about your behavior at the picnic yesterday."

"My behavior?"

"Yes. Your interference with Cal Foster."

"*Interference?*"

"Yes. I know that's a big word for you, but it means interrupt, intrude." The black of her dress accentuated the heavy liner around her eyes, underscoring her anger. "You knew darn well he was talking to me and you tried to steal him away."

"What are you talking about? Cal and I are friends from way back, same as you. Why, we were dancing together only minutes before he saw you."

"Don't play coy with me. I know how you operate. You were flirting with him to steal him away from me. Well, I'm warning you right now—back off."

Lacy smacked palms to table and exclaimed, "Annie Grace, I was doing no such thing!"

Annie's eyes narrowed to slits. "You were and we both know it."

Aunt Frannie walked up from behind and put an arm around Annie's shoulders. "Annie, honey, is there something I can help you with?" She glanced around the restaurant. "You're making a scene, sugar, and I'll not have you continue."

"Sorry, Frannie, but Lacy has it coming."

"Not in my diner, she doesn't." Nudging her from the table, Frannie steered Annie a few feet away and hushed her voice, "Your daughter is sittin' over there in the corner, all by herself. Why don't you go sit a spell with her and enjoy lunch on me?"

At the sight of her daughter, Annie's gaze splintered. Alone in the corner, Casey looked like someone stole her puppy. Lacy's heart fell.

Annie turned back to Lacy, her earlier anger diffused. "Don't let it happen again, Lacy, or I swear I'll let you have it." Pivoting, she turned and headed for Casey's table.

Frannie watched her go, then asked, "What was all that about?"

Lacy wanted to cry. Her sister hated her. Growing up, Annie had always been better at everything than Lacy. She could do hair and nails, ride better, swim faster—even Daddy liked her best, always fussing over his oldest child, his pride and joy. Annie scored better in school, took the lead role in a school play, but she had never been very good with the boys. For Lacy, flirting came natural, as natural as breathing. She enjoyed the company of boys and encouraged their attention. Was it her fault she connected with people in a pleasant fashion? Besides, she hadn't seen Cal since high school and she'd been happy to see a familiar face.

Glancing over at Annie, now seated with her daughter, Lacy understood all too well the value of having a friendly face in your corner. It took the edge off the lonesome. Yesterday at the picnic, she'd only wanted to show her sister that Cal liked her, and why couldn't Annie like her, too?

Tugging her focus from across the restaurant, Lacy replied finally, "Nothing. It was about nothing."

"Nothing?" Aunt Frannie wiped hands together and then across her apron front. "I've seen nothing and that ain't it."

Lacy looked up, met with a reproach tampered by love. "Annie hates me, pure and simple."

"Your sister doesn't hate you. She just needs time to re-adjust to your being here, is all."

"Hmph." Lacy slumped back against the booth. "You don't know Annie, then. That girl can hold a grudge longer than a dog with a rib bone."

Aunt Frannie patted Lacy's back. "Don't you fret, child. She'll come around, you watch and see." Staring down her nose, she added, "Now eat your okra, young lady. You need to put some meat on those skinny bones of yours."

Lacy nodded. Aunt Frannie returned to the kitchen and she returned to her plate of okra. If she had somewhere to go, she'd leave this instant. Storm right out of this restaurant and show Annie how little she cared about her silly outburst.

But she didn't. She had nowhere to go, and that was her problem.

"Mind if I join you?"

The deep masculine voice startled Lacy. She snapped her head up and found Malcolm Ward peering down at her with an easy, friendly smile. The shock of white hair still surprised her when she looked at him, so at odds with his pale blue eyes and tanned skin. His body was lean and fit, not appearing a day over forty. At the picnic he'd been dressed in navy linen shorts and white silk T-shirt. Today he wore blue slacks and a pressed gray shirt, a steel gray that underscored his hair and eyes. Clearly, in spite of his hair, Malcolm was young, vigorous, sleek and sophisticated.

"Looks like you could use some company."

Ignoring the jump of her pulse, Lacy gave a quick nod. "If you want."

"I very much want," Malcolm replied, and lowered himself to the bench seat across from her. Sliding the napkin-rolled utensils aside, he asked, "You okay?"

The earnest look in his eyes served to massage her spirit. "Why wouldn't I be?"

"I saw your sister. She didn't seem too happy with you."

"Annie doesn't seem to be happy, ever."

"Does she always take it out on you?"

"Yes." No. Lacy nibbled her lip. She could use an ally right about now. Reaching for her coke, she decided to share, "She's a bit stressed. We haven't seen each other in a long time."

"I remember."

Lacy paused. "That's right. You know Delaney."

"I saw you at the picnic yesterday."

A quiet understanding passed between them. Of course he knew everything. She stole a glance at him, then averted her gaze to the safety of her glass. He knew about her troubles with Annie, Jeremiah—everything. Witnessed her exchange with Annie and Cal Foster.

"I missed you after you left."

She stared at him. "Missed me?"

"You left rather abruptly. I was hoping we'd have some time together, maybe a dance or two."

A torrent of desire blasted through her, permeated by resentment. She would have loved to dance with Malcolm—if only Annie hadn't spoiled her afternoon. And Cal. He didn't even stick up for her. Lacy dropped her gaze. So much for that friendly face she'd been hoping for. He'd been friendly until Annie showed up.

"Ever find out what your friend Loretta and the boy were up to the other night?"

"No." Lacy looked up. "How could I? I was talking to you, remember?"

"I remember," he said, pleasure swamping his expression.

A thrill skipped through her breast. Lacy took the napkin from her lap and patted her lips, hiding the smile tugging at her mouth.

"But don't you two talk? You said you were friends, right?"

"In Atlanta," she said matter-of-factly, replacing napkin to lap.

"And that friendship doesn't extend to Tennessee?"

Lacy reached for her coke and sipped. "Oh, course it does, but it's like I told you. I've only seen her that once." And at the diner, earlier in the day, when Loretta must have been making plans with the boy. In case Lacy had missed the connection, Aunt Frannie sure had given her an ear full about it.

Malcolm interlaced his fingers, his well-manicured nails drawing her attention momentarily. Elegant hands, they appeared refined for a man. She wondered if he had them professionally manicured.

"Do you mind if I ask you a personal question?" he asked.

"No. What?"

"You seem pretty easygoing with your ex, Jeremiah. You're friends with his current girlfriend. I don't know too many women who would be."

Lacy gave him a queer look. "Why wouldn't I be?"

"Oh, I don't know," he ventured. "Bad blood, bad breakup, it happens."

"Oh, poo." She stirred the straw through her drink. "Jeremiah and I split six months after we arrived in Atlanta. He didn't care. I didn't care. Why be mad?"

Malcolm grinned. A group of businessmen passed by their booth en route for the lunch counter, each one stealing a glance at the woman seated across from him. She was definitely eye candy in her silk turquoise blouse, the V-neckline revealing her creamy white cleavage. Lips glossed in pink and her makeup applied to enhance the blue of her eyes. More than a looker, Lacy was a rare bird. And exquisitely rare bird.

"You never felt like he took advantage of you?"

"Heck, no," she tossed out. "I went with him willingly. I wanted to leave Tennessee back then in the worst way, and Jeremiah was my ticket out."

Malcolm nodded. He wanted to ask about her family, wanted to know what would drive a seventeen-year-old girl to run away, hook up with a man who slept with her sister only to leave him six months later. She would have been too young to work in the lounge at that age. How did she survive? From what he'd gleaned, looking into her history, Lacy had quit her job at the lounge to come here. Up and left, the manager said, without giving notice. He was not pleased about it, either, informing Malcolm there would be no referral coming from him.

Studying the woman across the table, Malcolm considered she might be at a crossroads in her life. None of his research into her background turned up trouble. No arrests, no drugs, no violations of any kind. Unless they were sealed in juvenile court, Lacy Louise Owens had no record with the law. She'd merely "popped" back home for a visit. Because her ex-boyfriend and girlfriend had decided to do so?

"So how long are you in town for?" Malcolm asked.

She hesitated, as though debating the answer. "Oh, I don't know. For a while."

"A while? Your boss back at the lounge okay with that?"

"You have a good memory, Mr. Ward."

He laughed at her cooled response. "I have to. Running a hotel chain demands it."

"Is it fun?"

"Is what fun?"

"Working in a fancy hotel? Aunt Frannie told me that you build really nice hotels."

Amazed by the quick spin in subjects, he nodded. "Remind me to thank her for the compliment, but yes, it's fun. One of those jobs I enjoy every day of the week."

"I bet I'd like working at a hotel, meeting new people all the time, talking to them about where they're from, what their hometowns are like..."

He smiled, intrigued by her guileless nature. It was as though he were discussing business with a child, a girl who had no idea about the world around her but seemed fascinated by it. Had Lacy ever been to an upscale hotel? She worked in Atlanta. He couldn't imagine she hadn't been exposed to the finer things in life. His gaze dropped briefly to her chest, the thin cotton material outlining her curves to perfection. Why, men would fall at her feet for a chance to show her the town.

Returning his focus to her, he said, "If you're interested, I could get you a job with Harris Hotels."

"You could?" she asked, instantly bubbling with interest.

He winked. "I happen to have connections."

Lacy realized he was teasing and withdrew her enthusiasm. "Oh, of course." She reached for her soda and sipped. "How silly of me."

And peculiar. Lacy couldn't be a neophyte when it came to life, yet she came across as naïve. It was a trait he continually had to wrap his mind around. Actually, what he wanted was to wrap his arms around *her*. "I bet the guests would love you."

That hit the mark. "I would love *them*," she said, almost starry-eyed as she re-emerged from her shell.

"Then it's settled. If you're here when Serenity Springs opens her doors, you have a job as the official guest-greeter."

"Serenity Springs?"

"That's what Nick and I have decided to name the hotel, after the natural springs on the property. Serenity is the feeling our guests will experience during their stay, take with them upon their departure."

"Serenity Springs," she repeated dreamily. "I like it."

"If Jeremiah doesn't succeed in interfering, that is."

"Jeremiah?"

"Yes, he's stirring up trouble, just like you said he would."

Malcolm watched the calculations fire through her brain, her mind whirring at high speed. "Can you stop him?"

"Sure, if we know where he's coming from, what his weak spots are."

"What do you mean?"

"As it stands, Jeremiah can challenge Felicity's ownership, though I don't think he'll have much success in court. If Annie joins forces with him though, he might have a better chance."

"How so?"

Malcolm glanced askance and lowered his voice to prevent eavesdropping from neighboring booths. One thing he did know about small towns was people talked. They listened, repeated and talked and talked and talked. One afternoon at the lunch counter and he learned more about the townsfolk than he cared to know!

"From what I understand, Casey is Jeremiah's daughter."

"That's what she claims," Lacy told him, "but it's never been proven. Jeremiah certainly won't claim her."

"No?"

Lacy shook her head, a hint of shame entering her gaze. "Jeremiah is as selfish as they come. He has no desire for children. None. Zippo. Not long after we moved to Atlanta, Annie tried to get him to acknowledge Casey as his daughter, but he shut her down. Refused her flat."

Nice guy, Malcolm mused but kept the observation to himself. Lacy didn't appear too pleased with her role in the matter, either. Perhaps she could redeem herself by helping him and Nick. If anyone knew how to get to Jeremiah, it would be her.

"Well," Malcolm pretended to think aloud. "If they do join forces, it might prove harder to defend. Now, if we had something on Jeremiah to use as leverage, it would be helpful."

"Leverage? What do you mean?"

"You know, something that could be held over his head as a reminder that he doesn't want to mess with us. I've looked into his background in Atlanta and he seems pretty clean."

Lacy's face lit up. "Oh, you won't find it in Atlanta—Jeremiah's problems are in Vegas!"

"Vegas?"

"Sure. He's got a bit of a gambling problem—in that he doesn't know when to stop."

Hope blazed anew. "Really?"

"According to Loretta, the man can't keep enough money in his pockets to leave a trail of pennies to the front door. He gambles and he gambles big. Actually, he owes money to a casino out in Vegas." Lacy pushed her plate aside and leaned forward. "And from what I can figure, it's a pretty fair amount."

"Jeremiah has an unpaid marker?"

Lacy shrugged. "I don't know about a marker, but he borrowed a lot of money from the casino so he could gamble and then lost it all. He can't pay it back."

Malcolm beamed. *God, he could kiss her right now.* An unpaid marker amounts to a felony which carried a prison sentence. Nevada was the only state to allow casinos the right to go after a guy for spending their money, and his friends took the privilege pretty seriously. They would hunt Jeremiah down until they got their money and if they didn't, they'd throw his butt in jail. Tapping back his excitement, he asked, "Are you sure about this?"

She nodded, seemingly unaware of the gold mine of information she was providing. "It's one of the reasons Loretta said they were coming to Tennessee. Jeremiah needs money."

Malcolm chuckled. It was beautiful.

"What's so funny?"

Staring across the booth at Lacy, he thought, *She's beautiful.* "You struck gold, Ms. Owens."

"I did?"

"You did."

Lacy's attention jumped to the door. "Don't look now, but we have company."

Chapter Twelve

Malcolm turned, expecting to see Jeremiah, but instead was treated to Tennessee's latest budding romance. Troy hung by the door, scanning the restaurant as he held it open for Loretta to pass through ahead of him. The boy's gaze stilled and Malcolm followed his line of sight, tracking his point of interest. *What do you know?* It was young Casey Owens.

Loretta spotted Lacy and waved. Lacy waved back, even as she quietly told him, "I hope they don't come over and sit with us. That's all I'd need, Annie thinking I'm cavorting with the enemy!"

Malcolm returned to the couple in question, unavoidably settling on Loretta's breasts. Ample cleavage spilled from the tight yellow shirt she wore, her legs long and lean as they extended beneath a short black skirt, her calves strategically enhanced by four inch heels. She was a good-looking woman, no two ways about it. "To tell you the truth, I don't think they have any interest in us."

"You're probably right," Lacy replied, but her blue eyes remained fastened on the duo's every move.

Malcolm watched them secure a table on the opposite side of the restaurant. Troy seemed uncomfortable, though he worked hard to cover it, squaring his shoulders as he steered his woman about. He avoided eye contact with anyone as he slid into the booth across from Loretta, his back to the wall.

"Do you want to order lunch?" Lacy asked him, drawing his attention back to her.

"Haven't you eaten?" he asked, indicating her plate of food.

"Not yet. That was only a snack my Aunt Frannie made for me."

Malcolm raised his brow. A snack left untouched. "Lunch sounds great. I'm always up for some good old-fashioned home-cooking."

She beamed. "Two orders of fried chicken?"

"You bet."

"I'll go tell Aunt Frannie. Can I get you a coke?"

"A soda would be great."

Malcolm watched Lacy swing out of the booth and breeze into the kitchen, his interest split between her body and Troy's lunch table. What was he doing here with that woman? Was the kid trying to broadcast his disrespect for the Ladd family around the entire town? First Whiskey Joe's and now Fran's? If Delaney or Felicity walked in and saw him, Malcolm didn't have to guess what would transpire next.

It was exactly the boy's audacity that concerned Malcolm. He pulled the cell phone from his pocket and dialed Nick's number. Add the new information he'd received on Jeremiah, and the two of them had to come up with a plan and fast.

Nick answered on the first ring and Malcolm dipped his chin as he spoke into the phone. "We need to talk."

Armed with knowledge of Clem's whereabouts, Jeremiah drove straight to the diner. If Loretta didn't have any news for him, so be it. He would find out everything he needed to know from one Clem Sweeney—though he still couldn't believe it. Clem kidnapped Delaney? By himself? Jeremiah chuckled. He didn't think the hound dog had it in him. But maybe things had changed since high school. Back then, Clem was as scrawny as an abandoned mountain dog and couldn't hurt a flea, let alone kidnap the feistiest female this side of the Appalachian Mountains. Had the world turned upside down since he left town?

Slowing to a stop outside the front door of Fran's Diner, Jeremiah noted the building hadn't changed a bit since the last time he'd seen it. Still had a curved entrance and block windows. The blue paint had faded, the red neon-lettered sign remained the same loopy style of the fifties. Did the old lady spend a dime on the place? Never did when her husband was alive and probably didn't spend a cent now. But Fran had always been cheap. When he and his buddies worked the kitchen, she'd paid minimum wage and disallowed overtime. There had been no argument, no room for discussion. She refused to pay the boys a nickel more. It was a wonder she'd stayed in business all these years.

Jeremiah ignored the yellow-orange "no parking" lines painted across the pavement and jumped out of his truck. *Tow the heap of garbage, if you want.* He smiled to himself. *I'll be getting a new one right soon.* Bells clanged loudly as he yanked the glass door open, forcing an elderly couple on their way out to move over as he passed them on his way inside. The joint was hopping, not a single table available. Several people waited by the hostess stand, a few more circled around the pie case. *Damn...*

Old Fran must he pulling in a mint with this place! In the back corner he glimpsed Annie, a teenage girl sitting across from her. Was that his kid? By the looks of her black hair and blue eyes, she resembled nothing of him, but he couldn't care less. He spotted Lacy, with a man in tow. Jeremiah shook his head. No surprise there. That one never did spend much time alone. The customer he was looking for was an obvious stand out, her blonde head of hair unmistakable, even from behind.

Jeremiah walked over and giving the Parker boy a cursory glance said, "Let's go, Loretta."

She whirled in her seat. "Jerry!" The boy hit him with a hardened gaze. "What are you doing here?" she asked, but wasted no time scooting out of the booth. Straightening her shirt, she glanced about their immediate vicinity as though someone might recognize her or overhear.

"I'm giving you a ride back to the motel." He smiled. "You can thank me later."

The Parker kid rose and stood eye-to-eye with Jeremiah. "You got a problem, mister?"

Overgrown brown hair, angular jaw, pumped-up muscles, the boy was like every other punk Jeremiah had come across in his travels. Get in the face and whip out the fists. "Yeah, that's right," Jeremiah said, raking him with a hot glance. "I'm here to pick up my woman."

The younger balked. "*Your* woman?"

Loretta placed a hand to his forearm. "Troy, it's okay. I'll explain later."

Jeremiah glanced between the two. "Have another date, do we?"

"I don't see how that's any of your business," Troy thrust.

"When you're making plans with my woman, everything's my business."

"*Jerry*! You said you were here to give me a ride, now let's get going." Loretta started pushing at him but Jeremiah didn't budge.

Troy looked to Loretta, seeking answers, but none came. "I'll call you, okay?" Fury lit his eyes.

Now you're getting the idea, Jeremiah mused, enjoying the displeasure of a man who's just realized he'd been conned. Loretta pushed past him and made a beeline for the door. Jeremiah paused and savored a private smile. If looks could kill, he'd be dead right about now. Which gave him a chuckle. Jeremiah patted the boy on the shoulder. "Sorry kid, maybe another woman will mean it."

The boy whipped his hand up and grabbed Jeremiah's arm. "Keep your hands off me," he growled.

Surprised by the swift move, the strength of his grip, Jeremiah was momentarily stunned. While he enjoyed watching the kid suffer, he wasn't interested in a fist fight. Around him, the din of restaurant conversation had hushed to rabid curiosity. "I'm not looking for trouble, kid."

"Too late."

With a jerk of his arm, Jeremiah freed himself from the kid's hold. "It's never too late. Or didn't your mother ever teach you that?"

Before the kid could respond, Jeremiah turned on his heel. Ignoring the stares, he tugged his shirt from his chest and made his exit. While he wouldn't mind going a round with the boy, Jeremiah wasn't about to give these people a reason to call the cops. Cops served warrants—warrants with his name on them.

Strolling outside, he found Loretta hopping mad. "What do you think you were doing in there?" She jabbed a finger toward the diner and cried, "I was making progress with that boy!"

Jeremiah brought hand to chin and eased the tension from his jaw. "Told you already."

"Did you think it was a good idea to let him know we're together? After I spent all that time getting him to trust me, convincing him I'm just a friend looking out for your best interests?"

Jeremiah brushed past her and eased into the driver's seat. "Well, if he's stupid enough to believe that, you might have been wasting your time."

Loretta opened her door and climbed into the truck. Pulling the end of her skirt toward her knees, she said sternly, "I said you were a *friend*, not my lover."

"Did you get any information?" he asked, inserting the key into the ignition.

"As a matter of fact, I did."

"And?"

Loretta's blue-green eyes stilled, flooding with emotion. "Your daddy is sick."

Jeremiah's hand paused on the gear shift. She might as well have sucker-punched him. "*Sick*? What kind of sick?"

"Sick. As in terminal sick." She reached over the center console. "Troy said he thinks that's why your daddy signed the deed over. He's dying."

She searched Jeremiah's gaze. If she was looking for sympathy, any feeling at all, she was wasting her time. Something inside him closed. Jeremiah didn't care about his father. In fact, part of him was glad the old man was dying.

"Did you hear me? He's dying, Jerry. Doesn't that mean anything to you?"

He snapped to life. "It's about time."

"Jerry!"

Jeremiah ignored the stricken look on her face and gunned the engine, pulling away from the curb with a hard acceleration. Tamping down the mix of emotions coursing through him, he said, "You're not the only one with news. I learned a few things of my own today."

Loretta didn't say a word. She only stared. If he had to guess, it looked to him like she was disappointed by his reaction. That she was upset, offended that he had the gall to not care. Why should she be surprised? Loretta knew how he felt about the old man, though a terminal illness was the last thing he'd expected. Jeremiah smiled, as if to prove he didn't care. "Don't you want to know what I found out today?"

Loretta turned away, shunning him with a haughty edge.

"Seems my neighbor Clem Sweeney has been getting pretty tight with my old man but ran into trouble with Delaney."

"What kind of trouble?" she asked, continuing to stare out the passenger window as they drove through the dump of a town.

Jeremiah savored the words as he said them, "Clem kidnapped her."

Loretta spun around to face him. "What? That poor woman! Did he hurt her?"

Jeremiah chuckled. "Didn't look like it from what I could tell. But I bet he had good reason."

"Jerry, what could *possibly* make kidnapping someone a good idea?"

"I don't know. But that's the part I intend to find out."

Chapter Thirteen

Malcolm and Nick tracked Delaney as she paced from one end of the cabin to the other. Both men sat pulled up to the butcher block island in her kitchen, patiently waiting for her to absorb the information. He and Nick had already discussed the situation, drawing up a set of their own plans to handle Jeremiah. But when it came to Delaney, Nick suggested they move slow, break it easy to her. Interesting concern, considering Malcolm had never seen Delaney take anything easy. She paced, she grumbled, she fretted and she questioned. She was knee-deep in emotion and Malcolm wondered if she could even *think* clearly, let alone understand the options at hand. But Ladd Springs was her land, hers and Felicity's, and she needed to be involved.

Delaney paused, a grave look hanging in her dark brown eyes. "This is bad. This is really bad. If Troy was with Jeremiah's girlfriend, he had to have told her."

"We don't know that," Nick said.

"Why else would they be together?"

Hot body, easy pickings. Malcolm exchanged a glance with Nick. None of which Delaney wanted to hear at the moment. Taking a deep breath, Malcolm focused on the more pertinent issue at hand. "It doesn't matter. Even if Troy did tell her, it doesn't matter."

"But he can sue us for duress!" she cried. "You said so yourself!"

"He doesn't have the money," he returned calmly, as though treading softly would help soothe the wild beast in her.

Delaney slid a hand over her head, resting it on a cotton hair band that held her long blonde hair back in a ponytail.

Thick and full, it almost could belong to a pony. "How do you know that?"

Without makeup, lines of worry scored her face all the deeper. Dressed in jean shorts and simple tank top, Delaney was thin as a rail. Malcolm understood worried, but she looked stressed as hell, almost to the point of becoming unhealthy.

"Lacy," he replied quietly.

The name chilled Delaney's demeanor. "She's not the most reliable source."

"She's proven right on so far," Malcolm defended. But he wasn't about to argue the point. Family feuds ran deep in this part of the country, and inserting himself between opposing forces was not a good bet. Especially female feuds.

Delaney brought a hand to her forehead, as though a headache were coming on. Malcolm sympathized with her plight. She had cause. If Jeremiah was successful on any level, it would jeopardize her ownership of the property and from what Nick told him, living on this land was the only thing that mattered to Delaney. If she lost that right, she would be devastated.

"What if Jeremiah finds out about the gold?" she asked. "What if Felicity told Travis and Troy about the gold?"

"Would she?"

Delaney dropped her hand and heaved a ragged sigh. "She tells them everything."

"But I thought you specifically told her to keep it under wraps."

"I did. But if Jeremiah finds out about the gold..."

Malcolm groaned inwardly. It was clear she wasn't certain her daughter would honor her wishes. Nick went to Delaney and took her in his arms. "He won't. We have a plan."

"A plan?" She looked up at him, then checked with Malcolm. He nodded. "What kind of plan?"

"According to Lacy, Jeremiah owes money to a casino in Vegas."

"He does? How would she know that?"

"She keeps tabs through his girlfriend, Loretta." At Delaney's puzzled expression, Malcolm explained, "Lacy and Loretta are friends. They worked at the same lounge in Atlanta. Loretta shared the information with her and she, in turn, shared it with me." And she had been so proud of herself for doing so, he thought, pleasure streaming through him at the memory, as though it were a most amazing feat. In the end, it might just turn out to be amazing. "It's all we need to take Jeremiah out of the picture."

"How is a debt he owes in Vegas going to help us stop him from taking Ladd Springs?"

Malcolm smiled. "An unpaid marker is a felony."

"What's a marker?"

Nick responded, "It's a loan. A line of credit. When a guy goes into a casino and wants to gamble, but doesn't have the cash, he can sign his name for a loan."

"But if he doesn't have the money, the casino can go after him," Malcolm finished.

"Like defaulting on a credit card?"

"Kind of," Nick replied. "Except that in Nevada, casino debt is a felony. Unlike your standard credit card, they can put you in jail for defaulting."

Delaney stood there, mouth agape.

"The casino boys take it pretty seriously," Malcolm told her. "They'll go after him."

"But I'm sure Jeremiah didn't give them his real address. What if they can't find him?"

"They'll have his ID on file, unless he used a fake driver's license. Either way, I guarantee you they know who he is. They'll have surveillance video on his every step through the casino. All we have to do is help them connect the dots."

"And they can go after him?" She shifted her gaze between the men. "Across state lines?"

"Yes, ma'am. The DA in Nevada will obtain a warrant for his arrest and it will be reported nationwide. Jeremiah can be picked up in any state, at any time."

Delaney paused. Still wrapped within Nick's arms, she settled her hands on his forearms. "How is it you two know so much about casinos and debts?"

They shared a smile. "Didn't Nick tell you?" Malcolm asked.

She peered up at him. "Tell me what?"

Nick grinned. "Mal and I like to gamble."

"It's like our home away from home."

"Are you addicted?" Delaney demanded flatly. Nick dropped his head back and laughed. She punched his arm and tried to pull free from his grasp. "I'm serious. Are you?"

Amused by the domestic squabble unfolding before him, the confirmed bachelor in Malcolm enjoyed watching his pal squirm.

"No, I'm not addicted," Nick said. "Why would you ask?" Delaney didn't reply and Nick's face changed abruptly. "I'm *sorry*, that was insensitive of me." Surprising Malcolm with his swift contrition, he kissed the top of her head. "No, I'm not addicted. I merely enjoy the entertainment."

"Why haven't I heard of this before?" Delaney asked.

"Because we've been together all of two weeks?" He flashed a grin to Malcolm then said to her, "I daresay there's a lot more to me you haven't learned yet."

Delaney seemed placated by the response and Malcolm stood. His business here was finished. Nick and he were in full agreement. Delaney didn't need to know any more. "Listen. I'll call our man out in Vegas and get the ball rolling. After that, we wait."

Nick nodded, communicating the unspoken half of their plan with his eyes. Malcolm nodded.

"But can they arrest Jeremiah for no reason?" Delaney asked.

"I don't call fifty thousand dollars 'no reason.'"

"He owes that much?"

"He owes that much," Malcolm said. "Confirmed it with a friend of mine which is why he'll be running scared when he receives a visit from the local sheriff." A visit he and Nick were going to provoke.

Malcolm walked to the door and Delaney blurted, "Where are you going? Aren't you staying for dinner?"

"No, ma'am. I'm going fishing at the local watering hole." Malcolm tipped an imaginary hat and let himself out.

Jeremiah sat in a plastic chair in the county jail visitation room. He tapped his toe on the floor, impatient to see Clem, but grateful he'd made it before visiting hours ended for the day. There was a young woman to his right, visibly agitated with the inmate sitting across from her and to his left a man sat bent over, repeatedly looking from side to side, as though plotting an escape and worried someone was listening. At a loud slam of metal door, Jeremiah looked through the glass partition to see Clem Sweeney being led over to him. Clean-shaven, thin, his jail garb was a washed-out gray, he shuffled his feet as he walked. He looked old, Jeremiah thought, much older than his forty years. But Clem's health and well-being were not his concern. His knowledge of Delaney was what mattered.

Clem dropped to a seat before him, curiosity glittering in his eyes beneath the glare of fluorescent lighting. "Jeremiah Ladd," he drawled, scrutinizing him as one would an appari-tion. "It's been a long time."

"Sweeney."

"I didn't believe it when they told me it was you."

"Sorry it has to be under these circumstances," Jeremiah said.

Clem shrugged. "What brings you to town?"

"Delaney Wilkins."

The name set fire to Clem's expression. "I reckon you know about what happened."

"Not really, but I've been hearing things."

Clem set his mouth in a grim line, his eyes distrusting. "What kind of things?"

"Things that I don't like, Clem." Jeremiah responded, reeling his catch in, slow but sure.

"Nothing to like about that woman, I'll give you that."

Jeremiah chuckled. "Aw, now, she wasn't so bad as a kid."

"She's trouble now." He cut Jeremiah in half with a hateful gaze. "You heard about her and your daddy?"

Jeremiah nodded and assumed the saddest look he could. Did Clem know his father was sick? "Don't seem right, her taking full rights to the property from him like she did. She could have at least called me."

Fury blustered through Clem's features and he hissed, "She don't care about nobody but herself!"

"People change, I reckon. But with my daddy feeling the way he does?"

"He don't like her none, I'll tell you that right now," Clem spat.

"I mean his health."

"His health?"

"He doesn't look well," Jeremiah said, hinting that he knew, that Clem could open up to him.

"I don't know about all that." Clem lifted his cuffed hands and laid them on the counter, the metal skidding across the Formica. "I only know that Delaney is a greedy little thing. She tricked him somehow, kept threatening him with court."

"Court?" This was the first he heard about Delaney going to court. "On what grounds?"

"Grounds?" Clem looked around as if he were searching for somewhere to spit his dip. "I don't know nothin' about grounds. I'm only telling you what I heard."

Jeremiah nodded. "She was probably trying to coerce him to sell."

"She ain't got no money!" Clem hollered, drawing a sharp glance from a nearby guard.

Staring at the man he'd known his entire childhood, the man who had never been very bright, Jeremiah doubted he'd get anything meaningful regarding Delaney's abuse of the legal system. Time to change direction. "Well, from what I hear, you and my dad were pretty close."

Clem stilled. His right eye twitched.

Hooked. Jeremiah paused for effect, then added quietly, "Thanks for looking after him for me. I know I didn't leave on the best of terms, but I was young back then, ya know?" He shifted his weight in his chair. "I didn't know the importance of family like I do now."

Clem pursed his lips, the wheels of thought spinning behind his eyes. He slid his hands down into his lap. "Have you seen him?"

"Briefly. He's still angry. I don't say as I blame him, but I still had to try."

Clem paused, as though finally catching on. He slid a wary gaze around the room before settling in on him. "What are you after, Jeremiah?"

Point blank. Jeremiah almost smiled. He respected a man who got right down to business. "The property," he said. "I want what's rightfully mine."

Clem smiled thinly. He licked his lips, glanced about and said, "I might be able to help you with that."

"Help me?" Did Clem think Jeremiah was going to cut him in? He almost laughed in his face, but held himself in check. He wanted to hear what came next.

Clem nodded. Knitting his brow, he rubbed his skinny chin and pondered who knows what. The nearby woman wailed at the man across from her, attracting a guard to their cubicle. "I know a secret about Delaney."

"You do?"

His eyes lit up with a wicked gleam. "I do."

Jeremiah wondered if it had anything to do him trying to kidnap her. "Tell me."

Clem visibly retreated and Jeremiah cursed himself for moving in too soon. Checking for unwanted attention, Clem said, "Not yet, not yet. I got to think about it a while."

What the hell was there to think about? It was *his* family they were discussing!

"Can you come back tomorrow?" Clem asked.

Jeremiahs' instinct was to refuse, but on account he had no other leads, he agreed. "What time?"

"Ten o'clock."

"Ten o'clock," he confirmed.

Clem's smile returned. "I think we may be able to work together to get us some revenge, you and me."

Chapter Fourteen

At the knock on the door, Annie clicked off the television set. Nine o'clock in the evening, no one should be calling on them at this hour. Casey was up and en route to answer it. "Are you expecting someone?" she asked, rising from the couch.

"No," Casey replied.

Annie took a brief survey of her apartment—a quick assessment of its suitability for guests—and judged it to be tidy. There wasn't a whole lot to the two-bedroom apartment, and with Casey spending most of her time in her bedroom or on the couch watching television, not a whole lot to mess up. "Check through the peep hole," Annie instructed. "It could be a stranger."

Casey did, then opened the door. "Hi, Candi."

A staccato of pulse erupted.

"Is your mom home?" Candi asked.

"Sure." Casey stepped aside, allowing Candi to enter.

But Candi stood locked in place. Hesitant, her brown eyes latched onto Annie, but she didn't take the first step.

"What are you doing here?" Annie demanded.

"Annie, we need to talk."

"I've said everything I have to say to you."

Casey gaped between them, obviously confused by the hostility between friends. *Ex-friends*. Annie had yet to tell her daughter about their change in status.

"Please," Candi pleaded, wary of Casey. "Two minutes. That's all I need."

Annie slanted a gaze toward her daughter. "Casey, will give us a minute?"

"Sure," she said, and meandered out, curiosity tearing through the sudden tension filling the living room.

Candi ventured inside, closing the door behind her. Annie stared at her, determined not to give her a second longer than necessary. Looking at her ex-friend now, she only saw a tramp, her naked body wrapped around Jeremiah's, the two laughing in their betrayal. Annie shut the images from her mind, crossed arms over her chest. The woman made her nauseous. "What do you want?"

"Jeremiah came by today." Shards of ice filled Annie's heart. "He mentioned he ran into you and that you were seeking rights to the property. I explained about Casey and he tried to say she was Clem's." The accusation found its mark, dead center in her chest. The two women went still. "So it's *true...*"

"Who I slept with is none of your business," she said, but she felt shamed by the shock circulating through Candi's expression. She'd never told her. Never once had she let on she had slept with her brother. But then again, Candi never mentioned her affair with Jeremiah either.

"But she *isn't*, Annie," Candi said quickly. Rooted in place, she shook her head vehemently. "She *can't* be. Clem is sterile."

Annie's emotions imploded. Disbelief streamed through her limbs, unwound her arms. "What?"

Candi nodded. "Clem is sterile. He can't possibly be Casey's father."

"How do you know that?"

"A girl once tried to claim he was the father of her baby. She was fifteen, he was eighteen. Her family was trying to get him on rape. Clem denied he ever slept with her, but the judge ordered him to take a test. Turned out, he was sterile. The girl had been lying the whole time."

Annie's world caved in. "Oh my...Clem is sterile."

"You get a paternity test and you'll have your proof positive," Candi said proudly.

"Jeremiah is Casey's father." It's what Annie had insisted all along, yet somehow doubted. *Clem is sterile. Jeremiah is Casey's father.*

"Just like you thought all along," Candi asserted.

"You mean to tell me that man who made a scene in the diner today is my father?" Both women whirled. Casey stood at the edge of the hallway, repulsion simmering in her gaze.

"How long have you been standing there, young lady?" Annie exclaimed, feeling none of the authority she was trying to display. The pain etched in her daughter's features broke her heart. Annie could feel her daughter's deep fury stir. It matched the shame churning through herself.

"Long enough to hear the truth."

"Oh, Casey, *I'm sorry,*" Candi burst out.

"Because that loser is my father? It's not *your* fault." Casey honed in on her mother. "How could you sleep with a man like him? How could he be my father?" Disgust spilled from her expression. "He's *not.* He's nothing but a sperm donor." Casey turned on her heel and fled to her bedroom.

"Casey!" Annie ran after her daughter a few steps but gave up. She dropped her face into her hands and muttered, "What have I done?"

Candi came to her, sliding an arm around her shoulders. Warm, solid, they were allies again. "She'll be okay. She just needs time."

Annie lifted her head and turned. Peering into the eyes of her best friend, a woman she had shunned only days ago but now needed more than ever, she asked, "Time to what— accept that her father is a loser? I think she's managed that quite well, don't you?"

"Annie."

"Well? It's the truth." Annie gazed off in the direction of her daughter's bedroom. "Jeremiah Ladd is a loser, with a capital L." Annie knew Candi wouldn't disagree with her. She couldn't. Coming from a family of bitter relations herself, it was a condition with which Candi was all too familiar.

"I'm sorry," Candi said.

"For what?"

"For everything. For Jeremiah, for Clem..."

The words fell away, leaving the two mired in the wake of their choices. A frivolous commercial flashed on the television screen, adults resorting to ridiculous antics for the sole purpose of selling clappable light switches. Totally inane in the scheme of life. Unlike trust. Trust lay at the core of life. Candi had done her friend wrong. Annie had done Candi wrong. But who had poor Casey done wrong?

No one.

"Can you ever forgive me?" Candi asked.

Candi had slept with Jeremiah behind her back. She had betrayed her in the vilest of terms—breaking the code of sisterhood. Women didn't sleep with their friends' boyfriends. That was out of bounds. Annie considered the notion. Was it okay if they slept with their brothers? In the sweep of one question, all the hurt and anger and shame were brushed away. "There's nothing to forgive." Candi hugged Annie. She hugged back, holding her friend like the lifeline she was, would always be. "I love you, Candi."

"I love you, too. We'll get through this," she whispered fiercely. "You watch and see."

Annie nodded. "But will Casey?"

Per Clem's instructions, Jeremiah returned to the jailhouse the next day, nursing a mild hangover after a night out with the old gang, anxious to discover whether or not Clem had anything real on Delaney. He said he knew a secret. Was it possible it was something big?

Waiting at the walled cubicle, Jeremiah looked around him. A girl sat pressed to the window, as though she could move through the glass and make out with her man. Another guy seemed to be talking to his mother. She was upset, he was asking for money, probably asking the old woman to put her house up for bond.

As Clem emerged from the back and ambled up to the window, Jeremiah centered on him. In reality, there was only one jailbird he was interested in. Yesterday Clem sounded like he really hated Delaney. It could have something to do with why he kidnapped her, but Jeremiah had yet to uncover that dirty little morsel of information. Would it be something he could use against her? Something that would help him take the property from her and Felicity? His father had signed over a life estate deed. Jeremiah didn't know anything about deeds, life estate or otherwise. All he knew is that it had to be overturned. A lawyer pal of his in Atlanta said it was doable. He only needed a reason.

"Sweeney," he said, impatient to begin.

Clem sat and bent forward, a quick smile forming on his lips. "So, you still wantin' to get after Delaney?"

"I am."

"Okay." He glanced from side to side, as though checking for eavesdroppers. As if anybody cared what Clem Sweeney had to say.

"What's the deal?" Jeremiah asked.

"Come here," Clem muttered harshly. "*Closer.*"

Jeremiah didn't like anyone barking orders at him. "Why?"

"Cause nobody can hear what I'm about to tell you."

Jeremiah doubted anything Clem had to say was *that* important, but obliged.

"But before I say a thing"—his mouth twitched like a rat—"I need to know what's in it for me."

"Revenge," Jeremiah replied evenly. "Isn't that what you said you wanted?"

"I want more than revenge. I want out of jail." Clem swiped a glance to his side.

"I don't even know why you're in jail."

"A phony kidnapping charge, that's why."

Jeremiah pretended surprise and, raising a brow, eased away from the window. "I can't help you with that, brother."

"Yes, you can. You got money." Clem eyed the expensive shirt Jeremiah was wearing, looked at the watch on his wrist. Jeremiah realized he was making an inventory of his wardrobe. "I need money to make bail."

"How much?" Jeremiah asked.

"Ten thousand."

Jeremiah blew out a low whistle. "That's a chunk of change." He pushed his chair back. "Sorry, but I can't help you."

"Yes, you can. I got a friend who works as a bondsman. He can help you."

"I *can't*. I don't have that kind of money."

Clem swept the surroundings with a guarded look and waggled his finger for Jeremiah to return to the window.

Growing tired of Clem's stalling tactics, Jeremiah leaned over and clipped, "What?"

"There's gold in Ladd Springs."

"*Gold?*"

"Hush your mouth!" Anger glinted from muddy brown eyes as he scolded, "You tryin' to alert the whole world?"

An anger of his own fired in Jeremiah's belly as he glared at Clem. If he was yanking his cord—"What the hell are you talking about?"

"I done told you. There's gold in the rocks in the woods."

"Where?"

Pleasure glinted in Clem's gaze. "That's the part I have to tell you."

"Tell me."

"First you got to agree to help me with bail."

Jeremiah wasn't sure there was gold, let alone how much, but he damned well knew he wasn't going to help Clem with bail. "Let's say I'll help you *if* there's enough of this gold you're talking about to spare it."

Clem scowled. "You're just as greedy as Delaney."

"Except you forgot one thing. It's *my* land."

Clem eased back into his chair. "Well then, I ain't gonna show you where the gold is."

Jeremiah leaned back in his chair, made a sweeping glance of the barren visitor's room and asked, "How are you going to show me anything?" He rolled his eyes around them and said, "You're rotting in jail."

"I got friends on the outside."

Jeremiah chuckled. Friends. His same cohorts from high school? Or had Clem upgraded his list of contacts? He returned to the window and said, "Okay. I'll help pay your bail." Whatever you need to hear, he mused. "Now where's the gold?"

Clem hesitated. "You swear?"

"I swear. Cross my heart," he mocked, gesturing across his chest.

"I'll have my friend Willie meet you at Bubba's Hideaway."

Jeremiah knew the place well. Bubba's Hideaway was a dive in the worst section of town. If you weren't looking for trouble, you kept away. It was a reality he knew all too well. He'd be lucky to get out alive, let alone find Clem's pal, Willie. But if there really was gold on the property... "When?"

"Today. Noon."

"How will I know who he is?"

Clem smiled, skimming over Jeremiah's clothes with a sneer. "He'll find *you*."

"Okay." Jeremiah stood. "You better not be wasting my time."

Clem rose. "And you better not double-cross me."

Chapter Fifteen

At twelve noon on the dot, Malcolm strolled into the diner, the smell of greasy grilled food increasing tenfold as he entered. As usual, the restaurant was packed, the clamor of kitchen activity evident from here. Pleased to find Lacy ready and waiting, he smiled. Malcolm liked punctuality in a woman, and liked her in black boots. At least the way Lacy wore them. Combined with a short blue denim skirt and a fitted white tank, she was sexy as hell. He could see the outline of her pink bra beneath the white cotton and chuckled. Either she had no mirror or the girl had gumption. Both of which suited him fine and blended perfectly well with his khaki shorts and navy T-shirt. His hiking boots were a tan pair he'd purchased to get him through the Brazilian rain forest and Australian Outback.

Her hand possessively guarding a brown paper bag, Lacy was a standout among the crowd, men and women dressed conservatively and milling quietly about as they waited for a table. Good thing they weren't standing in line. Malcolm doubted they'd be sitting any time soon. "Good morning, gorgeous," he said, and pecked her cheek with a kiss.

Lacy giggled. "Good morning, yourself."

"You ready for our picnic?"

"Sure am." She tapped a large paper bag sitting on the cashier's counter. "Aunt Frannie packed us a lunch and everything."

Malcolm peeked into the bag, his nose inundated with the warm moist scent of fried something. But Fran fried a lot of things. "It smells good. What's in it?"

"Fried chicken and okra, biscuits and cornbread, two slices of peach pie, some pig ears for snacking on..." Lacy batted her eyelashes. "She wasn't sure what you'd want, so she included everything."

"I love your Aunt Frannie." Though he could do without the pig ears. "Think she'll adopt me?"

"Probably. Aunt Frannie's a pushover when it comes to handsome men."

That surprised him. "She is?"

Lacy nodded, adding a mischievous wink. "Must be where I get it from."

Malcolm liked what he heard. Dodging a man standing close to Lacy, he grabbed the bag and extended an elbow for Lacy. "Shall we?"

She looped her arm through his and said, "We shall!"

Malcolm had missed Lacy at Whiskey Joe's last night. He'd gone there in hope of running into her but after two hours, abandoned the effort. Disappointed but not about to give up, he called Nick to see if Delaney could get Lacy's number. No problem, he'd been told. Between Fran and Ashley, one of them was bound to have Lacy's contact information. Within ten minutes he had Fran's number and called Lacy first thing this morning.

"So where are we headed?" Malcolm asked, opening the passenger door to his truck for her, assisting her as she hopped in.

"Zack's Falls."

"Zack's Falls?" he asked, placing the bag of food in the seat behind her.

"You said you wanted to go to my favorite picnic place."

Closing the door, he grinned at her through the half-open window. "Yes, but I didn't know we were going swimming."

"You want to?" she asked with a sudden eagerness.

He frowned. "No suit."

"No need," she replied, a naughty tickle in her gaze.

He laughed and said merrily, "I think I'm in love."

Climbing into the driver's seat, Malcolm drove the short distance to Ladd Springs. Nothing but blue sky and balmy temps, it was a great day to be outside. Unlike California in the summertime when the hills turned golden, Tennessee was green and lush. Veritable forests lined the roads—open roads, country roads—and flowers abounded. From a proliferation of wildflowers street-side to the manicured borders and window boxes around houses, colorful blooms were everywhere. Branches suspended their leaves over the road creating a lush canopy of shade as they drove. Here and there, mailboxes poked out from private drives, most homes hidden from sight behind a wall of trees. Tennessee was different than any other place Malcolm had been. Trees and forests he'd seen, but driving these quiet country roads filled him with a sense of peace and tranquility, completely unlike driving through the jungle, where the senses fired to eight cylinders on watch for natives and wildlife, hair pin curves that weren't announced. The rocky coastline of California offered the crash and thunder of the Pacific Ocean where here the water flowed rapid and rhythmic through rivers and creeks.

And then there were the springs. Nick had given him the grand tour and it was amazing. Out of nowhere, water would spurt from the ground and begin a stream that traveled down the mountainside until its path became blocked, detoured or re-routed. Delaney's father had built a wishing well around a spring off Ernie's cabin. It was a plain wooden structure, used for aesthetic purposes only, but the spring it concealed was a gift of nature. More than drinking the spring water, Malcolm imagined showering in it—heated, of course—but showering from water cleaner than any city in the country, any land in the world.

Malcolm was content to simply drive around these parts. No doubt, something his guests would enjoy as well. But today wasn't for scenic drives. Today was for outdoor hiking, a vigorous jaunt to Zack's falls, a part of Ladd property he had yet to tour. He gazed over at his passenger, the beautiful brunette staring out the window as though she were mired in thought. He hoped it was all good.

Lacy broke the silence. "You don't have a wife you're hiding somewhere, do you?'

"A wife?" Startled, he reached over the center console and patted her arm. "Not on your life."

She looked at him queerly. "You don't want a wife?"

The comment caught him on the chin. Did she want to become one? "Well, I'm not against the idea per se," he slid out noncommittally. Actually came close once, but the woman turned out to be a manipulative liar. She'd been conning him the whole time, only interested in his money. After he caught her making plans to buy a condo in Colorado—one he knew nothing about—the deal was off. Investment opportunity or no, a married couple was supposed to discuss these things ahead of time. Now, Nick Harris was about the closest thing he had to a wife. Malcolm chuckled. And not a very pretty one.

"Good," Lacy retorted, as though the issue were settled. "We can go swimming, then."

Amused by her logic, Malcolm asked, "So tell me, Ms. Owens, when do you plan on returning to Atlanta?"

Her exuberance dimmed. "Why?"

"I want to know how long I'll have the pleasure of your company." She smiled at the reply, but it was a joy that didn't seem to penetrate completely. "Is there a problem? You sort of dodged my question at the diner."

"No." Lacy pressed the button to fully lower her window. "It's such a beautiful day out, isn't it?"

"Dodge number two."

She turned to him. "If you must know, I don't really have any reason to go back to Atlanta."

"How about a job?"

"The lounge?" She waved him off. "Oh, poo. That's not important."

"It puts money in your pocket."

Lacy expelled a sigh and thrust her attention back out the window. "Money isn't everything, you know."

"True." Malcolm considered the woman beside him, the shift in mood. "You could always consider my job offer for the hotel, though you'll need something in the interim. Maybe they're hiring at Whiskey Joe's."

"Oh," she blew out her breath, "I don't want to be in the bar business anymore. I think I'd like a day job."

"Well then we need to find you a day position. Until the hotel's built, that is. Because after that, you're mine."

Lacy latched onto him with a grin—one that stirred him more deeply than he expected. Malcolm realized he was beginning to really like this woman. Beyond her looks, Lacy was like no other woman he'd ever met. She was beautiful, yes, with a body that could rock a man's world, but she had spunk. She was fresh and candid. She didn't lie or hide things, she didn't play games—other than her affinity for flirting. She seemed utterly transparent, as though her closet was bare, no secrets or skeletons in sight.

But Malcolm wasn't fooling himself. A girl who ran away at age seventeen with an eighteen-year-old young man certainly wasn't an innocent. Landing on the sidewalks of Atlanta, forced to fend for herself after the breakup, she had to have been exposed to the sleazier side of life. How was it she didn't bear the scars?

"We're almost there," Lacy announced, and shifted in her seat.

Malcolm could tell she was excited. "How long has it been since you last visited Zack's Falls?"

"My word!" She flattened a palm to her breast. "Since I was a kid, really." Her blue eyes turned fluid with memory as he watched her mentally calculate time and distance and her life since then. The excitement of recollection that had opened her expression slowly closed. "It's been a *long* time..."

Sounded to him like she missed the place, a sentiment he could fully understand. This area was beautiful. It was peaceful, homey, a great place to raise a family—if one were so inclined. But kids were never part of his plan. Not because he didn't like them, but carting them from hotel to hotel didn't appeal to him. Kids needed stability, sameness. Like his childhood in California, kids needed a community and a world they could rely on to stay consistent, parents to be there for them as they navigated their way through life. Malcolm's lifestyle was anything but.

Pulling onto the property, he rolled over the wooden bridge and said, "Let's make this afternoon memorable."

Lacy squeezed her hands together and rewarded him with a delicious smile. "*Yes*, let's do."

Parking next to Nick's sedan, Malcolm jumped out and circled the hood to collect Lacy and their picnic bag. Grabbing the blanket he'd snagged from his hotel, he slung it over his arm and held out his free elbow. "May I?"

Lacy took his arm he closed the door behind her. "You thought of everything, didn't you?"

"While I'm no sissy, sitting in the dirt is not my idea of fun."

She laughed gaily. "Are you sure you're going to make it through the woods? There are spiders and bugs, you know."

Malcolm liked her tease. Running his gaze slowly down her legs, landing on her black boots, he considered them next to the hiking boots he'd opted for and retorted, "If you can make it, I can make it."

"Let's do it!"

"By all means," he said, "let's do."

Lacy led the way through the meadow adjoining the Ladd homestead, pointing to the meadow, the river, the mountains beyond as she explained to Malcolm that it was all part of Ladd property, only this section was more gentle than where they were headed. The falls were part of the property in the area of forest that bordered the USFS. Public land, Malcolm had learned, woven between private parcels throughout the Appalachian Mountains. Ladd Springs had scores of trails and creeks, and if you didn't know where you were going, it was easy to get lost. Higher up the river was her favorite spot—and according to Lacy, the biggest water-falls for a hundred miles—Zack's Falls.

"It's definitely a beautiful tract of land," he said. "From what I've seen on my hikes with Nick and Delaney, it's a real treasure."

"Brings back so many memories for me." She stopped, crouching down to admire a pretty purple flower, yellow lines running down the length of its narrow, droopy petals. Cradling the orchid-like bloom in her fingers, she said, "My momma used to grow these in her garden."

"Is that an iris?"

Sporting a wide grin, she looked up at him through squinted eyes. "Now how does a man know anything about flowers?"

He's given enough of them away to know what he's paying for. But Malcolm wasn't about to introduce the image of him and other women to Lacy. That was the furthest thing he wanted from her mind. "I'm a man of education. In fact, that's the Tennessee state flower," he told her, recalling the page from the airline magazine, an article detailing facts about the state as his plane touched down in Knoxville.

She stood. "You're right."

Hitting the trail, they wound through a forest of trees and bushes, the temperature several degrees cooler now that they were out of the sun. For the next half-hour, Lacy entertained him with stories from her youth, memorable moments she shared with Jeremiah and Delaney when they were kids—before the trouble started—from horseback riding to jumping from the falls. Once they hit high school, everything changed. Annie and Delaney went to war, Jeremiah turned tomcat and began hanging with a bad crowd, and running stir-crazy down the same old dusty country roads, she'd been itching to break free of it all. Apart from the forest, there'd been nothing for her here and thus, she left.

Navigating the fairly level trails was easy and Malcolm enjoyed the exercise. It wasn't until they arrived at the river that things became tricky. He heard the water before he saw it. About fifty feet wide, the river was littered with rocks and boulders. There were a few decaying trunks jutting over from the sides, a few tangled in pools of water. After a slight drop off, ripples of white water rode the surface as the river ran free and fast.

Malcolm reveled in the sound of rushing water. "It's beautiful."

"Told you!" Lacy trotted over to the water's edge and tugged off her boots.

Whoa, did he miss a sign? *Skinny dipping begins here.*

She set the pair of boots aside, high and dry on a large, flat surface of a boulder. Standing bare-footed, she pointed at his feet. "You'll need to take off your shoes."

"Is that all?" he joked, hoping it wasn't.

She giggled. "For now."

Desire zipped through his loins. Lacy sounded serious.

Setting bag and blanket on a different rock, he quickly removed his boots and socks and set them alongside hers. The stone was uneven and grainy beneath his bare feet.

"You might want to roll up your jeans," she advised.

"Am I going to be wading through the river?"

"Climbing," she clarified. "But many of the cliffs have pools of water within them." She shrugged. "It might easier, is all."

"You're the boss," he said—much to her delight—and rolled up his pant legs.

"Let's go!"

In amazement, Malcolm watched as Lacy hopped up the rocks, climbing from boulder to boulder agile as a deer. Despite himself, his gaze searched for a glimpse up her skirt, but none came. She was too quick and now too far away. "Wait up!" he called after her.

Lacy traversed the rocky terrain swiftly, while Malcolm managed the climb with no small degree of effort. It wasn't that he was out of shape, more like he feared losing his grip as he scaled one rocky ledge to the next. Add the bag and blanket in hand—the blanket now stuffed inside the bag—and he had his work cut out for him. But if getting naked next to Lacy in the waterfalls was his reward, then the trouble would be worth it. *Worth every second.*

Climbing for what seemed like an hour, Malcolm seized hold of a triangular-shaped stone and hauled himself up a narrow passageway between two massive boulders. Creating a foothold in a jagged crevice—heart hammering—he coordinated his movements and hoisted himself up, invigorated by the heavy pound of water above.

Sweating, muscles pumped, he glanced up to see Lacy staring down at him with a pert smirk. "You gonna make it?" she asked loudly, her voice competing against the roar of water.

Malcolm grunted. "I'll tell you in a minute," he muttered, pushing up from his knees. Clearing the wet, gray stones to reach her level, he surveyed the surroundings and let out a low whistle. "This is some kind of beautiful."

"Isn't it?" She spoke as a proud momma would of her baby.

"It is." He turned to her, captivated by her eyes. Sunlight lit up the intricate blue layers, happiness took care of the rest. "The guests will love it, if they're able to manage the climb."

Lacy giggled. "No problem." She turned and pointed. "The trail is right over there. They can walk up, if they prefer."

Malcolm seized upon an exposed section of the trail. It paralleled the river bank. *Was she kidding*? He turned. "And you made me climb up rocks? Carrying a bag of food and blanket for your soft tush to sit on?"

She laughed and held up her hands, as though warding off an oncoming beast. "Now wait a minute—you said you wanted to explore my favorite picnic spot."

"I didn't say I had to climb myself to a near heart attack to get there!" He went for her, but she darted away from him. Malcolm backed her to the edge of the rock.

With no place left to run, she dished out a quick pout. "Are you mad at me?"

"No." Malcolm pulled her close. "But I will exact my revenge."

She covered her mouth with both hands and laughed.

Drawing her hands away, Malcolm leaned down and kissed her smack on the lips. Nothing involved, he simply wanted a taste of her incredibly fun spirit. "You owe me."

Lacy's eyes shuttered. "I do?" she asked breathlessly.

"You do." He gave her a brief kiss but pulled himself away. Now was not the time.

Malcolm scanned the landscape. The crashing water reverberated inside him, energizing every cell in his body. Unable to see upriver past the falls, he turned and inhaled the view downstream. From this elevation, it was a picturesque panorama. The river cut and turned as though carving a swath through the forest. Rocks looked as if they had been carelessly tossed in the river's path and now lay stuck within its hold. Beyond the wall of trees on either side, blue filled in the sky above. Malcolm could spend some time in a place like this. Quiet, peaceful, yet rugged and challenging. He turned and took in the woman beside him, her expression wistful, dreamy. He could spend that time with *her*.

"Fond memories?" he asked.

"Yes," she said quietly. "A lot of them."

"You'd make a great hiking guide."

Lacy tilted her chin up to him. "You think so?"

"I do. You know the land, you climb it well. And you love it. It's the perfect combination in a guide." In a woman, as well, he mused, but kept that observation to himself.

She cocked her head to the side and said, "Maybe I'll apply for the job of mountain guide instead of guest-greeter."

"You do that." Ready to settle in for their visit, Malcolm checked his watch. It was almost one-thirty. *Already*? Hot, sweaty, he was tempted to jump in and cool off right here. "How much further?"

"None. We're here. This is my spot."

He grinned. "Best news I've heard all day."

Lacy chose an area off to the side, close to the deepest pool of water but out of the direct spray from the falls by several yards. Partially shaded by the trees, the rocks were level, the spot semi-private and affording them a nice view of both the gorge of waterfalls crashing through a V in the boulders and the river below. Invigorating sound of water to his right, calm and winding scenery of river flow to his left, he'd have to remember this spot. It would make the perfect location to make love to her.

Sitting back against a rock with her legs extended and crossed, Lacy wriggled her toes. Painted apple red, they shone brightly in the sun. Digging into the paper bag, she pulled out a drumstick and handed it to him.

Sprawled out beside her, he replied, "Thanks." He could eat this one and ten more after the hike up here. Malcolm bit into the round end and groaned with pleasure at the mild spice of fried coating mixed with moist meaty flesh. "This is delicious," he said through a half-closed mouth.

"It's Aunt Frannie's specialty."

"What isn't her specialty when it comes to cooking?"

Lacy laughed. Pulling one free for herself, she said, "So you never told me where you're from."

"California."

"Really? What part?" she asked, then bit into her chicken.

"Southern California. Plenty of beaches, plenty of desert, not a lot of green. Basically nothing like Tennessee." He paused. "Which is probably why I like this place so much."

She frowned. "Did you not have a nice childhood?"

"Oh, I had a great childhood. I surfed, I played music, hung out with my friends. I was simply ready for a change of scenery."

Holding the chicken before her lips, she gazed at him. "Is that why you travel a lot?"

"I travel because it's my job. Nick and I have properties in ten different cities, three different countries."

"Wow, I've never been anywhere," Lacy murmured, and took another bite.

He could see her mind digesting the revelation, probably conjuring up exotic beaches and beautiful people. What she didn't see was the poverty of South America, the slums of the Caribbean, the hardship of the Outback in Australia. Life wasn't as pretty outside the hotel boundaries as inside. Nor in his hometown. Most people heard the word California and imagined Hollywood, movie stars, but there was a whole lot more to the state than the film industry. Maybe one day, he'd show Lacy.

A flash of red caught his eye. Malcolm fired a hand to Lacy's mouth, pressing it to her lips. She blinked and he held a finger to his own lips, motioning for her to be quiet. Her eyes grew wide. Malcolm's attention shot to the trail. As he lowered his hand from her mouth, she followed his gaze. Two figures were traveling down the trail, partially obscured by tree trunks, leave-filled branches, and a massive boulder that jutted up between the trail and river.

"Oh!" she cried under her breath. Lacy's eyes glistened as she stared.

"Shhh..." Malcolm warned, a bad feeling seeping into his gut. Jeremiah just ran past, followed by a skinny, ragged-looking fellow. What the hell were *they* doing up here?

Malcolm was surprised they didn't see him and Lacy, but the two men seemed in a pretty big hurry. His first instinct was to follow them, but that would leave Lacy exposed. With no weapon, no way to defend herself, she would be in jeopardy if he left her.

"What are *they* doing up here?" Lacy whispered.

"Don't know." But he was damn sure going to find out.

"And who was that man with Jeremiah?"

"You don't know him?" Malcolm asked.

"Never seen him before in my life."

"We need to tell Nick and Delaney. This could prove to be a wrinkle we don't need."

"A wrinkle? Right now?"

As much as he hated to do it, he nodded. "Time may prove critical on this one." The dash to her mood was quick and severe. Malcolm tilted her chin up to face him, taking pleasure in the fact that her current pout was genuine. "Don't worry. I'll make it up to you. But right now, we need to go."

Chapter Sixteen

Once in the privacy of Delaney's cabin, Nick and Delaney stared expectantly as Malcolm let loose with the news. "We've got trouble."

"What's up?" Nick asked, standing by Delaney's side at the kitchen island. A thick black iron skillet of cornbread sat on a heat pad on the butcher block surface, the aroma saturating the interior. It made Malcolm hungry for the picnic he'd abandoned, but for good reason. He could eat later. They needed to talk *now*.

Lacy hovered by Malcolm's side, meek as a kitten, almost as if she feared being in the same room with Delaney and in *her* room at that. He had to admit, the razors thrashing through Delaney's gaze were not the most welcoming sight, and they were *definitely* aimed at Lacy.

"Jeremiah was on the trail!" Lacy blurted.

Delaney recoiled. "What?"

Way to ease it out, Malcolm thought, though he wasn't angry, only learning her ways. "It's true. We saw him by Zack's Falls, headed down the trail."

Delaney clamped a hand to Nick's arm. "He knows." Her voice was a barely controlled panic as she hooked her gaze into her man. "He must have talked to Clem."

"Clem Sweeney?" Lacy asked, then glanced about. "What's he got to do with all this?"

Nick covered the hand on his arm and drew Delaney close. "We don't know that for sure. There could be a dozen reasons why he was there." He looked to Malcolm. "What do you think?" he asked, though both men knew better.

Jeremiah Ladd in the forest near the site of the gold? Not a coincidence. "He was with another man and the two seemed in quite a hurry."

"I've never seen the man before in my life," Lacy added eagerly. "He's nobody we know."

Ever the helpful one, Malcolm mused, noting Delaney's displeasure wrapping itself around Lacy like a python. But if Lacy's lack of familiarity helped narrow down the man's identity, then so be it. Let her chime in all she wanted.

"What did he look like?" Nick asked.

"Thin, scraggly," Malcolm began. "Definitely a local type, but one who looked pretty hard up."

"Was he wearing a hat, special clothes?" Nick probed.

"He had a ratty black hat, maybe a band of metal around the crown." Malcolm looked to his trusted eye-witness for assistance, but when Lacy remained quiet, he said, "I can't be sure. Like I said, they were in a pretty big hurry."

Nick and Delaney shared a knowing glance. "Willie," she said to Nick, then to Malcolm, "Did they see you?"

"I don't think so," Lacy replied. "We were sitting by Zack's Falls, on the far side by the old rope swing tree. Remember it, Delaney?"

Malcolm sought Delaney's response but none was forthcoming. If she did remember, she didn't concede the fact. "I'm willing to bet they would have said something if they had."

"I agree." Nick turned to Delaney, still clinging to his arm. "Jeremiah must have talked to Clem. There's no other way he could have known."

"He's going to steal it!" Delaney cried.

"Delaney." Nick took her gently by the arms. "At this point there's nothing he can do."

Anger slinked into her brown eyes. "Other than rob us blind."

Malcolm remained mum. It wasn't his place to reveal the presence of gold on Ladd Springs. Delaney wanted to remain pretty tight-lipped about the subject and with good reason.

Word would spread like wildfire, most folks heading in for a look-see themselves, probably leaving with a souvenir or two, for their time.

"It's not like we can stand guard, shooting any looters on sight—" Delaney stopped as if a thought just occurred to her. "Or can we?" She looked to Malcolm, then back to Nick. "Maybe that's *exactly* what we should be doing. We should stand guard and make sure Jeremiah doesn't get anywhere near it, shooting him on sight if he tries."

"Near what?" Lacy asked.

Delaney, claws exposed and ready to pounce, honed in on Lacy. "Nothing."

Lacy looked to Malcolm. It was clear she didn't believe Delaney. "Nothing?"

"Nothing your ex-lover should be anywhere near," Delaney jabbed at her.

"Delaney, please," Nick said calmly and pulled her back. "Lacy has been helpful so far. She's not conspiring with Jeremiah."

"I have *nothing* to do with Jeremiah, I told you. I'm here to visit family."

Lacy was so earnest, so genuine, but Malcolm could see Delaney was losing control. The stress was unraveling her before their eyes, and if he and Lacy stayed much longer, all hell could break loose and tie these two in one mess of a fight. Malcolm ushered Lacy toward the door and, with a hand to the knob, stated, "The point remains. If Jeremiah knows, he's not going to let it go without a fight. We need to keep our defenses up."

Surprising Lacy, the four of them left the cabin together, Nick and Delaney deciding they had to search the woods this instant, while Lacy and Malcolm chose to finish their picnic. Too bad it was interrupted in the first place, Lacy thought, although she had no idea why. What was Delaney so worried about Jeremiah stealing? Was it in the woods? Were they hiding something?

Following Malcolm step for step down the steep trail, Lacy couldn't shake her curiosity. Her brain kept peeling back the layers like a sweet Vidalia onion knowing there had to be a reason Delaney was wound up tighter than a fur ball. It was so unlike her, it had to be something big.

One after another they filed down the narrow wooded path. Hitting the small clearing, they crossed the bridge. Lacy worried the deteriorating structure would collapse beneath their weight, dumping them into the cold creek water rushing below. Several boards had been replaced, but in her opinion the whole bridge should be redone. It plumb wasn't safe!

"Looks like we've got company," Malcolm said, slowing.

Lacy's pulse quickened as she caught sight of Jeremiah, his bright orange shirt more like a hunter's vest than fashion statement and a stark contrast to the dilapidated old cabin. Standing on Ernie's front porch, Jeremiah was banging on the front door something fierce. Lacy feared he might break it. Next, he grabbed the door handle.

"If he thinks he's going to alert Ernie to his little discovery, he's in for a surprise," Nick commented.

"What discovery?" Lacy asked. And why wouldn't they tell her? Nick and Delaney were acting more secretive than the FBI.

Malcolm and Nick traded looks. Divulging nothing they kicked into action and headed for Jeremiah. Delaney was right behind them.

"What's going on?" Lacy wailed under her breath, trailing close at their heel. This was ridiculous and so unfair! After all, she was on *their* side.

As they neared Ernie's cabin, Jeremiah spotted them and stilled. The look on his face was pure evil, even from this distance, and the quickest way to ruin his otherwise handsome face, Lacy. Jogging down the front steps, he waited for them.

"Trying to break in?" Malcolm asked, leading the pack.

"As if anyone would try and steal something from this rat hole," Jeremiah pitched back. Although he acknowledged

Lacy, he was more interested in Delaney. Circling around her in a conceited swagger, Jeremiah held her in his gaze. "You thought you could get away with it, didn't you?"

Delaney remained mute, Nick and Malcolm standing guard to either side of her.

A wicked glimmer lit up Jeremiah's expression. "Does the old man know?"

"It's none of your business, Jeremiah. You don't own Ladd Springs, Felicity does—or will—and I'd advise you to keep off private property. I catch you trespassing again, I'll call the police."

He laughed. "Oh, Delaney, you floor me, you really do. You always were good at bluffing." Jeremiah set hands to his hips and said, "Remind me to invite you to Vegas on my next trip. I could use you by my side at the poker table."

"I wouldn't set foot in a casino with you."

He paused, staring at her with an odd look. It occurred to Lacy that Jeremiah still cared for Delaney—though he had a funny way of showing it. "The scowl on that pretty face of yours would prove distracting enough for my fellow players but it might distract me, too. Better we leave you home." Jeremiah glanced between the Malcolm and Nick. "So tell me, do your boys here know what you're hiding in the woods?"

"I'm not hiding anything," she replied, but Lacy noted a tinge of color rise in Delaney's cheeks. "And even if I was, it'd be no business of yours."

Jeremiah snickered. "So aggressive, Delaney. And here I'm the one who should be pissed off, what with you stealing my inheritance right from under my nose." He iced the men with a look of sheer contempt. "I hope she's paying you well for your trouble."

Nick stepped forward and growled, "I oughta cram that smirk straight down your throat."

Jeremiah's face twisted with pleasure. "Go ahead and try."

"Don't do it, Nick," Malcolm said, grabbing his arm.

Malcolm stood between Jeremiah and Nick and Lacy reveled in his courage. What Malcolm and Nick didn't realize was that Jeremiah had a black belt in karate. Add those ostrich boots of his and he could really hurt them if he wanted to. Yet look at them, brave as soldiers. Lucky for Delaney. She was thin as a twig and Jeremiah could break her in two, if he had a mind to do so.

A flash of sunlight glinted off the windshield of an incoming truck, its tires pummeling the gravel as it sped in. Lacy looked to see who the driver was, wondering why they were in such a hurry, but a puff of dust obscured her view as the red vehicle turned and stopped. Then Ernie Ladd jumped out and she gasped. My gracious, he was thin. He'd never been a big man, but he was half of what she remembered!

"Well, if it isn't the man of the hour," Jeremiah said, turning only slightly, maintaining a wary eye on Nick and Malcolm. Jeremiah had always been clever when it came to his adversaries. Lacy had seen him fight for less than a blink back in Atlanta, but never did she know him to be sucker-punched. He was too smart. Deviously so.

All eyes were on Ernie as he hobbled over on his cane, though at a pretty good clip, with legs that weren't much bigger than his cane. Ernie didn't have a spec of fat on his body, and instead reminded Lacy of a walking skeleton. His black boots were like cement blocks around his feet, his black belt cinched so tightly at his waist it was a wonder he could breathe. Even his ears stuck out from beneath his ball cap, like they were glued to a skull, one where they didn't belong. "Ernie looks so thin. Is he okay?" Lacy asked Delaney.

"Ernie is sick, Lacy," Jeremiah said, flicking a spiteful glance toward Delaney. "Or didn't you know?"

"Sick? Oh, heavens!" Lacy looked to Delaney for explanation. "Is he going to be all right?"

Jeremiah shook his head. "Afraid not. It's terminal."

He spoke gravely, yet Lacy didn't detect an ounce of sadness in his voice—only mockery—which angered her. She stole a peek at Ernie. Bless his heart, but he didn't look well at all.

Pushing the black-rimmed glasses up his nose, Ernie grimaced at Jeremiah. "What are you doing back here? Didn't I warn you off this property once already?"

"I came to tell you that your precious niece has been stealing from you."

Ernie didn't say a word, only continued to stare, like Jeremiah was some kind of dangerous varmint that might attack at any moment.

"Did you know you have gold on this property?"

Lacy's ears perked at the information. *Gold*? She flashed a glance to Delaney. The woman looked like a kid caught with her hand in the cookie jar. She checked with Malcolm. There was gold on the property? For real?

Malcolm nodded, but kept a wary eye on Jeremiah.

Oh *my*, Lacy thought. Didn't things just grow *worlds* more interesting? And folks in Atlanta thought small towns were slow and sleepy. If only they had a clue!

"I don't care nothin' about no gold," Ernie said, then jabbed a crooked finger in Jeremiah's face. "I want you gone. You hear me, boy? Gone. Right now."

Delaney came to life. "You heard the man. It's time for you to go."

"You're telling me you don't care that Delaney and her kid Felicity are stealing from you? Taking you for what could be hundreds of thousands of dollars?"

Ernie got in Jeremiah's face and snarled, "Don't you ever speak that child's name again, you hear me?"

Lacy pressed a hand to her mouth. Ernie's eyes looked like they were about to pop out of his head and clear through his glasses! Was the gold worth *that* much?

Jeremiah's posture stiffened. "Nobody tells me what to do, especially not you." He whipped a glance around the group and said, "You're a fool, you let them run off with this property. But not me. I'm entitled to what's mine and I aim to get it. And I'll take it from Delaney any way I can. Or her stupid daughter."

Ernie shoved Jeremiah and Lacy's heart caught. Jeremiah raised his hand, but Malcolm and Nick were between them in seconds—Malcolm taking Jeremiah, Nick taking Ernie. Lacy watched in horror as Ernie tried to fight his way free from Nick's grasp, shouting at Jeremiah.

"Ernie, stop it!" Delaney hollered. "Don't let him get to you!"

Lacy couldn't move, couldn't think. Jeremiah would hit his father? His sick father? Really? She closed her eyes. It was too horrible a thought.

"Get your hands off me," Jeremiah yelled at Malcolm.

Lacy opened back up to see Jeremiah break free from Malcolm. That's when she saw Albert Ladd. Ambling toward the house, his body larger than she remembered his pear-shaped figure to be, Albert looked like he was trying to mind his own business, passing by the scuffle like he was invisible, his eyes riveted to the scene nonetheless.

"You need to go," Malcolm commanded Jeremiah.

Jeremiah spit on the ground, then yanked the orange paisley shirt away from his body. "You are insane if you think I'm going to walk off and let Delaney have this property without a fight—a fight I intend to win." Lacy swore Jeremiah was about to spit on Malcolm, but he didn't. "It ain't gonna happen, cowboy. This here land is mine and I'm going to get it, one way or another."

Standing several feet from Ernie, Nick said, "This property goes to Felicity. It's a done deal."

"There's no such thing as a done deal where I come from." Jeremiah glowered at the group of them, with a brief glance to the passing Albert Ladd. "Never heard of challenging a deed?"

Lacy bet they had. Malcolm and Nick were smart. But Jeremiah was conniving. She frowned. Did they understand what they were dealing with when it came to Jeremiah?

"Whatever I have to do, I'll do it." Jeremiah pointed at Delaney. "Watch your back, sweetheart. You've messed with the wrong man."

"I'll kill you, you come back here again," Ernie declared.

Delaney flinched. "*Ernie!*"

He smacked her with an angry glare and repeated, "I'll kill him, I tell you. I'd kill him with my bare hands if I had to."

Jeremiah's hazel brown eyes grew black as night. "I'd love for you to try."

A chill raced down Lacy's spine. Her gaze went quickly to Nick. If there was a hothead in the bunch, it was him. But this time, he remained in place and merely watched Jeremiah walk away. All of them trailed his figure as he climbed into his truck, started the engine, and tore out away, tires skidding as he hit the street.

Ernie shuffled toward his cabin and Lacy caught her breath. *Kill* Jeremiah? She turned to Delaney. "You don't think he's serious, do you?"

"He's not going to let this go without a fight," Delaney muttered.

"I've only known Ernie a few weeks and I wouldn't put it past him," Nick put in.

"Why the love fest?" Malcolm asked, smoothing a hand through his hair. "I've seen bad blood, but this mix is lethal."

Delaney stared after her uncle. Lacy thought she looked torn. Did it hurt her heart to hear her uncle speak that way about his own son? His own flesh and blood?

"Jeremiah caused Ernie a lot of grief before he left," Delaney said, her gaze settling on Lacy who shrank under the spotlight of attention. Delaney took on a tough-girl stance, setting hands to her jean-clad hips. "He stole money and guns from Ernie. The money, so he could run off to Atlanta with his new squeeze," Delaney's eyes spit knives toward Lacy, "the guns because he was traveling with a rough crowd at the time. In fact, the night they left, there was a shooting down-town and word had it Jeremiah was involved."

"I didn't know anything about any shooting!" Lacy cried, genuinely stunned by the accusation. "He never said a thing to me about it." She sought Malcolm's reaction, her heart suddenly in her throat. "*Honest.* I swear on my mom-ma's life!"

Malcolm moved to her side. "I believe you," he said softly and slid a protective arm around her shoulders.

"Did they ever arrest anyone for the shooting?" Nick asked.

"Albert's son, Billy."

Malcolm let out a low whistle.

"His other boy is on the run," Delaney added.

Lacy had no idea! "Robby? What did he do?"

"Held up a liquor store."

"Oh, *no*..." Billy and Robby both? And they had been so nice to her in high school. A little rowdy, but she never imag-ined they'd turn into criminals.

"They're both worthless," Delaney said without care, as though she weren't speaking of two men's lives, of two liv-ing, breathing human beings.

"And both blood relatives to Ernie," Malcolm said quiet-ly.

Delaney stilled.

"You understand that under Tennessee law, both Al-bert's sons are equally as entitled as Jeremiah to ownership should he challenge the deed and win."

Nick dropped his head back. "Perfect."

Delaney buried her face in her hands, then fell against Nick's chest. He wrapped his arms around her and held her close. Why, if Lacy hadn't witnessed it with her own eyes, she wouldn't have believed it. Delaney Wilkins falling help-less into the arms of a man? She shook her head. Unbelieva-ble.

About time, if you asked *her*. Women needed men. Lacy's eyes went to Malcolm. Strong, brave men who would look after a female the way a man should. She smiled at him and he smiled back giving her a light squeeze. It was their job. After all, God made men strong and brave, and women sweet and beautiful and in need of protection and love. It's what kept the world spinning in harmony.

Startled by the sight of a white sedan pulling in, Lacy peered at the driver. *What in tarnation is she doing here?*

Chapter Seventeen

Lacy watched with displeasure as her sister drove over the bridge. Was Annie following her? Was she here to ruin her afternoon with Malcolm? If Aunt Frannie was to blame, Lacy would pinch her ear. She was only enjoying a picnic with the man. Her aunt didn't have to spy on her.

The white car rolled to a stop next to Malcolm's truck, and Annie hopped out. Clad in her usual salon black, she marched straight toward them with nary a concern to her shiny black heels.

Nick nudged Delaney and she straightened. "What now? More threats?"

Annie Owens pulled up front and center and stopped. After gathering the group of them in her gaze, she sized Lacy up with a suspicious look. "What are you doing here?"

Lacy gave a flippant shake to her hair. "I'm *visiting*, if it were any of your business. What are *you* doing here is the question."

"I've come to have a word with Delaney."

"We've said our words, Annie. There's nothing left to discuss."

As though it required great effort, Annie cleared her throat, glanced about and stated, "I've come to inform you that my lawyer is seeking a court-ordered paternity test from Jeremiah to settle the matter of Casey's birthright once and for all."

"You sure you want to do that, Annie?" Delaney asked.

Lacy was surprised by the venom tone. It was clear Delaney didn't believe Annie's claim for one second. Truth be known, Lacy wasn't quite sure of it herself. Annie had been with more than a few boys back in high school. Casey could belong to one of them.

"I'm sure," Annie replied. "And when you learn the truth, I'll expect you to do the right thing and split the property between the two girls."

Delaney's mouth fell open. "Split the property?"

Annie nodded with what Lacy found to be an imperious flair, like she was some kind of queen, or something. Good for her, she privately cheered. Delaney had no right to keep Ladd Springs from Casey if she really did belong to Jeremiah.

"At this rate, Felicity will be lucky she doesn't get run off the place entirely!" Delaney exclaimed.

Annie took a step back as though struck off balance. Her blue eyes rounded, confusion warring with suspicion. "What are you talking about?"

"The *father* of your baby may take everything."

"Don't blame *me* for Jeremiah's behavior." Annie flung an intimidating glance toward Lacy.

The hair on Lacy's neck stood on end. Don't blame *her* for Jeremiah's presence, either. She followed *him*, remember? It wasn't her idea to come back home. It was Jeremiah's!

"The hell I won't!" Delaney waved an arm through the air and skewered Annie wither gaze. "You're the one who called him in the first place!"

"I did not!"

"Oh, no?" Delaney derided angrily. "Did he appear out of thin air?"

Safely out of Delaney's firing range, Lacy wished she could help Annie. She looked sincere in her denial, but unfortunately, Annie didn't want anything to do with Lacy, help or otherwise.

Nick stepped forward. "Delaney, *stop*. This isn't helping."

She whirled on him, her long ponytail whipping behind her. "How can you be so calm? You have a lot riding on this, too, you know. I can't believe you're going to let her stand there and tell you what she's going to take."

Nick ventured a glance toward Annie then gazed down at Delaney. "This is not the time or the place to work through the details. First, we need to devise a plan."

"Plan? What kind of plan are you talking about?" Annie demanded. "There should be no plans put into place without *my* input." She thumped her chest like a momma gorilla.

"The only input you're going to give is—"

Nick closed a hand over Delaney's mouth and practically dragged her away. "Let's go," he said, and hustled her away. Dwarfed by his size, Delaney could fight all she wanted, for the good it would do her. That man was in *charge*.

Lacy giggled at the sight of Delaney's shrieks beneath Nick's palm as he led her to his car. For so many years, Delaney had been bossing the lot of them around like a steer in a cow pasture that it was gratifying to see someone take charge of that little vixen.

"Jeremiah is Casey's father," Annie declared.

"If he is, your test will prove it," Malcolm replied with a measured tone.

"It will, you'll see." Then to Lacy, she said pointedly, "I hope you're not here aiding and abetting the enemy."

"*What*? I'm doing no such thing," Lacy snapped.

"That woman at the diner yesterday, she's Jeremiah's girlfriend, isn't she? *Your friend*," Annie said in what felt like an accusation. "Frannie told me you two know each other from Atlanta."

"So?"

Annie served up a melting glare, but addressed Malcolm, "Watch yourself with her, Mr. Ward. She's a known backstabber."

Lacy bristled. "Annie Grace—how *dare* you."

Annie shifted her gaze to Lacy. "I'm only speaking the truth."

Her gallant Malcolm stood strong. "I don't have any concerns, Ms. Owens, I assure you. As far as I've seen, Lacy has proven herself to be nothing but helpful and courteous."

"See," Lacy snipped, pleased that Malcolm had rushed to her defense. She twirled the hair at her ear and thought, if that didn't quiet Annie, Lacy didn't know what would, though her pleasure was fleeting. Annie still hated her.

"You don't know her as well as I do. Now, if you'll excuse me," Annie said and stalked off to her car.

Lacy sighed and wriggled her fingers. "Toodles, Annie." If only she wasn't so hateful. If only she would come around. Lacy could use some sisterly love and she only had the one sister. The one who despised her.

Malcolm curled a finger beneath her chin and tipped it upward. "How about you and I go finish our picnic?"

Tickled by the suggestion, she replied, "Delighted!"

"Shall we?" Malcolm bent his elbow and she slipped her hand through. He pulled her close. She luxuriated in the smell of him, the feel of him. His cologne reminded her of the department store, the men's fragrance section where she used to idle and sample and dream of the day when a handsome, charming man would sweep her off her feet. She'd tested each and every cologne, debating which she'd want her dream man to use. Malcolm's choice was divine. She inhaled deeply. It was woodsy, spicy and smelled expensive. The fragrance of a man of the world. It was nice having a man next to her, particularly one as chivalrous as Malcolm.

Annie's car peeled out of the driveway and Lacy crinkled her nose. "My sister is so angry these days."

"She's fighting an uphill battle," he remarked, leading Lacy toward the main bridge and back toward the forest trail. "Being a single mother isn't easy, and she just wants to do what's right by her child."

"You sure are giving her a lot of credit," Lacy said, gently bumping her shoulder against his arm as they strolled. His browned skin was shades darker than her own, reminding her she needed to get out more, soak up the sunshine, stretch out by the falls and sun herself. It's what she used to do and would do so today.

"I'm only giving her proper due." Malcolm stopped by his truck and turned to her. "And I'm surprised to hear negative remarks coming from you—you who sees the best in everyone and can't hold a grudge if it were handcuffed to her wrist."

Lacy smiled. She liked that Malcolm saw the good side of her. "Well, she has been alone for a long time. According to Aunt Frannie, Annie's lucky to get an annual date, if that."

He chuckled. "Don't hold it against her. Not all the girls are as pretty as you, with men willing to stand in line in a desert's heat."

"You do go on," she said, enjoying every minute of it.

"Hungry? We can break open that food and eat it right here, if you'd like."

The food and blanket sat in the backseat of his truck. Lacy shook her head. Suddenly, she was in no mood for food. Deep down, she wished she and Annie could be on the same side. She wished the two of them could meet Delaney head on and challenge her for Casey's right to Ladd Springs. If the test proved Casey belonged to Jeremiah, wouldn't that make her claim correct? Lacy looked up to Malcolm. A tuft of white hair fell over his brow, his blue eyes intent upon her own. Gentle, quiet, he had an air of wisdom about him. "What if Annie's claim about Jeremiah turns out to be true? What if he really is Casey's daddy?"

"Then what Annie said is true."

She knew it. "Are you sure?"

He nodded. "Felicity and Casey are cousins. Their parents are both Ladds."

"Yes, but Susannah married Harry Wilkins. Wouldn't that make Casey more entitled than Felicity? I mean, she'd bear the Ladd name and all."

Malcolm returned a knowing smile. Nice try. "The two girls share equally in the Ladd bloodline. According to Delaney, Ernie promised her mother that he would will the property to Delaney and Felicity. There was no mention of Jeremiah."

"Not Albert, either?"

"I don't think Albert would know what to do with the property if he had it," Malcolm said, his tone very diplomatic.

Lacy nodded, closing off the possibility in an instant. The Albert she remembered was about as sharp as a dumpling. "You're probably right, there."

"But you're correct in that as sole owner, if Ernie had died without a will, the entire property would have gone to his son, Jeremiah."

"The entire thing?"

"Yes. But Ernie signed a life estate, giving Felicity the property upon his death."

"What's a life estate?"

"It's a simple way to transfer ownership for someone approaching the end of their life. With the swipe of a pen, you give your entire rights of ownership to one of your family members. Doing so while you're still alive eliminates a lot of hassle for the heirs. In the meantime, Ernie retains his right to live on the property but ensures Felicity receives ownership upon his death. She and Delaney will have to pay the back taxes," he said, "which are no small amount, but after that, it's theirs, free and clear."

Lacy and Malcolm crossed the bridge, the creek below a maze of rocks and moss and sand blurred beneath a crystal clear flow of water. Lively and quick, Lacy thought it pretty, even more when the sun's rays tumbled over the surface, setting life to the stream. "How come Jeremiah keeps talking like he's going to get it, then?"

"Because he can challenge the validity of the deed."

"Huh?"

He chuckled. "It's complicated. Suffice it to say, Delaney and Felicity are not out of the woods yet." He slid a glance toward the meadow, the mountains beyond, rounded hills of green. "And speaking of woods, let's say you and I go back to Zack's Falls."

Lacy shook her head. "Uh-uh."

Surprised by her refusal he replied, "Uh-uh?"

She nibbled her lower lip. "I have a better idea." Lacy tugged on his arm then pulled away, darting off ahead of him. "C'mon. Follow me!"

Wondering at the mischievous look in her eye, Malcolm chased Lacy through the meadow to the trailhead, surprised by how much effort it required. She ran through the tall grass like a deer, while he felt like a stampeding cow on a mad dash for his life. But the sight of her short skirt and curvy figure prancing ahead of him propelled him forward. She stopped short of the trail's opening, waiting for him to catch up.

Within seconds, Malcolm reached her. Dropping hands to knees, he leaned forward to catch his breath. He couldn't believe how winded he'd become from the quick sprint. She, on the other hand, stood there with only the mildest of deep inhalations. "You're in good shape," he commented.

Lacy beamed at the compliment. "Thank you. I do yoga."

"Yoga keeps your heart and lungs in shape?" He shook his head. "Never heard of such a thing."

She giggled. "I swim in the summer."

Malcolm nodded and pulled his body to an upright position, still struggling to calm his breath. "Now you're talking. Swimming is the one sport that will prove a body out of shape quicker than bathroom scale."

"You're not out of shape."

He shook his head. "You're kind, but I am. The proof is panting in front of you."

Lacy laughed. "Are you old?"

Such an odd question, he thought, but replied, "Forty-five."

"That's not old," she said. "I'm thirty-four."

"And in damn fine shape for your age," he said. Regaining control of his heart and lungs, Malcolm admired her shapely legs up close, creamy white between her denim skirt and black boots. Keep chasing this little pixie and he might end up flat on his back from a heart attack! But taking another gander at her legs, her narrow hips and full breasts in the white tank, he decided it would darn well be worth it. "So you don't want to go back to the falls?" he asked.

She shook her head. "I'd like to see the gold. Do you know where it is?"

Malcolm's instincts swooped in. Lacy wanted to see the gold? She wasn't even supposed to know about its existence, let alone see it up close and personal! "Why do you want to see the gold?" he asked, rubbing his lower back.

"I've never seen real gold before."

Malcolm raised a brow. "Somehow I find that hard to believe. Men drape girls like you in the stuff. How is it that the shiny metal passed *you* by?"

Lacy laughed gaily and waved him off. "No, silly. I mean in the rock, in its natural form. I've only panned for it as a child, but there were never anything but glittery flakes."

"And that wasn't enough for you?" he teased.

"I didn't believe they were *real*. Same as the rubies we used to pan for over the summer." She flicked the thought away like a nuisance fly. "My folks used to tell me I was panning for treasure, but it didn't look like anything but dirt and dust to me."

It was Malcolm's turn to laugh. "I shudder to think of the trauma you endured. By all means, a girl has got to experience the real thing as least once in her lifetime, doesn't she?"

"She does," Lacy agreed heartily.

Malcolm motioned for her hand. "Mind if we walk the trail instead of hike the rocks this time?"

She batted her eyelashes. "If you prefer."

"I most certainly do," he replied and, closing his hand around hers, marveled at the softness of her skin. Add her slender figure and fine features and she seemed delicate, almost fragile—until you tried to keep up with her. Malcolm was still in awe at her athletic ability.

Entering the trail, he kept the pace easy and slow. He wanted to enjoy Lacy's company for as long as he could. He found her spontaneity fun, her guilelessness sweet. She seemed genuinely hurt by her sister's accusation, yet the next words out of her mouth were directed to help Annie. It was a feud different than any others he'd seen around town, where the enemies were well-known, territories distinctly marked. Malcolm didn't get it. Lacy was clearly disliked by her sister, yet she continued to press forward, as though she missed the signs. Danger. No trespassing. Keep Out.

"Do you think Delaney will share the property with Annie?" Lacy asked.

"That's hard to say. So far, she's been staunchly opposed to the idea."

"But if Annie proves it? Wouldn't Delaney do the right thing by Annie and give her half?"

Malcolm glanced down at Lacy. It was beginning to feel like she had a vested interest in Annie and Casey prevailing in this deal. "Right' can be a relative term. Is it right for Jeremiah to have it when he's suspected of murder?" he asked, watching for her reaction. Did she truly not know about the incident Delaney spoke of? Was it possible? "And how about Albert. Is it right for him to be cut out completely? And what about his sons?"

"Billy and Robby," she murmured, dropping her gaze to the dirt path ahead of them. "They're blood kin, too, which means they're entitled to a piece, aren't they?"

Malcolm heard distress in her voice, as though the thought of Albert's boys getting a piece of Ladd Springs was not what she wanted to hear. "It's convoluted to say the least," he acknowledged, unwilling to let talk of family feuds and property rights interfere with their time together. "But in the end, it will all work out."

She angled her face up to his. "You think so?"

Taking in her pert little mouth and beautiful blue eyes, he replied, "I do. I much prefer to believe in the positive, don't you?"

Lacy smiled, as though realizing she knew he was on to her and gave a gentle tug to his hand. "I do."

Passing the time in quiet for a while, Malcolm thought hiking through the shade of the forest was like traveling another world. From a floor of clay and rock to walls of earth and trees and a ceiling of leaves, it was secluded. Cut off from society. The forest smelled rich and clean, no trace of smog or fumes, nothing like the busy world he normally inhabited. The trail was totally private, insulated from stress. This land promised a spectacular retreat for Harris Hotel guests. It would make for a memorable stay in sensory experience. Malcolm's mind went to Lacy's hand in his and felt this place was becoming memorable for a different reason.

He was beginning to look forward to spending some time here, designing the hotel, building it, and hanging out with the woman by his side. As far as he could tell, Lacy had no plans to return to Atlanta, nothing pulling her away from him. She was free and easy and it was his job to see that their relationship stayed that way. Observing a large rock at the curve in the trail up ahead, Malcolm knew they were getting close. Not far beyond was a valley of brush and a creek which would help him locate the "golden rock" with ease. "We're almost there," he informed her.

Her blue eyes widened. "We are?"

"Yes. But before I show you the rock, you must promise me you'll keep this a secret. Delaney doesn't want the entire world to know about it—"

"'Cause they'll come in and get it for themselves," Lacy finished for him. She nodded. "I understand."

"Good." He stopped. Cupping her face, he gazed into her eyes for any hint of deception. "I can trust you, right?" She nodded and linked hands behind her back like a dutiful child. "You wouldn't want me to get into trouble, would you?"

"Of course not."

Malcolm smiled. "Me, neither. Delaney can be a viper when she wants to be."

"You don't have to tell me—I grew up with her!"

"Point taken," he said. Sliding a hand behind her back, he unwound her arms and entwined his fingers through hers.

Holding her hand was nice. Simple, easy. His heart skipped a beat. Really nice. "This way."

Malcolm led her to a large tree trunk, a tight passageway cutting through rocks and roots as it forged a path to the forest floor. Twenty yards and they would be face-to-face with the gold.

"Where is it?" she asked, scanning their vicinity.

"It's over there," he said, pointing to the cluster of boulders, then looked down. "Are those your good boots? It's a bit muddy down there and I'd hate to see them ruined."

Lacy laughed. "These are cowboy boots. They're made for getting dirty!"

Malcolm felt a quick rise to his cheeks. "Of course. Why didn't I think of that?"

"Because you're a beach boy, not a country boy."

"You got me there," he said, and gestured a hand. "Ladies first."

Without hesitation, Lacy scooted between bushes and rocks, hardly touching a single branch for balance or support. Like a rabbit, she scampered down in seconds and waited at the bottom while he made his descent.

Steady as she goes, Malcolm mused, hoping he didn't slip and slide his way down. He wasn't sure his ego could stand the hit or his clothing the stain But to his pleasant surprise, he made it without issue, leaping from rock to trunk, then jumping down to within feet of her. His thigh muscles felt the burn—probably still recovering from his mad meadow dash—feats for which he'd pay dearly tomorrow. Definitely time to renew that gym membership, he mused.

Guiding Lacy toward the gold, Malcolm was careful not to trip over large stones jutting from the ground beneath him. Small underbrush and ferns were matted in places, trampled from the recent slew of foot traffic, he presumed—something they'd have to put a stop to and soon. Delaney was right. There was nothing preventing Jeremiah from waltzing in here and taking the gold for himself. Other than a shotgun.

Malcolm walked around the far side of the boulder, motioning for Lacy to join him. "It's there," he touched a finger to the cold gray stone before them. There was a distinct segment of discoloration, a scraggly mark across the surface. "You see this line? That's the gold."

Doubt wrenched her features. "*That's* it?"

"It is," he replied, lowering near her, the scent of her hair distracting as he hovered inches from her.

"Wow," she murmured, mesmerized by the exposed precious stone. She ran a finger along the jagged section, tracing the gouges. "It looks so...so..."

"Anti-climactic?"

She popped up and frowned. "*Smarty pants.*"

Malcolm chuckled. "Looks a lot better in jewelry form, if you ask me."

A shadow fell across her face. "Me, too."

At her disappointment, he asked, "Not what you expected?"

"Not really. I thought there would be huge chunks of it, like the whole rock would be gold-filled."

He lifted shoulders and hands and said, "Sorry to dash your hopes."

She turned to him. "Is there a lot here? I mean, is it worth a lot of money?"

Lacy was back to twenty questions—questions he didn't have answers to or the authority to give. "Don't know. Nick is the one looking into it. They want to make arrangements to have it mined."

"Mined?" She gaped at the stone. "Why do they have to mine it, can't they just chip it out?"

He grinned. "Manner of expression. Yes, I'm sure they could chip it out, but they believe there's a heck of a lot more underground."

"Huh."

"Huh?" Intrigued by her response, he asked, "Why does it look as if your mind is working on warp speed right now?"

Lacy snapped the lens to her thoughts closed. "It's curiosity, is all. I've never seen real gold. It's... interesting."

"Interesting." Amused by her choice of words, he suppressed a chuckle. "Well, have you seen enough?"

"I have," she quipped. "Now let's get back to that picnic you promised me."

"I'm all yours." Lacy trotted off, easily climbing up to the main trail. As usual, she was yards ahead of him, standing at the top waiting, tugging the ends of her skirt back in place. She brushed the back of her skirt, shaking back and forth, and suddenly Malcolm wanted a taste of her, a feel of her body next to his. With a punch of energy, he made it up the steep path in no time.

"Do you want to go back and get the food?" she asked, heading back the way they came.

He shook his head and moved toward her. "I'm not hungry."

"You're not? But you hardly touched your chicken. It's already three o'clock."

He smiled. "How about dinner? I'll be hungry then."

Blue eyes blinked in confusion as Lacy walked sideways along the trail with him. "Dinner?"

"Dinner. You know, restaurant, ambiance, food."

It dawned on her what he meant and a slow smile crept onto her lips. "Mr. Ward, are you asking me out on a date?"

"I am."

With a new skip to her step, Lacy moved a few feet ahead of him, though her gaze remained steadily fastened on his. "Where are you going to take me?"

"Where do you want to go?" he asked, playing along.

"Well, we've been to Whiskey Joe's," she said, toying with him, keeping two steps ahead.

"They serve food?" He shook his head as though surprised by the revelation, subtly lengthening his strides to close the space between them. "Huh. Didn't notice."

She smiled and continued, "We've been to Aunt Frannie's..."

Malcolm grinned. "Seems we're getting around, you and I."

"How about Lily Swan's?"

"Sounds perfect," he said and lunged for her.

Lacy shrieked, hurrying to dodge him, but Malcolm wrapped her up in his arms and she cried, "Let me go!"

"No way. You might run off and leave me in these woods. I'd never catch you then."

Snuggling up within his embrace, she asked innocently, "Is that what you're trying to do? Catch me?"

Malcolm peered down at her. Short tendrils of shiny black hair framed her cheekbones, but it was her flirtatious twinkle that captured his full attention. "I absolutely am."

Lacy giggled and wriggled within his arms. Desire fired through him as she tilted her mouth upward. No more hard to get? When she closed her eyes, his loins pulsed. Malcolm brushed his nose against the side of her face, inhaling the scent of her, a mix of floral fragrance and light perspiration, then slid his lips over hers. The supple quality of her mouth was almost too much to stand. He kissed her. She was soft and pliant, hunger and desire drove him harder, deeper.

Lacy gasped and pulled away from him, her mouth soft and swollen from his. "Whoa."

Searching for disapproval, Malcolm found none.

"That was some kind of *wow*."

Pleased, Malcolm smiled. Moving her back against the flat expanse of a large rock, he interlaced his fingers with hers and swept her arms above her head, pinning her in place.

Lacy gazed at him, her gaze fluid, attentive. "But what about dinner?"

"Dinner can wait. You can't." Malcolm pecked her forehead, her nose, then stared into the depths of her eyes. Lacy stared right back. He savored the sight of her, the feel of her curvy body beneath him. "I've never met anyone like you before."

She smiled, as though this were old news.

"I can't get you out of my mind."

"That's good, right?" she asked.

"It's better than good. It's phenomenal." Malcolm gently pressed into her. He kissed her again, only this time it was more caress than kiss. He wanted to immerse himself in the sensation of her, his building desire, and thoughts of bringing the two together as one. He wanted to think about Lacy and the way she made him feel. Her exuberance, her spirit. He wanted Lacy so bad right now he could take her right here. Touching his forehead to hers, he drew her arms down her sides and held her close. He nuzzled his nose against hers. *Dinner. Must hold back until dinner.*

Chapter Eighteen

Lacy waved goodbye to Malcolm as he walked out of Aunt Frannie's diner. "Toodles!" she called out, her heart singing. Malcolm had kissed her today, kissed her right out in the open and here at Frannie's, too. Trailing him through the front windows as he walked back to his truck, Lacy sighed. Malcolm was so wonderful. Handsome, smart, and he shared the gold with her. Gold. On Ladd Springs. How thrilling!

"Hey, sugar!"

"Hey, Aunt Frannie!" Lacy hurried over to meet her aunt and was instantly enveloped in a hug, Shalimar perfume permeating her senses with a dose of nostalgia. The fragrance reminded Lacy of her momma. She used to wear the same perfume, and breathing in the scent of Frannie's made Lacy long for her mother. After she reconciled with Annie, Lacy decided she should call her momma. It'd been too long. Much too long, and it was high time the family had a reunion. Maybe her momma would come back home for a visit!

"Did you have fun at your picnic?" Aunt Frannie asked.

"I did."

"Oh, good. That man is as handsome as they come. I might of taken a shine to him myself, if I hadn't met Deacon first. Course, he's dead and gone and plumb plugged my heart closed, but you know my eye wanders on occasion." She winked. "It's a natural affliction I was born with."

Lacy clasped her hands together. "Oh, Aunt Frannie, this one is divine."

"Divine, is he? I like the sound of that!"

"Oh *yes*. He kissed me today—out on the trail."

Aunt Frannie scowled. "Now don't you go giving away your milk 'til he buys the carton."

Lacy stuck out her lower lip and served up her best pout. "Aunt Frannie, my clock is ticking. Besides, he asked me to dinner and I made him wait. Wouldn't be right if I gave in so easily." That, and she wanted to tell Annie about the gold right away.

"What do you call a kiss?"

"If I don't encourage him, he might move on and leave me an old spinster."

Frannie fanned herself, exclaiming, "Lord a'mercy! I expect you to wait long enough to give your child a right proper daddy. If you haven't learned a thing from watching that sister of yours, I don't know what I'm going to do."

Annie. Yes. That was exactly who she wanted to talk to, this minute. "Do you know where Annie is?"

"Child, I'm not her keeper! Only recently became yours." Frannie eyed her like a nuisance bunny in her flower bed. "Now tell me, do I have to instill a curfew for you and this young man of yours?"

Young man? Lacy almost laughed, but thought better of it. No sense getting Aunt Frannie all worked up over her interested in an older man. She might go so far as to forbid it! Lacy forced a serious expression onto her face. "No, Aunt Frannie. I'll behave."

"Promise?"

Lacy slipped a hand behind her waist and crossed her fingers, same as she did with Malcolm in the forest. "Promise." Everyone knew it wasn't a sin to break a promise when your fingers were crossed. Lacy checked her watch, a slim silver band at her wrist. Three-thirty. "Now, do you think Annie will still be at work? She must work until five, right?" Aunt Frannie simply stared at her. "What?"

"What mischief do you have up your pretty little sleeve, young lady?"

"Nothing."

"Nothing?" Frannie shook her head and stuffed strands of red hair back into the base of her hair net. "You and your 'nothing' are becoming a pattern around here."

Lacy enclosed her palm over Frannie's forearm and assured her, "I promise, Aunt Frannie." And this time she meant it. Lacy wasn't out to cause any mischief. She was out to help Annie by letting her know there was gold on Ladd Springs. Gold on Ladd Springs! But she had to hurry. What if Jeremiah tried to go back there and steal it all? "Toodles!"

With a kiss to her aunt's cheek, Lacy breezed out the front door, chimes singing her exit. Annie would have to forgive her now—once she understood Lacy was willing to help her get Ladd Springs. And when she told her about the gold, she'd be begging for help. Spinning in place, Lacy caught sight of Annie's daughter farther down the sidewalk, accompanied by a brown-haired boy. Lacy waved. "Oh, hey there!"

As the girl walked toward her, she glared at Lacy with sharp blue eyes underscored by heavy black pencil. Add her long black hair and ivory skin and Lacy thought it gave her a vampiress look. The resemblance to Annie was striking— though where Annie was mature and attractive, the child was plagued by a case of acne, spots that stood out against her pale skin. There was a time Lacy had faced the same battle, and knew Casey's would pass, too. The boy with her was pure country—jeans, boots, good-looking and well-built. As they neared, Lacy realized it was the same boy she had seen with Loretta at Whiskey Joe's.

Startled by the realization, it was nothing compared to their reaction to her. Neither teen was friendly, both cold as river snakes. Oh—they must not know who she was! Lacy put forth her best smile and said, "Hi. I'm your Aunt Lacy."

The girl hardened her stare but said nothing.

Sullen, moody, Annie had been no different at that age. She'd get annoyed with Lacy for breathing back then, as if she could do a thing to stop it! The teenagers passed. *Well go on and be grumpy, see if I care*. Lacy was too busy for drama—she had a relationship to mend! She called after them, "Have a nice day, kids!"

Casey Owens watched Lacy as she hurried down the sidewalk, dubbing her short skirt and black boots a bit young for her age. That was her aunt? How embarrassing.

"Who's that?" Troy asked, opening the door to Fran's.

"My mom's sister."

Troy gaped. "For real?"

Casey nodded. Entering the diner, she was hit by the same old aroma. Fried chicken, fried fish, fried potatoes—everything was fried. Other than biscuits and pies, the menu was fried to a crispy brown. Casey didn't like any of it. She only came here because she received free food.

"How come I've never seen her before?" Troy asked, choosing a booth in the corner, away from prying eyes and nosy neighbors.

Casey slid in across from him and replied, "She's back in town."

"Where from?"

"Atlanta, I think. My mom doesn't talk about her much."

"How come?"

Casey shrugged. "Never said." All she knew was that the two of them had some kind of feud going on. She glanced around the restaurant, recalling her run-in with Delaney Wilkins a month or so back when Casey told her straight to her face that she knew Delaney hated her and that's why she working to get Ladd Springs for Felicity. But then again, who *didn't* have a feud going on? "My mom says she's staying with Fran."

Fran pulled up to the table and glanced between her and Troy. "Hey, sugar. Did I hear someone callin' my name?"

Casey nodded. "I was telling Troy about Lacy."

Fran smiled. "It's great to have her back, isn't it?" When neither Casey nor Troy responded, she let it drop. "Two cokes for you kids?" Both nodded. "Are you hungry?" They looked at each other and shook their heads in unison. Smiling all bright and happy, Fran tried, "How about a biscuit? Just made a fresh batch."

"No, thanks," Casey replied and checked with Troy.

"No, ma'am. I've already eaten lunch."

"All-righty. Two cokes, coming right up."

Once Fran had moved out of earshot, Troy hunkered over the table and said, "I hear your mom is trying to get you a share of Ladd Springs, on account of your inheritance and all."

Casey grimaced and sank back into her seat. "She says it's for me, but I think it's more for her."

"Why would you think that?"

"Because she hates Delaney, she wants money, I don't know."

"That doesn't sound right."

"Tell *her* that. I bet if she does get her hands on it that land I'm never gonna see any of it."

Emotion stormed Troy's expression. "But you're the rightful heir, not her. You're the one who deserves it, especially since she made you live without a daddy."

Casey looked away. She didn't want to hear about her miserable life, especially not from Troy, the kid with tons of money, the one with awesome parents. The Parkers spent time with their kids, took them on vacations, went to their school functions. Her mom didn't hardly do any of that stuff, let alone care about whether or not she had a father in the house. No matter. Her mom would probably embarrass her if she did show up. Spotting Fran on her way with the cokes, Casey dumped her gaze to the table.

"Sorry," Troy mumbled.

"Two cokes," Fran announced and slid them on the table. Setting straws alongside, she prodded, "Those biscuits back there are warm and moist. You let me know if you change your mind about food, you hear?"

"Yes, ma'am," Troy replied. "We will, thank you."

Casey's gaze tracked Fran's black-soled comfort-wear as she walked across the black and white checkered floor. Normally a fan of the biscuits, Casey didn't feel like being a fan of anything at the moment.

"Listen, I wanted to tell you that I'm leaving this summer."

Jerking her head up, Casey shot forward. "What?"

"I'm going to work with a horse trainer outside Murfreesboro."

"Murfreesboro? Who? How?"

"Some guy my dad knows. He runs a ranch up there and I called him about a job."

"You *told* your dad?"

Troy stilled. "Naw, not yet." He tore open the straw and stuck it into his coke. "I wanted to be sure I had someplace to go first." Chucking the balled white paper toward the ketchup container, he picked up his drink and dragged a long sip.

Casey slumped. "Wow."

"I want us to keep in touch, though."

"You do?" she asked, instantly feeling foolish.

His mouth tipped into a small smile. Troy shook the overgrown bangs from his eyes and asked, "Why do you always act so surprised when I say stuff like that?"

Because she couldn't believe it. Because he'd never said it before. "I don't know." Casey shrugged and evaded him with a glance toward the kitchen. "I always thought you kinda liked Felicity." Then there was that older woman he was with yesterday, the one her "daddy" came in and made a scene over.

"Aw, dad gum. Felicity's only a friend. She likes Travis, anyway, not me."

Casey's attention intensified. "She does?" When he nodded yes, she detected a hint of sadness in his eyes. Did it upset him? Did Troy want Felicity to like him, instead?

"I like *you* Casey."

Anxious excitement pumped in her chest. Fine time to tell her—he was leaving.

"I wanna have some fun before I go." Sipping again from his coke, Troy held her in his gaze. Nerves rippled and frayed. "Do you wanna go out tonight?"

"Go out?" Like *out* out, as in boyfriend, girlfriend? she wanted to ask, but didn't dare. There was no way she was sticking her neck out *that* far.

"There you go again, acting all shocked." A boyish grin seized hold and he asked, "Is there something wrong with me?"

"No—not at all. I just..." Involuntarily, she glanced at the booth he'd been sitting at with the blonde woman.

Troy whipped his head around and his eyes lit up with the realization. "You worried about that woman you saw me here with yesterday?"

"No." Casey shrugged again but refused to look at him. Of course she was worried about that woman. What were they doing together? Wasn't he the one acting all interested in her welfare, yet he was cavorting with the enemy? She didn't understand him. Though she wanted to, in the worst way.

"She don't mean nothing to me."

Casey stared at him, distrust pricking at her heart. "Then why have lunch with her?"

Anger thundered beneath his voice as he replied, "Listen. That woman means nothing to me. I was only using her for information."

"Information? What kind of information?"

"You don't worry about that," he said firmly, closing the subject with a dead-bolt. Troy reached over and tried to grab her hand, but she withdrew it, depositing both hands into her lap. Displeased, he repeated, "Do you wanna go out with me? I can pick you up. We can talk," he added, as though that would convince her.

Did he have other intentions? Or was he only after friendship?

When she hesitated, he persisted. "C'mon, Casey, don't play like this."

Play like what? she wondered. Play like she didn't want to be with a guy who was obviously interested in someone else? He was, wasn't he?

"I'll follow you around if you don't." A light smirk curved his mouth to one side. "I'll make you're momma think I'm crazy." The imagery tugged a smile from her as she watched him beg. It was warming to her ego. "I mean it. You don't agree, she'll make you, just to get rid of me."

Casey doubted that but enjoyed how hard Troy was working. It made her feel good. Maybe it was true he didn't like that woman. Her heart dipped. But Troy was leaving. Right when they got together, he would be gone. It wasn't fair.

Troy acted like a sad puppy dog, his brown eyes pleading. "I'm waiting."

Shouldn't she take every second she could before he was gone? "Okay. I'll go." Of course she would. Casey would take Troy any way she could get him.

Chapter Nineteen

Eager to speak to his friend Willie, Clem Sweeney pushed through the heavy metal door leading to the visitation room. He wanted to know what happened with the gold, if Willie showed Jeremiah like he told him to, and did he follow him afterwards. Clem didn't trust Jeremiah, but he was the only man he knew with any money who could help him make bail. He spied Willie at the first cubicle, his ratty black hat and grubby clothes unmistakable, looking like somethin' the dog'd been keepin' under the porch. Clem surely wasn't gonna get a dime out of *him*. He only trusted Willie not to steal the gold because the man was dumb as dirt. Didn't have two brain cells to rub together and, besides, Clem had the goods on him. He happened to know for a fact that Willie was involved in a certain robbery that took place on the Baxter Farm. Old man Baxter was madder than a wet cat covered in mud, and both knew he'd pull out his shotgun before he dialed the first number to the police.

Shuffling to a stop before the cubicle, Clem eyed Willie. "Well?" Willie looked from side to side, then scooted real close as Clem sat across from him. Cigarette smoke seeped through the small holes in the window, giving Clem an itch for a cigarette. "Did you find out anything?"

Willie withdrew a toothpick from his mouth and muttered, "Jeremiah is a dog, Clem."

Clem's gut tightened. "What do you mean?"

"I mean, I showed him where that gold was, just like you told me, and then he done went and told his buddies about it!"

Clem scowled. "How do you know that? You followed him like I told you?"

"Yeah, Clem, you know I did!" Willie fidgeted with the toothpick in his mouth. "I followed him all the way to Bucky's place."

Jeremiah wouldn't let Willie get within ten feet of him. How did he overhear what was going on? "Did you hear it with your own ears?" Why would he go talkin' about it with you right there, listenin'?"

Willie snatched his toothpick. "What do you take me for—a *fool*? I ain't no fool. Course I was watchin' from across the bar. He went to Bucky's place and I hid in the corner. I could tell by the looks on them there faces of his pals. They got all serious like and started lookin' around." Willie snuck a gaze around the visiting room and whispered, "You know how folks get when they hear about gold."

Lightning bolts ripped through Clem's midsection. Willie might be as clueless as a blushin' sow on butcher day, but Jeremiah was a snake. "That no good two-timin' double-crosser." Willie nodded like a bobble doll. "Who does he think he is?"

"Jeremiah Ladd?" Willie offered.

"Shut up," Clem snapped. He lashed his gaze around the lobby, his thoughts unraveling. Jeremiah wasn't gonna pay his bail. He was gonna take the gold for himself, with the help of his buddies. "I got to think a minute."

Willie sat, his face twitching, fiddling with the chewed-up toothpick as he stared at Clem.

Clem should never have believed Jeremiah when he said he'd help him with bail, out flappin' his lips faster than a preacher caught with his pants down, already out tellin' everybody in town about the gold. How was there gonna be any left for him by the time he got out?

"What we goin' t'do, Clem?"

He set his lips in a firm line. Jeremiah had another thought comin' if he figured on double-crossin' Clem Sweeney. He might be locked up, but he wasn't powerless. He had friends on the outside. Loyal friends. "You've got to call Harley."

Willie nodded. "Harley."

"You've got to tell him I need to see him."

"Okay, then what?" he asked eagerly, pleased Clem had a plan.

"You tell him come see me. I'll take it from there."

With a determined step, Lacy filed through the forest at a virtual race walk, recounting her steps from yesterday with Malcolm through the fading light. Misty air cooled her skin as she travelled, the rich scent of earth filing her nose with familiar scents and memories old and new. Running wild through these woods as a child had been glorious but so was her hike with Malcolm. He was glorious, she mused. The only dim spot in his journey was Malcolm's call for an early dinner this evening. She had refused him—again—claiming Aunt Frannie was fussy about spending too much time with him. Lacy professed the need to placate her aunt, all of which was true, but this expedition was the real reason she had declined. Recalling the disappointment in his voice, Lacy smiled. She really liked him and would love to be dining with him this very instant, but the job of convincing Annie was taking longer than she had anticipated.

Last evening, when Lacy had gone to Annie's salon and revealed the news, Annie had shut her down. *You're lying.* But Lacy heard insecurity in her objection. Annie wasn't sure. She wasn't sure what to believe and wanted to see for herself. Lacy had been thrilled! It was the opening she needed. She was telling the truth and the sooner Annie realized it, the sooner the two could mend their broken fences and start acting like a family again. Unfortunately, Annie had been working the late shift and the forest would have been too dark last night, but today was a new day. A new day for discovery and forgiveness.

So now, like two thieves in the night, they were charging through the shadows of green and brown. Stepping over a root, Lacy sighed and looked over her shoulder to make sure Annie was still following her. Not the most athletic person, her sister was struggling to keep up. But if they didn't keep up their pace, the blanket of night might just smother them to a standstill. "C'mon, Annie, we're almost there!"

The path was easy to remember. All she had to do was find the rock where Malcolm kissed her and then look for the group of boulders near a low-lying creek just beyond. Simple. She'd remember that rock anywhere. Sticking out from the mountain, it was a flat panel of stone where he pushed her— trapped her with his body—and kissed her. A squiggle of delight scurried low in her belly. It had been the best kiss *ever*.

"Slow down," Annie hollered at her from behind. "You didn't tell me it was this far!"

"It's not that much farther," she encouraged, clueless as to how much farther it really was—but they had to be close. She and Malcolm hadn't hiked for *that* long before they made it to the spot. *The spot*. Her insides tingled again. Malcolm's mouth on hers had been so gentle, his body so warm and hard and delightful... "There!" Lacy cried, elated to have found the rock. She ran up to it, inspected the wall of earth around, skimming her palm down the center where she had stood only hours before. Stood. Leaned back against. Been pushed into. A swell of desire rose inside her. This was the rock where they kissed, no question. Lacy pivoted and searched off the trail, scanning the forest floor to their right. *Yes.* "Those are the rocks where the gold is!"

Annie came to a stop at Lacy's side. Staring in the direction Lacy pointed, Annie surveyed the landscape. "Where?"

"It's in one of those rocks over there. You see that group? It's the one on the right, *I think*."

"You think?"

Lacy dismissed the fresh swarm of doubt in Annie's expression. "It's there, I'll show you," she said and confidently trotted down the same narrow path she had taken with Malcolm. She only hoped Annie could see the yellow hue of the stone. In this waning light, it might all look gray and drab.

Traversing the soft forest floor, she breathed in deeply. The air was infused with a musty scent of wet clay and decaying plants and her senses wallowed in the moist smell. She loved it out here, always had, though as a child it was all about the adventure, the freedom of roaming the forest outside the watchful eye of her parents. Then she'd moved to Atlanta and the opportunity to lose herself in the woods, in the middle of nature, all but evaporated. There was always the chore of shopping or laundry, work or dates—something that interfered with her desire to get outside and find a hiking trail. Stumbling over a rock on the ground, Lacy inhaled again and thought, yes, she loved the forest with every fiber of her being.

Annie stomped a branch in half as she trekked behind Lacy who slowed, circling a group of boulders, their surfaces blotched with patches of white fungus and smiled. "See. There it is!" she declared proudly. "Gold on Ladd Springs."

Annie looked at the rocks, but clearly saw nothing. "Where," she demanded.

"Right there." Lacy motioned for Annie to come closer. She tapped a finger on the ragged line cutting across the gray stone. "See it?"

"Oh, my..." Annie's breath expelled in a rush as she inspected the dusty lines in the rock. She touched them, fingered them, outlined them as if to prove to herself she wasn't seeing things. All trace of displeasure erased, she stood mesmerized.

"I told you I was telling the truth."

Annie gaped at her. "I can't believe it."

Lacy nodded. "Now you know. So when you get the property rights for Casey, you'll be sure to include this as part of the deal." Annie didn't say a word, only stared, moving her gaze slowly between Lacy and the streak of gold in the stone. "This will help, won't it?"

"Yes, but..."

"But what?"

"But I'm sure Delaney will try and keep this section for herself. She won't let Casey get anywhere near it."

Disturbed by the declaration, Lacy frowned. "But who's she to say? Shouldn't a judge or someone important like that be the one to make the decision?"

Annie fixed her focus on Lacy. All edgy hate and anger had dissolved, softening her sister's features into those of the girl she grew up with, the one who used to braid her hair and paint her nails. This was her big sister, Annie Grace, the girl Lacy had looked up to her entire life. "You don't understand," Annie said. "It's more complicated than that."

"Why?" Lacy asked, refusing to be discouraged. "Because of Jeremiah?"

"Because of Jeremiah, Felicity, Ernie..."

"Jeremiah doesn't deserve the property, after everything he's done. The man has become so hateful. Why, you should have seen the way he treated his daddy today."

"The law doesn't care about his personality, Lacy. It only cares about the rules."

"Can't Ernie tell him no? Can't he give it to you and Casey instead? Along with Felicity, I mean, seeing's how she's already on the new deed," Lacy added matter-of-factly.

Annie slumped against the stone, an utter sense of fatality settling into her gaze. "Ernie already signed it over to Felicity," she repeated, as though reminding herself of the facts.

It occurred to Lacy there was more to getting the property than proving Casey was Jeremiah's daughter. And it dashed her enthusiasm. Why should doing the right thing be so hard? "Well," she said flatly, "I'm sure we'll think of something. We have to. It isn't right for Casey not to get her share."

Annie crossed her arms and brought a hand to her mouth. She massaged her chin, glanced at the rock, the trees. She seemed so intent, Lacy was certain she was coming up with a solution this instant. Then Annie tightened her gaze around Lacy and said, "Thank you." Lacy's pulse jumped. "Thank you for telling me about this. I appreciate it."

Nerves fluttered beneath Lacy's breast, trapped, anxious. For the first time since Lacy had arrived in town, her sister's hatred showed signs of thawing. "Even if you can't get it?" she asked, desperately hoping Annie would say yes, even then.

Annie offered a smile, small, but genuine, embracing Lacy with a warm gaze. "Yes, even then."

"Oh, Annie Grace!" Lacy threw her arms around her sister and hugged her as tightly as she could. There were no words for the gift she had just received. No words for the first step her sister had taken toward her. Lacy would do whatever she had to do to help Annie get Casey's share of Ladd Springs. The epiphany of her predicament slammed home. Even if she had to take sides against Malcolm, she would. For Annie, she would.

"Are you two here to steal my gold?"

The shouted question iced Lacy's exuberance. *Jeremiah.*

Annie sprang from her embrace. "Jeremiah!" she cried under her breath.

Standing up on the trail, the green of his shirt blending in with the mountainous landscape, his mocking leer slapped them with accusation. "Now you know I don't take kindly to thieves."

Lacy's mind scrambled for reason. How did he know they were out here? Had someone told? But who? No one knew. She hadn't even told Malcolm where she was going.

I can trust you, right? You don't want me to get into trouble, do you?

Oh, silly fool! Why had she broken her promise to Malcolm? And now she stood face-to-face with Jeremiah on her own!

Annie took charge. Gesturing for Lacy to stay behind her, she walked toward him and demanded, "What are you doing here, Jeremiah?"

"Collecting what's mine," he said snidely, then jogged downhill through wooded brush.

"Nothing here belongs to you," Annie informed him.

Jeremiah cocked his head. "Aren't you all high and mighty these days?"

"I'm relating the facts, Jeremiah. Nothing more and nothing less."

Lacy's breathing grew shallow. She didn't like the mean-spirited look flashing in Jeremiah's eyes. It reminded her of the day she left him. He'd been so callous, so awful, announcing that he wasn't giving her any more money. His days of supporting her were over.

She'd only been seventeen! She had no savings, no experience. How did he expect her to go out on her own? Jeremiah didn't care. Just like that, no warning, no leeway, he'd strolled through their front door and told her she was on her own.

Jeremiah slanted a glance toward the rocks behind them. "I see you know about the gold." Annie didn't respond. Lacy kept mum. "Who else knows?"

"Unfortunately you do," Annie returned evenly.

"Watch your tongue, Annie," he said, jumping at her. Annie shrieked, causing him to laugh. "Not so tough are you?"

A bomb went off in Lacy's heart and she hollered, "Shame on you, Jeremiah!" The man was infected with the devil, that's what he was—pure evil and she was leaving this instant. She turned on her heel, but he grabbed her arm.

"Where do you think you're going?"

"Let me go!" she cried and yanked her arm. His fingers dug into her skin like bear claws. "You're hurting me!"

"I'm gonna do a whole lot more, you walk away from me like that again."

"What do you want? I don't have anything for you."

"You never were a very bright one, were you?"

Lacy took offense at the comment, but worse, she was scared. Jeremiah had hurt her. He was acting crazy. She could see Annie thought the same, her eyes hollowed by fear. But surely Jeremiah wasn't going to do anything serious to them. Why would he?

"Now, you two are going to stand there while I collect a few chunks of my gold, and then you're going to walk out of here with me."

"For what purpose?" Annie asked, anger firing her voice back to life.

"Because I said so. And after I'm finished here, you and I are going to have a little talk about this paternity test you keep screeching about."

Annie's expression erupted into anger, but she kept a lid on it.

"That's right," he said, serving up a nasty look. "You are going to back off that stupid stunt of yours and accept the facts. I'm not paying for your illegitimate kid."

"You have no say over what I do or don't do."

"Don't I?" He pulled a chisel from his back pocket and walked over to the rocks. Running a hand over the gray surface, he located the strands of gold and paused, gazing at Annie. "Let's just hope for your sake you don't need the kind of convincing my friends specialize in."

"Jeremiah!" Lacy couldn't take this another instant. He was threatening her sister!

Annie's demeanor grew remote, colder than the rain on a foggy winter day. Lacy's pulse scattered as Jeremiah began stabbing away at the stone. "What are you doing?"

"What does it look like I'm doing?" he asked, whaling on the rock without pause. *Chling. Chling.* The high-pitched sound echoed through the trees.

With each swing, Lacy raged. "You can't do that!"

"Lacy." Annie warned her off with a quick shake of her head.

Lacy willed her sister to understand. He's stealing the gold! He's taking it and there will be none left for you and Casey!

Jeremiah kept digging until a nugget fell away. Catching it he smiled, then held it up for them to see. But in the dusky light, it didn't look like anything but rock. Lacy hoped it was. She hoped Jeremiah couldn't see what he was doing and all he'd succeeded in taking was rock. Stone. Worthless pebbles. Shoving the piece into his front pocket Jeremiah continued chipping away for what felt like an eternity.

Lacy felt helpless. Annie's face had emptied of emotion, her eyes lifeless as she watched him chip away at her daughter's inheritance. It wasn't right, Lacy fumed. It wasn't right what Jeremiah was doing and someone should stop him. Deep in her heart of hearts, Lacy knew that if Casey were entitled to the gold, so was Jeremiah. But Jeremiah didn't deserve it. He didn't deserve anything good because all he put out into the world was bad. It was called karma and one of these days his would come around and smack him on the backside.

Wait until Malcolm heard about this—Jeremiah would get his due. Then it dawned on her. Malcolm. Lacy's spirits fell into her boots. Would he be mad she told Annie about the gold? Of course he would.

Finally, Jeremiah straightened. He slid the chisel back into his pocket and commanded, "Let's go."

"Go where?" Lacy asked.

"Out," he replied.

"I don't want to go anywhere with you!"

He chuckled. "Aw, Lacy, why do you have to go on and hurt my feelings like that? I thought we were friends."

"You are no friend of mine."

"Well, isn't that too bad, because I've decided to introduce you two ladies to a few friends of mine." Jeremiah targeted Annie and said, "Just to be sure we understand each other."

Annie silently urged Lacy to move. Go. Walk. *But it isn't right*, Lacy wanted to shout! They couldn't give in so easily. Who knew what Jeremiah had in mind. But with no man to protect them, Lacy understood they were helpless. Victims. And it angered her even more. "You're gonna get what's coming to you, Jeremiah Ladd!"

With one last look at Jeremiah, at Annie, Lacy reluctantly turned and headed for the main trail. Annie hiked alongside her, a powerful strength emanating from her. She was so brave, Lacy thought. Annie was strong and determined while she on the other hand was unable to shake the feeling of a criminal walking to the guillotine.

Chapter Twenty

Delaney sat rigid in the front seat as Nick drove the last stretch home to Ladd Springs. From the backseat, Malcolm could feel her turmoil. She was a woman of action, yet she was bound to her seat, immobile. Nick had explained to her that he and Malcolm were going out tonight, on business, and she had to stay home. It wasn't news Delaney wanted to hear. But after a scuffle of debate, the matter had been settled. Nick and Malcolm were going out, she was waiting at home.

Thoughts of Lacy came to mind. Visions of her lips against his, her body beneath him brought visceral pleasure. It turned out to be a good thing she cancelled on him for this evening. Jeremiah was becoming a problem—a problem that needed their immediate attention, putting killer curves and sex appeal on hold. Actually, as much as he relished her body, it was Lacy's spirit of sunshine and innocence that appealed to him most. Hiking up to the falls yesterday had been fun. It had been an easygoing, spontaneous adventure of frivolous, free-spirited fun with a woman who was the epitome of impulsive adventure. While they never made it to the skinny-dipping, the mere fact it had been an option tickled his fancy.

Malcolm sensed that Lacy was becoming more to him than a passing fancy. Perhaps it was because he was getting older, but he was tiring of the pretentious glamour and superficiality of the dating scene in Los Angeles. He spent much of his time in the company of beautiful women but never felt as if they wanted him for him. It was the prestige of being with an international businessman that appealed to them. The allure of his money, his experience. Malcolm was over it. He was ready for down to earth. He was ready for easy and fun.

Dare he say he was ready for commitment?

Nick turned left, driving over the bridge that was the entrance to Ladd Springs, but Malcolm's attention had been snagged by a white car parked near the trailhead. "Who's that?" he asked, as wood planks vibrated beneath the vehicle as Nick's tires rolled over the bridge.

"Who's what?" Delaney asked absently.

"That white car, over there by the trail," he said, his instincts jumping to life.

Delaney's blonde hair whipped around and she gasped. "What's Annie doing in the forest?"

"Annie?"

"That's Annie's car," Delaney spelled out for him, her tone rising with irritation. "But she has no business on the trail." She turned in her seat and asked Nick, "What do you think she's up to?"

Nick shrugged. "Don't know, but I'm willing to find out."

Malcolm had a bad feeling. Lacy knew about the gold. Lacy cared about her sister's hostility toward her. Did she go back on her word and tell Annie? Nick parked the car, and he and Malcolm leaped from the vehicle.

Delaney picked up the rear, but Nick warned her off. "Stay here, Delaney. I don't need the complication of your quarrel with Annie."

"What?"

"You heard me. Stay here. Go up to the cabin. I'll check in with you before I leave."

Crossing the field, Malcolm noted the setting sun. It would be dark soon. A woman alone in the forest at night was a bad idea. He picked up his pace, forcing his jog into a run. As they neared the car, Malcolm glimpsed a sight that tore his heart in two. Lacy's purse on the passenger seat. Chafed by her possible deception, he prayed it was coincidence. Anger warred with concern. If only he could believe in coincidence.

Nick ran the entire way, a fact that suited Malcolm just fine. Heart pounding, legs taxed, he had no interest in delaying the inevitable. If Lacy had gone behind his back and shared the location of the gold with Annie he needed to know—the sooner the better. He was having feelings for the woman and to discover she didn't deserve them was information better gained now, despite the fact it would hurt. As they ran past Zack's Falls, the certainty that Lacy had broken her promise penetrated like a stake to the heart. No woman lied to Malcolm Ward and preserved his confidence.

No woman.

Malcolm pushed forward against his labored breathing, catching a whip of branches as Nick cleared them from his path. As they ran, they continually scanned the forest, the rocks, and the ravine below. Hopefully they'd be at the site within minutes. Thoughts whirred through Malcolm's brain, logical explanations as to why Lacy was here with her sister and not the *cause* for the trip. Maybe Annie discovered it on her own and Lacy tagged along out of prurient curiosity. Maybe her sister asked her to come as cover, so she could blame it on Lacy when Delaney came down on her for trespassing. There were a million reasons Lacy could be here with her sister that didn't include deception. Only Malcolm didn't believe a single one.

Anticipation thudded in his chest as they passed the rock where he kissed Lacy. Shooting a glance toward the cluster of boulders, the gold vein, Malcolm saw nothing. No one. Ahead of him Nick had stopped. "They're not here."

Malcolm hauled up next to his partner and scanned the depths of the forest. Silhouettes moved eerily through the trees, trunks black and massive, bushes still. Nothing moved. There wasn't a soul in sight. Crickets sawed to life in a slew of noise around them. Misgiving clawed at him. He pulled the cell phone from his pocket and dialed Lacy's number. Nick watched pensively as Malcolm waited through rings.

"Voice mail." He ended the call and shoved the phone back into place. Raking a hand through his hair, he glanced around the forest, willing her figure to appear.

Where are you, Lacy?

With a hand to Malcolm's shoulder, Nick said quietly, "We'll find her."

Malcolm nodded but bit back his response. She had been here. Her purse was in the car. Her phone was probably in it. But why had she left it behind?

They had to find her. When they did, what would he learn?

"Back to Plan A," Nick said.

"Yeah." Plan A. Jeremiah Ladd.

Jeremiah drove Lacy and Annie to his motel. Sitting in the backseat, Lacy clutched her sister. To her relief, Annie didn't remove her claw-like grasp, simply held her hand like it was the most normal thing in the world. As they drove, neither woman said a word. They only stared—at Jeremiah, out the window, toward the road ahead. They were headed into town. Jeremiah didn't say why or where they were going. Simply that they were going for a ride.

In the beginning, Annie had tried to talk sense to him. She'd tried to convince Jeremiah that she and Lacy were of no use to him, and that if he had any chance to reclaim Ladd Springs, it wasn't by kidnapping them. Oh, but he thought that was funny and laughed and laughed.

"Kidnapping? Who said anything about kidnapping? I'm just taking my two old girlfriends for a drive. To the scenic part of town."

Lacy shuddered to think what he meant. Certainly not scenic, as in pretty scenery. Through the window, she saw the sky was turning a dusty blue, the fiery orange and red long since melted into the mountain ridge around them. Lamps came on in houses, street lights flickered to life along the lonesome county road. Night was upon them, darkness brewing. *As was her fear*. Lacy didn't like Jeremiah one bit anymore and wouldn't put anything past him these days. Jeremiah had become so mean and unpredictable, Lacy knew trouble would not be far behind. And soon as she could, she was going to tell her friend Loretta Flynn exactly what she thought of the man and advise her to run clear of him. Skedaddle, move on. Run for her life!

Until then she had to think of a way to get away from him. Think, Lacy. *Think.*

When nothing came, she turned to Annie, imploring her sister with her eyes to do something. *We have to do something!*

Annie shook her head in that frustratingly calm way and re-hooked her gaze to the windshield. They'd be to town soon. She'd do something then. Lacy stifled a sigh. Something—but what?

Jeremiah's phone rang. Grabbing it from his pocket, he answered, "What's up?" Lacy watched his eyes from her corner of the backseat and wondered who he was talking to. "I can't. I'm busy." Light brown eyes flicked a glance to the rearview mirror. Catching her looking at him, he sharpened his gaze. "Fine. I'll be there." Ending the call, Jeremiah said, "Change of plans. You're going to my place, instead."

The motel? Excitement mounted. Loretta would be there! She could help them get back to their car. And, oh, but wouldn't Lacy help her pack her bag, too. Heck, she'd pack it for her if Loretta would help them get away from Jeremiah!

Fifteen minutes later, Jeremiah dumped Lacy and Annie at his motel. He didn't drop them at his door, didn't lock them away inside. He merely pulled over, told them to get out and drove away. "Tell Loretta I'm going out for the evening," he said, as if Lacy would deliver any such message. Turning the steering wheel of his truck, he glared at Annie. "And don't forget what I said. Continue with this paternity business and you'll find yourself convinced otherwise—a convincing that won't be pleasant." His eyes skimmed her from head to toe. "It would be a shame to ruin your good looks. And you are a good-looking woman, Annie." He made a *tsk* sound with his mouth. "Too bad it didn't work out between us."

Jeremiah spun his tires with a loud screech, his truck hitting the road with a bump as he tore off into the night.

"I'm going to call the police, Jeremiah!" Lacy screamed at him then lashed out at her sister. "We have to stop him. We have to call the police. We have to do something!" Annie held her tongue. "What's the matter with you? How can you stand there and let him go?"

Cool, blue eyes iced the flames licking at Lacy's heart. A blinking red sign overhead illuminated her expression with a creepy glow. "What exactly do you want me to tell the police? Jeremiah gave us a ride to his motel? He was stealing the gold right before our very eyes?" She narrowed her gaze. "Or better yet, he picked us up while we were trespassing on Ladd springs."

Lacy blinked. She sealed her lips shut, outrage blasting through the seams.

"You understand, now? We have to work smarter. We have to beat Jeremiah at his own game. Running around like two scared hens won't solve a thing."

The imagery punctured her wrath. Beat him at his own game? How were they going to do that? Jeremiah was a *snake*. He was nothing but a no-good, downright, slithering varmint intent on spewing his venom. Is that what Annie wanted? Did she want to turn hateful toward Jeremiah and kidnap *him*?

"I'm going to call Candi," Annie said flatly. "She'll give us a ride back to my car."

"But...but..." Lacy stammered, unable to digest the detour her sister made so easily. *I'm going to call Candi. Back to my car.* Lacy didn't understand. She didn't understand how her sister could let Jeremiah go without a fight, without putting him in jail. It was maddening. Unbelievable, she thought, but obediently stomped after her sister.

Chapter Twenty-One

Jeremiah blinked, the light bright, painful. His head throbbed. His jaw ached. One eye felt swollen shut. Lifting his head, he dropped it back down. "Ouch!" he cried, the pain to his scalp quick and severe. Spreading, it began to pound. Miserably. He raised his arm, but dropped it. The effort was too great. *What the—*?

Rolling his head from side to side, he opened his eyes. *Where am I*?

He was lying on the pavement. In a parking lot. What the hell happened last night? Jeremiah wracked his brain—his throbbing brain. He'd been downtown, drinking with his buddies...drinking heavily. He blinked. Where had they gone? Bucky's? Leon's? He couldn't remember. He could only feel, and everything he felt hurt. His head was splitting open, his body pulverized. Closing his eyes, he willed the pain to subside.

One thing he did know, this was *not* a section of town he wanted to be in. Not even in the daylight. But Jeremiah couldn't move. Not without his brain tearing apart. Had he been hit by a car? A truck? He lifted a hand and forced it to his forehead. His shoulder was stiff, sore—really sore, like it had been hit with a metal bar.

Images flashed in his mind's eye. Men, arms, swinging objects. Yes, he'd been hit. Jumped. Jeremiah concentrated on the pictures forming in his mind. There'd been two men. They jumped him from behind...

Yes, one hit him across the back with something hard. The other whaled on him with his fists. Jeremiah groaned. His hand slid from his head, dropped outward to the rough grainy pavement. Damn, if they hadn't done a thorough job on him.

He couldn't remember who they were. He'd never seen them before. Didn't really get a good look at them, either. It was dark. He was outside the bar. Jeremiah opened his eyes and scanned the parking lot where he lay. Was it here? He didn't see his truck. But then again, he'd been at the bar. There was no bar in sight.

Closing his eyes, it came to him. They probably dumped him here after they beat the hell out of him. But who? Why? That's what he needed to find out.

Forcing himself to move, he winced, sharp jabs of pain plunging into his side. Son of a bitch— Jeremiah hugged his midsection. Did they break his ribs? It sure as hell felt like it. Rolling over to his knees, he took a second to catch his breath. The pain in his chest was bad, but his head hurt the worst, like someone had slit the thing wide open.

Fury rolled through him. Whoever did this was going to pay—dearly. Only first, he had to recover. Jeremiah noticed his watch was gone. Damn it. Automatically, he checked his back pocket. Then his front. Mother fu—

"Hey, *you.*" Jeremiah's heart stopped. The gravelly voice above him was laced with malice. "What are you doing?"

Staring up at the man, he wanted to shout, *Can't you see I'm trying to get up, you idiot*? But Jeremiah held his tongue. The guy was a vagrant. Torn pant legs, filthy shirt, missing two teeth. If he hadn't already been robbed, this man would gladly do the honors. The vagrant glanced over him head to toe, as though checking his person for any valuables.

"Already taken," Jeremiah grumbled. "I don't have anything for you to steal."

The man stood taller and scowled. Like Jeremiah had insulted him, or something.

Please, he mused bitterly. Get over it and move on to your next victim. Jeremiah pushed up from the ground, suppressing the urge to yelp. *Damn* that hurt. He shot a dirty look toward the man who then stumbled off. Good riddance. Slowly rising to his feet, Jeremiah glanced around, took a step and cursed. This wasn't going to be easy.

Three hours later, Jeremiah managed to make it as far as Fran's Diner. His motel was a good mile farther, but there was a chance Loretta would be here. When she wasn't chasing the Parker kid, it was her new hangout. Jeremiah didn't kid himself when it came to Loretta. There was one reason she was with him and one reason only—he had money. Used to. Didn't take long in Vegas to make a mint, or to lose one, he added ruefully. But after last night, his gold was gone too. Son of a bitch. Whoever took it was going to pay.

Loretta wouldn't be too happy to see him in this condition. He could smell the cigarette smoke and sweat that pervaded his clothing. The marks on his face would only add to his unsightly appearance, but too bad. With no wallet, he needed money.

As he swung open the door to the diner, the bells reverberated in Jeremiah's skull. "Damn it," he muttered. He was trying to keep the jar of pain to a dull minimum. Scanning the diner in short order, he found no Loretta. His attention caught on the couple in the corner. Well, look who was here. If it wasn't Loretta's Parker squeeze. And from the back of the head sitting across from him, Annie's daughter. His kid.

Jeremiah sauntered over, enjoying the ignition of concern in the boy's eyes. That's right. *Be concerned. Be very concerned.*

Casey followed Troy's abrupt fascination with something behind her and turned to look, but whirled back around quickly. It was Jeremiah Ladd—her sperm donor—and he was coming over!

She gulped, tamped down the sudden race of her heart and concentrated on ignoring the man. But how could she? His face looked *awful*, like he'd been beat up or something. Why would he be coming over to them?

When he reached their table, Troy, ever the brave one asked, "What happened to you?"

"None of your business." He glanced briefly between the two and demanded, "Where's Loretta?"

Troy scoffed. "How the hell do I know? Not my problem you can't keep track of your woman."

If he wasn't standing in the middle of Fran's diner, Jeremiah would have slugged the smirk from the kid's face. "Don't get cute with me, boy. As you can see, I'm in no mood."

"Don't matter to me what kind of mood you're in," Troy said defiantly, speaking more to Casey. "We didn't ask you to come over here."

Jeremiah looked at Casey and she averted her gaze. Not only did his face look terrible, it made him seem all the more scary. And he smelled disgusting. It was all she could do not to pinch her nose. How could he be her father?

Through her periphery vision, Casey saw that he continued to stare at her, the silent probe like a hot barb shredding her nerves. Was he going to say something to her? Should she respond?

But he didn't. "If you see Loretta, tell her I'm looking for her."

"I have no plans to see her." Troy looked at Casey and she yearned for him to say more, to mean more. After last night, she was beginning to feel like he really cared about her. "If you'll excuse us, we're trying to have a private conversation."

Casey held her breath. Was Troy trying to provoke him?

"You're a cocky son of a bitch," Jeremiah replied but stalked off just the same. No lingering at the entrance, no words for other diners, he went straight for the exit. Jeremiah may be right about Troy being cocky, but it had never felt better having him near. "That guy gives me the creeps."

Troy reached over and pulled her hand toward him. "Don't let him get to you."

His hold was strong, warm. Reassuring. Nerves tickled her neck. "I wonder what happened to him."

"Looks to me like he got what he deserved." A flicker of pleasure lit up Troy's dark eyes. "I only wished it could have been me."

Did Troy hate the man as much as she did? But he had been with that Loretta woman, hadn't he? Suddenly confused and uncomfortable, a bucketful of regret poured into her heart. She pulled her hand free. Last night she had let Troy touch her. He had touched that woman.

"What's the matter?"

"You were with his girlfriend."

"Loretta?"

Casey nodded.

"I told you, she don't mean anything to me."

Jealousy fired hot through Casey's veins. She felt cheap, easy. Troy had been with that blonde woman and then he smooth-talked her into going out with him, too. "If she doesn't, then why were you two together?"

Troy's rough exterior melted. "I was trying to help you."

The tide of anger broke. "Help *me*? How does being with that woman help me?"

"She was asking questions about Ladd Springs, said she was trying to get information about Delaney and Felicity. When she started, I didn't know she was his girlfriend. She told me they were just friends. She said he was here to re-claim his property rights. I figured if I helped her to help him get the property away from Felicity, you'd have a chance at getting your share."

Casey clung to Troy's every word.

"It's not right Felicity gets all of it. She don't need a thousand acres. You should have some, too." Emotion simmered in the depths of his gaze. "He is your daddy. It's right you should have it."

"You went against Felicity?" It was more than Casey could ever wish for.

He nodded. "Actually, more against Travis, but her, too." Troy lowered his gaze. "The both of them."

Last night had meant something to Casey. She and Troy went out drinking, a little too much, and kissed. He held her in his arms like he really cared about her and said sweet things. So many sweet things. Hope bloomed warmly in her breast. Did he really mean them? Was last night as important to him as it was her?

"Dad gum, Casey. I like you. I'm sorry if my being with her makes you mad, but I was only trying to help."

Casey didn't care. He wasn't with that woman anymore and it sounded like he didn't want to be with Felicity either. Casey smiled. "It's okay."

An hour later, Jeremiah pounded on the door to Ernie's cabin. He'd found Loretta at the motel sunning herself by the pool, reading some trashy novel. As expected, she wasn't pleased by the marks on his face, but that was too bad. He didn't care what she thought. He was there for money and a change of clothes—even spotted his truck outside a gas station on his way over. Parked off the side of the road, it looked as if he'd been driving, been stopped, yanked out of the driver's seat and hauled away. Beat the hell out of him was how it went down. He didn't remember the first detail. According to the lumps on his head, it wasn't a wonder.

At least they left the keys in the ignition. Jeremiah was surprised the vehicle hadn't been stolen but there it was, sitting pretty and waiting for him. Now he wanted to know who the hell was responsible for it all. There was no doubt it was planned, and the last person to threaten him was his old man.

Ernie swung open the door, shotgun in hand. Pointed directly at Jeremiah's head.

Jeremiah flinched.

Beady black eyes bore at him through the dusty screen. "You're not welcome here, boy."

Caught off guard by the barrel in his face, Jeremiah taunted, "You gonna shoot me, now?"

"I will if I need to."

"Haven't you done enough already?" he goaded, searching for signs of guilt in his father's face. Jeremiah didn't put it past Ernie to hire some local thugs to rough him up after their encounter yesterday. Between him and Albert, they probably had access to enough of them.

Ernie scrutinized Jeremiah's face, his injuries. "Too bad they didn't finish the job."

Jeremiah riled. "Too bad you're not *dead* already. Sure would have made taking this place from Felicity a hell of a lot easier."

Ernie thrust his gun into the screen between them. "Say her name again and I pull the trigger."

Jeremiah hesitated, his heart thumping against his rib cage. It was possible the old man was crazy enough to do it. Ernie Ladd, blowing his own kid clear off the porch with his shotgun. Glaring eye-to-eye, Jeremiah grimaced. "You're not worth it," he said, "but if I find out you had something to do with this," he said, pointing to his face, "I'll be back and give you a reason to use that gun of yours."

Ernie yanked it back and Jeremiah retreated down the steps, each foot fall a painful reminder he was not up for a fight. But he'd be back, that much was certain. There was gold on this land, gold that belonged to *him*. First, he'd have to nurse his wounds and get some more money. He might not have the cash to hire a lawyer, but he damned well had the brains to outsmart this bunch of hillbillies and get the judge to see things *his* way. And if that didn't work, he always had the power of persuasion. Jeremiah punched fist to palm. A persuasion he'd take great pleasure in using against them.

At the sound of a vehicle crossing over the bridge, Jeremiah cursed. Delaney and her boys. Well, talk about making his life easier. They were on the list of people he wanted to see today.

From inside the car, Malcolm glanced across the meadow. The white car was gone. Knots unwound inside him. *She must be okay*. Questions swirled anew. Where was she? Why didn't she return any of his calls last night?

Delaney spotted Jeremiah and pointed. "Oh my... What happened to *him*?"

Via the rearview mirror, the two men exchanged a glance. "No idea," Nick replied.

Abruptly, she whirled on him. "Did you have something to do with that?"

"No, ma'am," Malcolm said easily.

But the smile easing onto Nick's lips didn't help ease the worried look from her face. "If you're lying to me—" she said to Nick.

He put a finger to her lips. "I told you. I'm a man who believes in honesty. Mal and I had a meeting last night. We had nothing to do with Jeremiah's beating. We may have shadowed him for a while before our meeting," Nick allowed, "but we didn't lay a hand on him."

"You *followed* him? Are you insane? Don't you under-stand Jeremiah is not above using sleazy tactics?"

It was exactly those sleazy tactics Malcolm wanted to discuss with Jeremiah. All night long he'd wondered about Lacy. He'd wanted to confront Jeremiah about it last night, but Nick forbade him. *We're innocent bystanders here. We can't be tied to him in any way.*

Well, Malcolm had questions—questions he wanted an-swered. Before Nick placed the car in park, he jumped out, his eyes never wavering from Jeremiah as he approached. "Where's Lacy?"

"I have no idea."

"I don't believe you," Malcolm growled.

Jeremiah snickered, his one eye swollen shut. Up close and personal the bruises from his beating were dark and pro-nounced. Whoever did this to him had done a thorough job.

Delaney pulled up beside Malcolm. "What happened to you?"

"As if you don't know," he said snidely.

"Know? How would I know?"

"Ask your boys, here. They're responsible."

Delaney sucked in her breath but didn't ask a single question. Malcolm understood. She already doubted them. Once Nick revealed their plan from last night—part of it, anyway—she had no reason to believe they wouldn't have done this to Jeremiah. They had a will, they had a way. "That would be a waste of their time," Delaney defended, her conviction quivering beneath a fine layer of nerves threading through her voice.

"We didn't beat you," Nick confirmed. He grinned boldly. "Though I sure am glad someone did."

"Don't push me," Jeremiah cracked. He swiped a menacing glance toward Delaney and said, "You have people you care about that could get hurt."

Malcolm grabbed Jeremiah by the collar and wrenched him close. The stench of alcohol from Jeremiah's breath assaulted his senses, set a fuse to his temper. "You lay a hand on Lacy and I swear I'll kill you."

"Let go of me," Jeremiah said evenly, "or you'll be the one lying in the morgue."

Malcolm made a snap appraisal of the man's eyes. They were black as coal behind a veil of brown. Jeremiah Ladd would fight and he would fight hard—to the death if need be. He was a man on the edge, a man with nothing to lose. Malcolm's gut warned Jeremiah would prove a worthy opponent, too. Shoving him away, he thrust a finger in Jeremiah's face. It might be worth a go-round to find out. "Warning stands."

Four heads swiveled in unison as a blue compact car passed by the bridge, turning into the meadow on the other side. Malcolm's heart kicked. In the backseat sat Lacy. *Lacy.*

Malcolm took off running. The driver slammed the brakes, put the car in reverse and drove over the bridge heading straight for him. Pulse pumping, a thousand thoughts raced through his mind, emotions tangled in his heart. Lacy was okay. She was okay.

The car stopped suddenly and three women popped out of the vehicle. Lacy ran toward Malcolm. A sliver of fear entered her eyes as she noticed Jeremiah. Malcolm scooped her up in his arms and hugged her close. *God*, she felt good. "Where have you been? What happened to you?"

Lacy didn't reply, only squeezed him tightly. Annie Owens and a blonde woman came up behind her. "What happened to Jeremiah?" Annie asked. But rather than showing alarm, she seemed oddly intrigued.

"He got a beating last night," Malcolm told her, then released Lacy but kept her close.

"From you?" Lacy asked.

Malcolm shook his head. "I wish." Cupping her face in his hands, he searched her eyes for answers, meaning. "What happened to you? Why did you leave your purse in that white car by the trail last night? Why didn't you return any of my calls?"

Lacy's eyes hollowed, her lower lip began to quiver.

"We were in the forest," Annie explained. "Lacy was showing me the gold. We were on our way out—until Jeremiah showed up."

"Jeremiah?" Anger exploded inside Malcolm.

"Jeremiah thought it would be a good idea to threaten us," she said. "Drove us off the property and took us to his motel." Malcolm logged every syllable, each and every one stoking the embers of his fury. "Before we reached town, he received a phone call and that's when he dumped us at the motel. Up and drove off, leaving us with no car of our own, no way to get home." Annie's anger was palpable. She raised a hand to her side. "I had to call my friend Candi, to come and get us."

Malcolm registered the blonde and her timid wave, registered the role Jeremiah played, registered the fact that Lacy had revealed the gold—the truth unfurling in her eyes as clear as a written confession. Malcolm's heart ripped open. More hurt than he was prepared to be, he released Lacy. "How could you?"

Tears welled in her eyes. "I'm *sorry.*"

Malcolm spun around and charged Jeremiah.

"Malcolm!" Nick yelled.

Annie screamed. Delaney jumped out of the way. From somewhere in the background, Lacy shrieked his name. Back-stepping, Jeremiah threw a punch, landing it against Malcolm's jaw. He swung again, but Malcolm blocked it, undercutting Jeremiah's chin with a slug of his own. The man reeled and fell.

"Mal, stop!"

Malcolm ignored the plea from Nick. Yanking Jeremiah up, he hit him again. Jeremiah moaned in pain, the sound like a balm to Malcolm's pride.

"Malcolm!" Lacy cried. "Stop! Please, stop!"

Something inside him snapped. He no longer cared about the consequences of assault and battery. He no longer cared about a calm presence of mind. This parasite had it coming. Jeremiah lifted from the ground and Malcolm kicked him hard. His body fell limp.

Nick grabbed Malcolm by the arm, pulling at him. Malcolm resisted, staring down at the bloodied face, the body writhing on the ground. He reached down to haul Jeremiah up, but Nick dragged him away. "This is not a fight you want to have."

"Oh, but that's where you're wrong," Malcolm objected bitterly. He rubbed his jaw. *That's where you're wrong.* The pain building in his face had been worth it.

Lacy ran to him. "Are you okay?" she asked, examining his chin.

"I'm fine," he answered gruffly.

Lacy looked frightened as a kitten on a high wire. Tears spilled from her eyes. "I'm sorry." She glanced at Annie, Delaney, Nick. "I'm *sorry.* This is all my fault!" She took off running. Malcolm's instinct was to follow her, to chase her down and demand an explanation. But he didn't. He didn't move. Didn't take the first step. *Lacy had lied to him.*

Annie stepped forward, squaring her slender shoulders. The delicate lace trim of her blouse posed stark contrast to the authority in her voice. "She didn't mean any harm. She had no idea it would cause this kind of trouble."

"Lacy told you about the gold?" Delaney asked, incredulous at the turn of events.

"She was trying to help me."

"Help you? By telling you about my gold?"

"It's Felicity's," Annie corrected bluntly.

"Mine and Felicity's!" Delaney shouted.

"Ladies, please," Nick interceded, one hand clipped to the stirring Jeremiah.

About to retort, Annie closed her mouth. She turned to Malcolm. "Listen, Lacy acts first, thinks second."

"That she does," he agreed, tracking her fleeing figure. Lacy was running through the meadow in a direct line for the wooded trail.

"She's always been that way. She just doesn't think in normal terms. But if I had to be honest..." Shame trickled into Annie's blue eyes and Malcolm felt the pinch. "I'd say she was trying to do the right thing. The right thing by me and my *daughter*," Annie corrected, brazenly baiting Delaney with the comment. To Malcolm, she said, "Lacy thought that if I knew about the gold, it would help motivate me to fight for Casey's rights. As though I wasn't fighting hard enough already," she complained under her breath. "But Lacy doesn't act on facts. She acts on emotion. She was trying help." Annie's expression softened. "It's what she does, I think. She just tries to help."

"Ah, *hell*," Malcolm muttered. He cast a glance toward Nick, touched upon Jeremiah as he roused himself from the ground and asked, "Can you take care of this mess? I've got a mess of my own to clean up."

Nick nodded and Malcolm took off after Lacy, a mix of anger and want swirling in his heart. *Lacy was only trying to help*. It's what she did. A large part of Malcolm believed that to be true, but another part of him couldn't get past the lie. It was betrayal.

Chapter Twenty-Two

Lacy ran and ran and ran, the tall meadow grass scraping at her legs as she pushed forward. She had to get out of here. She had to get away from Malcolm and Nick and Annie—all of them! She should never have come back to Tennessee. She should have stayed in Atlanta and made good with what she had. She had a boyfriend. She had a job. But she wasn't happy. She wanted to be with her family. She wanted to be loved. Tears spurted from her eyes and she ran faster. Harder.

She wanted to be in love! She'd almost found herself a perfect man and then she ruined it. Ruined it. Smeared it into the mud. Lacy saw the look in Malcolm's eyes. She heard his words. *I can trust you, right? You don't want me to get into trouble, do you?*

He hated her. Malcolm hated her because she'd lied to him about the gold.

She should have settled for her manager. He had a steady job, made good money. He would have made a fine husband, taken care of her. But Lacy didn't love him. He was old and boring. He wasn't interested in fun, or kids, and he was about as spontaneous as a sponge. He was no good for her. Slowing to a jolty walk, she struggled against the pounding in her chest. She dropped hands to knees, her leg muscles pumped from the extended sprint. Looking over her shoulder, she saw that Malcolm wasn't coming for her. The knife to her heart was quick and deep. Another wave of tears pricked. There was no need to hurry. No one wanted her.

Lacy stood, inhaling against the rapid-fire of her pulse, ignoring the yellow and purple blooms dotting the grass with clusters of cheery color, the bright sunshine of a clear blue day, the hills plumped with green, mountains that reached to the sky. The beauty made her sad. She was alone, with no one to enjoy the scenery, the gorgeous weather. Up ahead, the forest would offer her shade, solitude. She could lose herself in the woods, erase her memory with the crash of water, the thunder of sound. The chilly water would refresh her, cleanse her soul, give her new direction. Time alone would clear her mind and help her think.

Breathing easier as the adrenaline wore off, Lacy plodded toward the trail. She'd spend the day at Zack's Falls and figure out what to do next. She halted, heaved a weighty sigh. Who was she kidding? There was no next step.

"Lacy!"

Limbs froze. Her pulse took off at a gallop.

"Hold up!" Malcolm yelled from a distance.

If she had an ounce of strength left, she would have bolted like a deer. But between her fatigue and the fresh shot of shock, Lacy couldn't move an inch. She wiped the tears from her cheeks. She looped her hair behind an ear, took a deep breath, threw her shoulders back and turned. She'd have to face him sooner or later. Stand up and face her sins like a woman. Wasn't the first time.

Every step closer he took twisted knots of anxiety through her heart. Malcolm was jogging, slowing his pace as he neared. "Lacy." Winded, his voice held a certain urgency.

"Malcolm," she said, forcing herself to sound strong, impenetrable. She'd faced her mistakes before and she could face them again—although trying to do right by her sister didn't feel like a mistake. It felt good.

"Are you okay?"

"Yes," she replied, but her bravado cracked at the compassion in his eyes. Malcolm looked genuinely concerned.

"I'm sorry. Back there"—he hiked a thumb over his shoulder—"I lost it."

Lacy wished he was sorry for hating her instead of for hitting Jeremiah. "I understand. You were angry."

"I was. Very." He dropped his head forward.

Lacy wanted to burst into tears. It was true. He hated her.

Malcolm blew out a heavy breath, raised his head and looked directly into her eyes. Hurt swam in his eyes. Lacy's heart squeezed at his tortured gaze. He looked beaten. And she had swung the hammer.

"Why did you say anything about the gold, Lacy? You promised you wouldn't."

You lied is what she heard. Loud and clear. Stung by the accusation, Lacy objected in a shaky voice, "But I didn't lie, Malcolm." His gaze turned dark and she added hurriedly, "Not really—I had my fingers crossed when I agreed." Confusion funneled into his gentle features and Lacy stepped back. "If you cross your fingers, Malcolm, it's not a lie," she insisted, and though she sounded foolish—even to herself—it was true. Sort of. In her heart, anyway.

The blue of Malcolm's eyes hardened to an impenetrable crystal. A wall rose behind them as he closed himself off from her. Beset with guilt, she stomped her boot and confessed, "Okay, I lied—is that what you want to hear? I lied, dang it! I wanted to help Annie and Casey. I wanted them to know there was gold, that they had to *fight* for it, that they couldn't let that mean old Delaney keep it for herself!" Lacy knew she was rambling, but she couldn't stop. Malcolm had to know. He had to know why she did what she did, and if he still hated her, then so be it. But she was going to tell him everything. "Casey is Jeremiah's daughter. She's entitled to her share of this property, same as Felicity. And just because someone doesn't like her daddy, or her momma," Lacy continued, fueled by anger, "that doesn't make it right to cut her out—"

Malcolm grabbed her face and kissed her.

Lacy squealed. The sudden move rocked her. She tried to think, tried to move, tried to—

Malcolm's mouth sank into hers and Lacy couldn't do a thing. He pried her lips apart and kissed her with a near violent greed. Her insides shivered as he probed, plunged. The kiss lengthened, grew needy, stirring swells of emotion within her. Powerful hunger wound deep and low in her belly, curled up and around her heart like a soft caress. Malcolm felt so good, so warm. He was solid. Strong. When he eased away, her heart lurched, yet his hands remained steady in their hold. Reaching up, she cupped her hands over his and searched his pale gaze for meaning, direction. "Malcolm?"

"No more crossed fingers. Ever."

Lacy's heart sung. Malcolm didn't hate her! He still cared. She still mattered. Relief washed through her. Slipping into a sheepish grin she replied, "No more. *Ever.*"

Malcolm wrapped his arms around her and pulled her near. He kissed her, hugged her—so hard, that Lacy feared the breath would burst from her lungs. Gasping, she pushed away. "Malcolm, I can't breathe!"

Lessening his grip, he grew serious. The fine black line of his lashes underscored the mellowing of his gaze. "I love you, Lacy. I knew it the second I saw you in the backseat of that car. If anything happened to you, I would have been devastated."

Lacy hated to laugh when he was pouring his heart out to her, but she couldn't help it.

He nodded, a mischievous gleam flaring in his gaze. "You think that's funny?"

"You *love* me. I thought you hated me."

"I did." Lacy stuck out her lower lip, hurt by his admission. "Until I realized why you did what you did."

She relaxed in his arms, adoring the way it felt to be held by him. "You understand? Honest, you do?" Lacy wanted to be on the same side as Malcolm. She wanted them to be a team. But Annie was her sister, and she didn't care what anyone said. It was true what people claimed, that blood was thicker than water. It connected you, bound you. It held you together as best it could. Of course family members had to do their share and not spill so much of it between them, but they were human. They made mistakes. Lacy reckoned both she and Annie had made their share and all they could do was move forward.

"I only wanted to help Annie," Lacy said, "but I want to help you too, Malcolm. I helped you with Jeremiah, remember?"

He smiled. "I do."

"But Annie's my sister. You understand I have to be with her first, right? Over you, she comes first."

He nodded. "She's the one who made me realize that fact."

Lacy balked. "Annie?"

"Annie. She said you were only trying to help her. That helping is what you do."

A cuddly joy enveloped Lacy's heart, snug as a child's fuzzy blanket. "She did? She said all that?"

"She did."

Lacy beamed. She felt bright as the afternoon sun. Glancing overhead at the blue sky, the temperature warming her skin, she suddenly ached for adventure. "Wanna go to Zack's Falls with me?"

Malcolm laughed. He hugged her tight. "More than you know!"

As Malcolm and Lacy lay side-by-side on an expanse of rock, a branch overhead shaded their bodies from the brunt of the heat. The thunderous crash of water invigorated him, misted the air with its cool spray. They hadn't skinny-dipped. They'd swum, but did so fully clothed. The wooded trail to their side was too unpredictable. First it had been Jeremiah and his cohort, who knew who might run past next time? Exposing Lacy's naked body to strangers wasn't a chance he was willing to take. He wanted that view all for himself. Restless, Malcolm rolled over Lacy's body, ignoring the dusty stone particles sticking to his back. He stared into her eyes, eyes that held a smile, a hint of mischief, and of course her tease that never quit.

"Have you warmed up, yet?" he asked.

"If I have, does that mean you won't stay near to keep me warm?"

"I'll stay near as long as you want me to," he replied, leaning down for a kiss. Lacy responded, as did his loins. He melted into her, desire surging. Lacy kissed him with a fluidity of motion that made him feel like they were the only two people on the planet. He cradled her head with his hand and delved his tongue inside her mouth. Moist and succulent, she was like candy, like juicy steak, like a drug, an aphrodisiac of the highest degree. Desire slid through him, detonating nerve endings in a surge of want. Malcolm lost himself in the sensation, in images of her body from their swim, the sky blue tank sticking to her soaking wet skin. Gliding a hand down her waist, her thigh, he thought she was beautiful, sexy, perfection in the female form. Hardening, Malcolm pulled away from her. "You have no idea what you do to me," he said huskily.

"It's all good, right?"

Malcolm smiled at her impish response. "It's all good. Everything you do is good."

She giggled.

The girlish reaction made him wonder yet again how she managed to stay so naïve, so fresh in her outlook. It was an odd outcome for a woman with her past. Brushing the short tendrils of black hair from her forehead, her cheeks, he marveled in her creamy skin, pink from the sun and their swim in the brisk pool of water beneath the falls. "Tell me about Lacy."

"About me?" she asked, as if startled by the question.

"I want to know everything about you."

She dipped her chin and peered up at him. "I'm not that exciting."

Malcolm laughed, trailing a finger down the length of her arm. "Oh, I completely disagree. You are most interesting, Ms. Owens." She smiled, but something in her changed. Her gaze lost its carefree tease, her smile lost a bit of its luster. "I want to know how you spent your days, your nights in

Atlanta. When you weren't working, that is. What did you do for fun?"

She heaved a sigh. "That was the problem. I didn't have much fun. I worked," she said, and slid her gaze down to his chest. "A lot."

"All work and no fun?" He tipped her chin back up, noting the blue of her eyes had deepened. "I don't believe it. Fun is your middle name."

Lacy rewarded him with a smile. "Not everyone is as fun as you, Malcolm. In fact, some people are downright stick-in-the-muds."

He chuckled. Dropping his elbow, he relaxed onto his arm, placing his opposite hand over her narrow hips. Her denim skirt was still damp, though her tank had almost completely dried. No pink bra today, it was beige and not nearly as charming. "Speaking from experience, are you?" Lacy nodded, but didn't elaborate. "Well, let's not dwell on the stick-in-the-muds. Tell me about the young and rebellious Lacy, the one who moved to Atlanta with Jeremiah in a mad dash out of town." Lacy frowned. "What? Do you regret it?" She stilled, and a fleeting shame swooped into her expression. Caught off guard by the change, Malcolm tensed. Brief, but it had been there, he was sure of it. Was she hiding something undesirable? "Lacy?"

"Do we have to talk about the past? I'd rather talk about the future, about Serenity Springs and all the new jobs you're going to offer me."

Malcolm tried to smile, but remained tripped up by her reaction. What had she done that she wasn't willing to share? Couldn't share? She had no record. There was nothing in her past with regard to arrests, no legal trouble of any kind that he could find. Not that he liked snooping on women, but Malcolm had been burned once, badly. Ten years ago, he'd fallen for the wrong woman and she had nearly taken him for everything he was worth. And it wasn't the woman's first time. California divorce records revealed she had three previous marriages and then there was the lawsuit for fraud—all readily accessible had he the presence of mind to search for them beforehand. But he didn't. Malcolm relied on her word and learned a hard lesson.

It was a lesson in testosterone, stupidity and youthful inexperience. A lesson he would not repeat. Yet oddly, Malcolm felt as though it were happening all over again. He delicately turned her jaw until he could look her in the eye. "Lacy?" She blinked. "It's not like you to clam up." A sadness swamped her gaze. "Talk to me. What happened in Atlanta?"

"Oh, *Malcolm*. Do we have to talk about Atlanta?"

"Is there a reason we can't?" She looked away and he swore she was about to cry. "I've fallen head over heels for a woman and she can't talk about her past?" Part of Malcolm felt the brunt of the statement like a kick to the gut. Another part of him was swimming in dread. The steady pound of the waterfall reverberated in his chest as he held his breath.

"Will you still love me if I'm not perfect?"

Spurts of relief erupted inside him. "No one's perfect, Lacy. We all make mistakes."

She pursed her lips, as though pondering whether or not she should divulge her particular mistakes, her secrets. "I wouldn't call them mistakes, exactly."

He cocked a brow. "What would you call them?"

"Pictures."

"Pictures?"

Lacy nodded and gnawed on her lower lip.

"What kind of pictures?" Tears filled her eyes, instantly tearing at his heart. "Are they bad?" Suddenly, he wasn't sure he wanted to know the answer to that question.

"Not terribly," she replied, her voice shaky. "I was young, they paid well. They weren't vulgar or anything and they helped me save—"

Malcolm pressed a finger to her lips. He didn't want to hear anymore. *Pictures.*

For a moment, they only stared at one another. Water rushed and crashed as the past flowed over them, between

them, down the river. The power of nature, the quiet of solitude. One man, one woman, choices swept away, cleansing
the air between them. Malcolm had always known there was
something. Without roommates to split the cost of living,
minimum wage would barely scrape the rent for a modest
one-bedroom apartment in Atlanta. He tried to imagine what
had been going through her mind as she posed, why she
hadn't decided to return home, instead. But second-guessing
the past was a fool's game. He'd made his share of mistakes,
decisions he'd wished he could take back, emotions he'd
wished he never experienced. But that was life. You lived,
you learned, you did the best you could. You tried to keep
your eye on the ball, keep the ball up in the air, but sometimes it dropped.

Lacy was clearly upset by her choices. It was a part of
her life she'd rather forget. But she had survived. She'd survived the city and done so with minimal scars. An amazing
feat really, when he thought of everything that could have
happened and didn't. Posing for pictures wasn't illegal. It
might prove haunting, but not illegal. Malcolm couldn't help
but wonder if the pictures had been widely distributed. Would
he run across them one day? In a magazine, on the internet?

As he traced Lacy's cheekbone, her jawline, she remain
transfixed. Malcolm wondered if she ever thought the same
thing. Would those pictures show up when she least expected
them? Would they upset her? They wouldn't upset him. Lacy
Owens was a beautiful woman. He bet her pictures were gorgeous.

Lacy drew his hand from her face and whispered, "Do
you hate me?"

"No." He shook his head, pained by the naked fear in her
eyes. It was unnecessary. "I couldn't hate you, Lacy."

"Not even for what I did?"

"You did what you had to do." Tears pricked his eyes.
He hated to think she had been put in that position, but once
there, she'd done what she had to do to survive. "I admire
you for that." He paused. "Unless, there's something else

you're hiding from me." Shock peppered her expression. "You don't have a husband you're hiding somewhere, do you?"

Realization slammed into her eyes and she punched him. "I most certainly do not."

"Then I don't hate you." He grinned and pecked her nose. "I love you."

Relief unlocked her joy with a genuine smile. She wrapped her arms around his body and cried, "Oh, Malcolm, I love you!"

He laughed. "It's about time!" He'd said the words, but this was the first time Lacy had said them back. As he gazed into her eyes, Malcolm's heart swelled. Words he believed she meant. "C'mon." He pushed up from the rock. "I'm taking you home."

She looked up at him. "Home?"

"Well, maybe not *home*." Lacy was staying with her Aunt Fran but Malcolm wanted her all to himself. "We have a dinner date to make up for, remember?" Lacy squealed with delight as Malcolm offered a hand, pulling her to her feet. Her red toe polish snared his attention. Lively red for a lively girl. And though Lacy felt more girl than woman, he believed that deep down she was every bit as woman as any other, perhaps more so. He chuckled. She simply kept her wise old woman hidden in her back pocket, preferring to cater to the child in her—which suited him just fine. He like spirited and spontaneous.

"Can we go dancing?" she asked.

"Absolutely. Twirling you around the dance floor is something I've wanted to do since the picnic." Then he'd twirl her around his hotel room for even more fun.

Chapter Twenty-Three

Nick and Delaney sat huddled together on the leather sofa in her cabin, the space quiet and comfortable between them. Nestled warmly in the crux of his arm, Delaney found the rhythmic rise and fall of his chest soothing, the muscular wall of his body reassuring. Nick was on her side. He was in her corner. He wanted what she wanted. Granted they were her decisions to make, but he was here to support her in those decisions. Decisions. Seems like that's all she'd been doing of late—making decisions. From deciding how to convince Ernie to stand by his promise to figuring out a way to keep Annie and Jeremiah's greedy hands off the title, the decisions just kept coming.

Jeremiah concerned her the most. He'd fight for the entire thousand acre tract, then kick the lot of them out. He wasn't interested in tradition or family. Back home for less than a week and he was already threatening everyone from her and Annie to his very own father—his *dying* father. Images from the encounter earlier curdled in her heart. Jeremiah was a disgrace. He only wanted Ladd Springs for the money. He'd sell it to the highest bidder so he could pay off his gambling debt. Years of family and history would be gone. In the scratch of his signature, Jeremiah could end the Ladd legacy.

Delaney dropped her head back onto Nick's shoulder. Life had become a mess of decisions, and she was tired of making them. Though there remained one decision she couldn't ignore. Staring at the wooden beams above, the rough-hewn slats of the ceiling sloping steeply from the peak, she said, "Annie sounds pretty sure of Casey's paternity."

"That she does," Nick agreed.

Delaney's gaze lowered, glazing over as she stared out a side window. "With him in town, I think she'll finally get that paternity test."

"Easier when he's in jail."

Delaney grunted. "And if he sues us for the deed to Ladd Springs?"

"With no money?"

"What if he gets the money?"

"Law suits require money and they require grounds for challenge," Nick said, stroking her hair. "If Jeremiah decides to take it to court, then he's got two years to do so." Nick's hand stilled and gently squeezed her arm. "But Ernie signed the property over to Felicity in a life estate. It's a done deal. He had every legal right to sign it over to whomever he chose and he chose her. In the eyes of the law, once Ernie passes, Felicity is the owner of Ladd Springs. Your only concern at this point is paying the back taxes."

Delaney heaved a sigh. "Which I need you for."

He gave her a mild shake. "I thought we were in this together?"

"We are." She blew out her breath, the breath she hadn't realized she'd been holding. "I'm just worried about Jeremiah interfering."

"He won't," Nick said firmly. "We won't let him."

The thought gave her pause. If they were successful in stopping Jeremiah, there was still the issue of Casey. If she really was Jeremiah's daughter, it would make her Ernie's granddaughter, same as Felicity, and every bit as entitled to Ladd Springs. Shutting her out didn't seem right. "Casey shouldn't be penalized because of her parents," Delaney remarked quietly.

"I agree."

Nick's voice was faint, like an echo of her thoughts. Had he been thinking the same thing she'd been thinking? "But Annie is another thing," Delaney said defiantly. Where she may feel Casey equally entitled to Ladd Springs, she did not feel that way about her mother. Delaney was a Ladd. Annie was not.

"What do you want to do about it?" Nick asked.

Her gaze shot to the ceiling. "I don't know. I haven't gotten that far in my thought process."

Nick chuckled. "Give it time. I daresay we're not in a hurry. From what I witnessed today, Ernie is still in prime fightin' condition. A paternity test will take time. I say we pay the taxes and take it from there. Malcolm and I can draw up site plans, architectural designs and when the day comes, we'll be positioned to put them into action."

Good thinking. Steady, calm, Nick was fast-becoming Delaney's rock.

"Don't look now," Nick announced softly, "but we've got company."

Delaney jumped. "What?" Her gaze latched onto the dark figure walking across her porch. She twisted to him. "The police are here."

"I see that." He rose, gently guiding her up with him.

Staring up into Nick's dark gaze, she asked, "Do you think they arrested Jeremiah?

"I think we should answer the door and find out."

The rap was quick and succinct. Delaney hurried to answer, hopeful the police had Jeremiah in custody, but nervous it could be something else. Nick and Malcolm seemed a little too cool when Jeremiah asked about their involvement. They told her they'd been out on business last night. Could that business have had something to do with Jeremiah? Delaney tamped back the quick patter in her breast and exclaimed, "Hey, Gavin." Recognizing Ida Shore's son instantly, Delaney was relieved for the friendly face. "How can I help you?" she asked, standing aside to let him in.

"Hey, Delaney," he greeted with a smile, followed by a nod to Nick. Gavin was fair-skinned and boyish-faced, his receding blond hair the only outward indication to his almost forty years. Thankfully his hazel eyes were friendly, suggesting no ill intent for his visit.

"Gavin, this is my friend, Nick Harris. Nick, Gavin Shore."

"Nice to meet you," Gavin said and extended a hand. "Your uncle told me to come up here and talk to you about this." He pulled out a worn black wallet and handed it to her.

Delaney flipped it open with a sharp intake of breath. *Jeremiah's.* She looked at Nick, then Gavin. "This belongs to Ernie's son, Jeremiah."

"That's what I thought. I only know of one Ladd family around these parts and that's yours," Gavin said pleasantly. "When did he get back in town?"

Delaney's first instinct was to explain it wasn't a friendly visit, but she hesitated.

"Where did you find the wallet, officer?" Nick asked.

Gavin straightened and clicked back into business mode. "Downtown. I was concerned, because it was found in an area known for criminal activity." Gavin turned to Delaney. "Is Jeremiah okay?"

She wanted to shout, "No, he's a troublemaker who deserved the beating he got!" But fearing that would make her look guilty, she nodded, brushed her hair behind an ear. "As far as I know. I saw him earlier today," she said, checking with Nick to see if she was on the right track. He discreetly encouraged her. "But I haven't seen him since."

"Hmm." Gavin opened the wallet and furrowed his sandy brow. "Looks like he was robbed. There's no cash and no credit cards."

"Nothing less than I would expect, if you say you found it in a rough part of town," she replied. "Would you like me to give it to him if I see him again?" She had no plans to see him, but she wanted to sound normal. Helpful.

"Thanks, but I'd better keep it. We're running the fingerprints on it now."

"Good thinking," she said, her mind zipping through potential pitfalls. Were there any? She flashed a glance at Nick. Like maybe his or Malcolm's prints showing up?

Gavin smacked the wallet against the heel of his palm and said, "Well, when you see Jeremiah, tell him not to make a stranger of himself." He chuckled. "I wouldn't mind seeing the old boy again."

Delaney thought, *Think again. Jeremiah isn't the same kid they grew up with.* But she murmured respectfully, "I will."

She waved Gavin goodbye and closed the door before turning to Nick. "What do you think?"

"I think they'll find the fingerprints of whoever robbed Jeremiah of his wallet." Delaney's thoughts balled into a knot of curiosity. Nick took her face in hands. "It wasn't me, so wipe that suspicious look off your face."

"What?'

"You heard me." Nick leaned down and kissed her, soft and sweet. "You need to have some patience. The police will get Jeremiah in due time, and they won't be arresting me along with him." He grinned and winked at her. "Shame on you to think otherwise."

Troy gunned the engine of his truck and accelerated, spinning the steering wheel in a tight reverse out of his parents' carport. Casey was waiting for him at Fran's Diner. They were going out again tonight and he didn't want to be late. Casey was cool. Sweet and pretty, she didn't judge him. She believed in him. He swiped a glance at the upstairs window. It was more than he could say for anyone else around here.

As expected, his parents hit the roof when he told them he wasn't going to college. He explained his plan, laid out his vision, but all they did was try and talk him out of it, as though forcing him to go to a college and get a degree he didn't want was a smart idea. It wasn't. It was stupid and it wasn't going to happen. Picking up his cell from the center console, Troy dialed Casey's number. Bringing the phone to ear, he slowed. A police car emerged from around the wooded curve, heading in.

"Aw, crap." Casey answered and he said, "I'm running late, but don't leave, okay?" Troy watched the squad car near, the officer's eyes pinned on him. "I'll be there," he clipped, "so don't go anywhere, hear?"

Troy and the police officer veered to the opposite sides of the driveway, splitting the difference. What the hell were police doing on his property? The officer rolled down his window and looked up at him. "This the Parker home, right?"

"It is."

"I'm looking for a Troy Parker." The blonde officer squinted slightly, as though recognizing him through a fog. It was getting dark Troy thought, but not that dark. "Do you know where I might find him?" the man asked.

A sudden flood of nerves cut across his midsection. "I'm Troy Parker. What's the problem, officer?"

Glancing toward the home behind him, he said, "I have a couple of questions, if you don't mind."

"Naw, I don't mind," he said politely. Troy slid the gear into park and jumped out of his truck. The police officer emerged from his vehicle more cautiously. Angst zipped through him. Was he here to arrest him? Had he somehow found out about last night?

"Do you know a Jeremiah Ladd?"

Troy nearly crapped his pants. "Yeah. What about him?"

"He was robbed last night."

Beaten, too, but Troy kept his mouth shut.

"He said you might know something about it?"

"*Me*? I don't know anything about any robbery," he exclaimed. "Why's he bringing my name up?"

"That's what I'm here to find out." The officer glanced up at the house again. "Are your parents home?"

Yes, but this is a really bad time. Any more bad news and they might throw him out! "They don't know anything about it, either."

The officer smiled, as though to say "nice try." "Maybe we should be having this conversation with them."

Stuffing his doubt deeper, Troy squared off. "I'm eighteen. They don't have any reason to be involved."

Appearing amused by Troy's response, the officer nodded. "Okay." He rested his hands along his gun belt and asked, "Where were you last night?"

"Out."

"Out with whom?"

"Myself."

The man raised his brow. "Eighteen-year-old boys go out by themselves these days?"

Troy didn't like the man's insulting tone. "I don't need anyone to hold my hand."

"Where'd you go?"

"Bowling."

"Bowling?"

Troy nodded. He did stop by the bowling alley on his way out of town with Casey.

"There's only one bowling place in town, son."

"I know it."

"You have someone there who can verify your story?"

"Dad gum, it ain't no story. Why don't you go ask them and see for yourself?"

"This isn't a joke, boy."

"I didn't say it was." Troy's pulse quickened at the sight of a taxi cab pulling in behind the police officer. He watched the car roll to a stop and stared at the back door as it opened. His stomach pitched. What the hell was *she* doing here?

The officer turned and watched Loretta Flynn strut over, the dirt driveway proving tricky for her four-inch heels. Wearing her infamous combination of short skirt and skintight top, tonight's top a leopard print, she hurried to Troy's side. Concern ripped through her features. Her heavily made-up blue eyes rounded. "Honey, are you in trouble?"

The officer crossed his arms and broadcast his surprise at Loretta's presence.

"No, Loretta. I ain't in no trouble. What are you doing here?" he asked, mindful they were being watched.

Loretta slid a hand up his arm and smiled. "I came to see you."

"Isn't she a little old for you, son?" the officer asked with a smirk.

Troy wanted to punch him in the face. Loretta's smile broadened, apparently taking it as a compliment to her.

"This your boyfriend, ma'am?"

"I wish," she said.

Troy cursed under his breath. "She's a friend," he insisted, peeling her off of him—which was a challenge, the way she kept sidling up to him, all clingy like. Then to her, Troy repeated, "What are you doing here?"

"I came to tell you that I'm leaving. I'm leaving Jerry and I'm going back to Atlanta."

Troy groaned inwardly. *Way to go*, Loretta.

The officer perked at the mention of the name. "Jerry? Would that happen to be in reference to Jeremiah Ladd?"

"Yes," she answered. "You know him?"

"He was robbed last night," the officer said, suddenly taking a keen interest in her. "Were you with him when it happened?"

"No. I wouldn't have anything to do with that man."

"I thought you said you were leaving him."

"I know. I'm the one who said it," Loretta snipped. "You might want to get your hearing checked if you're still confused."

The officer's face reddened, his anger easily readable in the golden light of sunset. Time was ticking, and Troy was itching to get out of here. "Well, if you're though with me, I'll be going."

"Troy?" Loretta asked, her voice pinched with hurt. "Aren't you gonna say goodbye?"

"Goodbye, Loretta." It's not like they were an item, or anything. She had used him and he used her. There was no reason for emotional goodbyes.

Loretta grabbed his face and planted a wet kiss on his lips, leaving half her shiny pink gloss on his mouth. "Bye, Troy. I'll miss you."

Don't. Troy wiped the sticky lip gloss from his lips. *The feeling isn't mutual.*

Loretta strolled back to her cab with what Troy would swear was an exaggerated swing to her hips, hopped in her cab, and the vehicle backed out.

"You sure you weren't angry with her boyfriend?" the officer pressed, smoothing out his tone as if he was on Troy's side. "Fights over a woman happen every day."

"I didn't beat up Jeremiah."

The officer angled his head. "Now that's interesting. I never mentioned anything about him receiving a beating."

"He did. A bad one. I saw him this morning over at Fran's Diner."

The officer nodded that he'd heard but didn't seem convinced.

Troy asked again, "If you're through with me?" He wasn't stupid. He knew he had rights. No police officer could interrogate him without a lawyer unless he agreed to answer the questions.

"Don't go anywhere, kid. I might need to ask you a few more questions. We're running prints on the guy's wallet. You better hope they're not yours."

They ain't, he thought, and with a glance toward his house, spotted his father staring out the upstairs window. Great. He climbed into his truck. Tomorrow was gonna be a *great* day.

Chapter Twenty-Four

Malcolm and Lacy joined Nick and Delaney for breakfast at Fran's. Sunlight saturated the interior of the restaurant, lighting up the red vinyl booths, the black and white checkered floor. A floor that was gleaming, Malcolm noted, polished and ready to handle another day of heavy foot traffic. Perusing the laminated menu, Malcolm felt the nine-thirty food call was a bit early. But without Lacy in his bed, there was no sense in wasting the day. Last night after dinner and dancing at Whiskey Joes, she had refused his invitation for a nightcap at his hotel. Something about milk and cows which made no sense at the time, but eventually he got the gist. No sex. She was holding out for marriage these days. "Cup of coffee, black."

"Coming right up," Fran replied, scribbling on her petite notepad, then headed for the kitchen.

Sitting by his side, Lacy turned in the booth. "Black? No cream, no sugar?"

"Black, like the strands of your hair," he replied, raking the top of her head with a hot, hungry glance. They should be in bed right now, ordering room service.

Lacy smacked him lightly on the shoulder. "Be serious."

"I am. I like my coffee black. I like your hair black. I like your black boots. I'd like you in anything black," he added, struck by thoughts of her in lacy underwear.

Lacy giggled. Malcolm caught a glimpse of Nick and Delaney, staring. Delaney's face was wrenched in disgust while Nick's bore the spark of amusement. He didn't care what they thought. He was happy. "Any word on Jeremiah?" he asked Nick, ignoring their prurient curiosity.

"None," Nick replied, clearly enjoying Malcolm's new friendship with Lacy.

"Shouldn't take them this long," Malcolm grumbled.

"They have to find him first."

"Speak of the devil." With a flick of his eyes, Malcolm indicated the front door.

Nick and Delaney turned in unison to see Jeremiah Ladd walk into the diner. Hanging by the cash register, he glanced around, the brightly-colored paisley of his shirt out of sync with the traditional red and white country-style around him. Once he spotted them, his forehead smoothed and he made a bee line for their table.

Delaney turned her back while Nick tracked Jeremiah's every step toward them.

"Well, well, well, what a cozy little group we have here," Jeremiah said, sarcasm oozing from his voice. "What happened to my invitation?"

"What do you want, Jeremiah?" Delaney snapped.

"I want my gold and my land back."

"It's not yours," she replied.

"So you've been saying. But I've spoken to a lawyer who says otherwise. In fact, you'll be hearing from him soon."

Delaney's expression reflected the hit. She was obviously still worried about Jeremiah making headway with regard to the title, but Malcolm didn't see that he stood any real chance. Duress was a hard case to prove, the life estate deed a logical choice for a sane, terminally ill man to make. "Why don't you do a magic trick for us and make yourself disappear," Malcolm cracked.

"Funny man," Jeremiah jeered. "Feeling all big and strong because you've hooked up tight with my little lady?"

Lacy clutched Malcolm's hand under the table. "Back off, Jeremiah," Malcolm warned.

"Or what? Gonna finish what you started?"

Lacy gasped. "Malcolm had nothing to do with your face!"

"Oh, didn't he?" Jeremiah glanced to Nick and added, "With a little help from his friend, which is the only way this pretty boy could manage it. I have my sources. I'll get to the bottom of it and when I do, you'll be sorry you ever messed with me."

Malcolm and Nick both held steady. And quiet.

Which Lacy found odd. Peering over at Nick, she wondered if they had something to do with it. After all, Malcolm had not been with her that night. Lacy looked over at Delaney, who seemed to be wondering the same thing.

"See," Jeremiah said. "No denial."

"As much as I'd like to take credit for your beating," Malcolm replied, "I can't. I had a business meeting with my partner, here."

He did? Lacy considered the revelation. So that's what he did instead of dinner with her.

"Great alibi," Jeremiah mocked. "Tell the police." He lowered and came very near to Malcolm's face. "I suggested they might want to come and talk with you gentlemen. They'll be happy to listen to you explain your whereabouts and check out your flimsy alibi."

"Jeremiah—you leave him alone, this instant!" Lacy cried. "You have no business throwing accusations around."

"Does your new boyfriend know about your old hobbies, Lacy?" He flicked a glance to Malcolm. "Your money-making hobbies, I mean?"

"Hush your mouth, Jeremiah!"

Malcolm slid out of the booth and stood. Jeremiah took a step back but Malcolm leaned close, his tone raw and gravelly. "I'd suggest you get out of here right now, before your little fishing expedition sinks."

Jeremiah chuckled. "You should ask her sometime. It's real riveting stuff."

Lacy hated the suspicion crawling in Delaney's eyes. She was so judgmental, and she didn't even know what Jeremiah was talking about but simply went straight to the most horrible thing she could think of.

Malcolm remained doggedly in place, and it occurred to Lacy that he was defending her honor. Like a warrior blocking Jeremiah's path, Malcolm knew what Jeremiah was referring to and there he was, fighting against any and all insults. Lacy gazed up at Malcolm. Sleek white hair, silky black shirt, inky black pants—he was gallant, elegant, more attractive than any southern man she knew. It didn't matter what Delaney thought, or her boyfriend Nick. It only mattered what Malcolm thought, and he thought she was wonderful.

Aunt Frannie came up behind Jeremiah and hovered near, her tray of coffee and orange juice held close in hand, a stern look steeling the blue of her eyes. "You aren't welcome here."

"I wouldn't eat here if you paid me."

Frannie held her ground, and Jeremiah seemed to think twice about adding another retort. To the group he cracked, "Have a nice breakfast." Turning, Jeremiah strode down the aisle and clear outside the restaurant. Lacy watched him through the window to be sure he really left.

Aunt Frannie swooped in, dishing out coffee cups, creamer and juice. "That man is meaner than a wet cat spittin' mud." Pouring coffee, she grumbled, "Why, I have a mind to call the police next time he comes cavorting around here."

"I don't think you'll have to worry about a next time," Malcolm said.

"Well if he does, I'm bootin' him out."

Lowering to his seat beside Lacy, Malcolm slid a protective hand to her thigh. She intertwined her fingers with his and squeezed. "Thank you."

Malcolm leaned over and kissed her neatly on the lips. "You're welcome. I'm sorry you had to listen to any of it, at all."

In that instant, Lacy knew the love she felt for him was real and true. Any man who would stand up and defend her honor was a man who loved her and one she would always love in return. Forever.

"Nice restraint," Nick commented, raising his coffee cup to Malcolm in toast.

"Oh, *believe* me I would have taken great pleasure in finishing his beating if I didn't think he was already wrapped up in a pretty box and on his way to Vegas."

Delaney drew back. "Finishing?"

"We didn't do it, Delaney," Malcolm said flatly and brought coffee to lips, sipping slowly.

"Well," Aunt Frannie piped in, "as far as I'm concerned, next time he's here it'll only be a pit stop on his way to jail."

Lacy didn't hear a word Aunt Frannie said. Annie's daughter walked in, accompanied by the Parker boy. Should she go over and talk to her? Talk to them? Annie might get mad, see it as interfering. But now that she and Annie were making amends, Lacy wanted to get to know her niece. Maybe she should ask Malcolm.

"Lacy? Child?" Aunt Frannie stared at her. "Blow the cotton out your ears and tell me what you're fixin' to have for breakfast."

"Oh!" Her cheeks flushed. "The usual, Aunt Frannie."

"Eggs, grits and biscuits, coming right up," she said and departed their table. Aunt Frannie stopped and talked to Casey, leading her and the boy to a table on the opposite side of the restaurant.

Breakfast was served, eaten and cleared without any more disturbances. Lacy found it strange how Delaney continually looked over her shoulder, checking on Casey and Troy. What was so interesting over there? Otherwise, Lacy was grateful for the fact that Delaney was being nice to her. Probably because Malcolm was Nick's business partner and she didn't want to look bad for being rude, but Lacy wasn't fussy. She'd take what she could get when it came to peace in the neighborhood.

"So, while I hate to ruin a lovely breakfast with business," Malcolm said, tucking his napkin alongside his plate, "we need to get the ball rolling on the hotel. I can have a lease drawn up in a week," he said to Delaney. "You can have your attorney look it over, and we can go from there."

"Can we sign it, though?" Delaney asked. "I mean, between Ernie and Jeremiah and..."

Malcolm silenced her with a hand. "As far as I see it, nothing's up in the air. Once Ernie passes, Felicity owns the property. The two of you will need time to look over the lease, make sure it's in line with your expectations, and we'll sign when appropriate. Until then, Nick and I have a lot to do," he said, drawing Nick into the conversation. "Belinda has some preliminary drawings, but we'll need a site plan, a topography study. We also need to get the architects here as soon as feasible to work their vision into ours. The potential for working the hotel in the natural scope of the land is incredible."

Lacy thought Malcolm sounded intelligent, commanding. He *had* to be the brains behind the business.

"Have you thought about layout?" Nick asked. "Any changes you want to make?"

"I have." Pitching elbows to the table, Malcolm continued, "I agree with you on the main hotel location, but I say we add a restaurant along the river for a little al fresco dining. I want to hike the property a bit more before I agree to anything specific, especially for the Meditation Trail location." Malcolm looked to Lacy before adding, "I need to scout for the perfect location before I can decide on anything final."

"Sounds good." Nick leaned back into his seat, an outstretched hand lingering on his coffee cup. "I think the back meadow is the spot for the stables."

Malcolm nodded. "It'll be an easy walk from the hotel location. A short buggy ride if the guests prefer. In fact, I think we should—"

"*Stop*." All eyes turned to Delaney. "We can't decide *any* of this yet."

"Why not?" Nick asked.

"Because." Lacy thought Delaney looked panicky, her brown eyes nervous, unsettled.

"Because why?" Malcolm asked.

Delaney glanced over her shoulder. "Because I need to speak with Casey, first."

A knowing gaze sank into Nick's expression, but Malcolm simply appeared confused. "Casey?"

Delaney looked like the saddest dog Lacy had ever seen, but she held her breath hoping Delaney was about to say what she thought she was about to say. "Casey may be entitled to half of the property."

Lacy's insides cheered. She could *kiss* Delaney—if she wasn't wearing the face of a possum, that is. Delaney was really going to give Casey a chance! She was going to consider giving her half. Annie would be thrilled. Lacy was thrilled! Glancing about the table, Lacy decided Annie would *have* to appreciate her now.

"Is this because of the paternity suit?"

"If Casey is really Jeremiah's daughter," Nick interjected, "legally she's no different than Felicity. Children of unmarried parents—once paternity is proven—can claim a share of the parent's estate."

Malcolm turned to Lacy with a small smile. "I know someone who will be happy."

She could hardly contain herself. She grabbed his arm. "Isn't it great?"

He nodded, but when he looked away, Malcolm groaned. "So long happy days, hello misery." Lacy's pleasure collapsed. She thought he was happy for her. "Don't look now, but trouble just walked in."

Lacy's gaze dashed to the front door. Nick and Delaney followed suit. A dark-skinned woman stood at the entrance. She was tall and slender, raven black hair falling in a glossy sheet behind her. She slid off a pair of oversized black sunglasses and surveyed the restaurant's interior.

Who was she? Lacy's insides buzzed and popped. Did Malcolm know her?

Nick dug a hand through his hair. "Aw, hell."

"Who is she?" Delaney asked.

"Jillian Devane, Harris Hotels arch enemy."

Malcolm chuckled. "That's a little rich, don't you think?"

"Who's she a problem for?" Lacy asked.

"Jillian is a problem for everyone," Malcolm replied.

When the woman spotted them, a smile pulled at her mouth. With a gentle shake to her shiny hair, the Jillian woman headed straight for them. She walked like a runway model, Lacy thought. And her eyes were hypnotic, amber gold on brown skin, her brows manicured into well-defined, dramatic arches.

Malcolm didn't look happy to see her. Was this an ex-girlfriend?

Jillian Devane paused tableside. She took in the four of them and smiled, the sheen of the plum lipstick she wore almost liquid in its gloss. Hers wasn't a happy smile, quite the opposite. In fact, Lacy found it rather condescending.

"Hello, Nick," Jillian said, her soft-spoken voice thickly accented. "Malcolm."

"What brings you to Tennessee, Jillian?" Nick asked casually, as though it were normal for a foreign woman to stroll into a country diner in Tennessee.

She flicked an insulting glance toward Delaney and said, "Business."

"So I hear," Malcolm put in. "How'd you find us?"

"Small town, two gentlemen who don't belong...it was quite simple."

Don't belong? Lacy huffed silently. They sure do belong here!

"You're wasting your time," Nick told her. "We're two steps ahead of you."

Jillian tapped Lacy and Delaney with a snooty look and said, "Yes, it appears you are."

Lacy stiffened. She didn't like this woman one bit.

"Well, I wanted to tell you in person, *amorzinho*, that I will not be beaten."

Huh? Lacy looked to Delaney. What the heck was she talking about? Delaney ignored Lacy, clearly engrossed by the woman standing before them.

"I will be located not far from you," she said, adding with a catty smile, "so I can keep an eye on you. You know how well we work together."

Lacy gulped. Delaney's temperature was heating. It seemed this Jillian might be intimately familiar with her man. This very attractive Jillian. Lacy circled a palm around Malcolm's bicep. She was only glad Jillian was speaking to Nick and *not* Malcolm.

"We don't work together," Nick corrected. "Hang around if you want, but it will only underscore your second place status."

A wicked pleasure lit up her dark eyes. "Conceited as usual, I see. Well..." She smiled. "I only wanted you to know that I'm nearby. My number is the same." She bent slightly and, with very full lips, blew Nick a kiss before walking off, swaying her hips with a lethal swagger.

Delaney's cell phone rang. Although torn between the strange woman and the blaring ring tone at her waist, she lifted phone to ear. "Hello?" Her face paled.

Lacy stiffened by Malcolm's side. Nick's antennae shot up.

The hand holding the phone slid down from Delaney's ear.

"Delaney?" Nick probed.

With a faraway look, she whispered, "Ernie's in the hospital."

Chapter Twenty-Five

Malcolm left a fifty dollar bill on the table, and the four of them slid out of the booth. Fran refused to give them a bill, but a free-loader he was not. Malcolm helped Lacy rise, Nick and Delaney easing out behind them. A busboy hurried by them with a gray tub in hand. The restaurant had filled since they arrived, the crew handily clearing tables for the next patrons.

Nick paused by the hostess stand and placed a hand to Delaney's lower back. "Can you get a ride back to the hotel? I need to drive Delaney to the hospital."

Malcolm turned to Lacy. "I can drive him," she replied soberly.

"Thanks."

Delaney stood shell-shocked, quiet as a post. The normal flush was gone from her complexion, replaced by the lifeless look of distress. *Ernie was in the hospital.* The news wasn't completely unexpected, but she seemed to be hit pretty hard. Malcolm imagined Jillian's appearance couldn't be helping matters.

"I'll call Lanny," Malcolm offered, more to Nick than anyone. Lanny was their business lawyer. He'd draw up the lease and get it ready for signatures. To Delaney, he said, "Once you decide what you want to do about Casey, we can go from there." She nodded dumbly. "Call me if you need anything." In the meantime, Malcolm had other plans. A rush of nerves skated through him. Big plans.

Officer Gavin Shore walked in, his posture alert, watchful, as though he were on the hunt. Surprised by his appearance, Malcolm wondered if he had any news for them.

"Hey, Gavin," Lacy said.

He smiled, strolling to a stop before them. "Howdy, Lacy. Long time no see."

"Any word on Jeremiah?" Nick asked.

"Not yet." The officer turned from Lacy. "I questioned Troy Parker about it, though."

The comment poked Delaney back to life. "Troy? What's he got to do with it?"

"Jeremiah gave his name as a possible suspect. Said he's been stirring up trouble for him since he's been in town, and could have had something to do with the robbery."

Nick cursed under his breath. Malcolm shared the sentiment. Bastard. Luckily, Troy and Casey had left about ten minutes ago.

"Troy wouldn't have anything to do with Jeremiah," Delaney declared.

Gavin raised his brow, hooking thumbs to his belt. "Except stepping out with his girlfriend."

"How do you know that?" she asked.

"Paid the boy a visit last night." Gavin slid a wary glance around the restaurant. "While I was there, Jeremiah's girlfriend showed up to say goodbye to Troy."

"Goodbye?" Nick questioned.

Malcolm agreed. Jeremiah was still in town. Why would Loretta have left without him?

"You say Loretta left?" Lacy asked.

Officer Shore nodded. "She seemed pretty sweet on the boy, too. Said she was fed up with old Jeremiah but wanted to say goodbye to *him*." He snickered.

"She didn't even call me to say goodbye," Lacy complained.

"You knew her?" the officer asked.

"Yes. We worked together in Atlanta."

"But you—" The officer cut himself off, as though embarrassed to finish his sentence.

Lacy glared at him. "Doesn't mean we can't be friends."

Delaney looked devastated, but Malcolm thought it was a good sign. Jeremiah had alienated his one ally in town. He was alone, with no support when he needed it.

"Well, I can assure you," Delaney said, "Troy had nothing to do with Jeremiah's mugging."

The officer returned a skeptical gaze. "I'm not so sure about that." Treading lightly, he glanced around the restaurant, settling on no one in particular before whispering, "I hear he's been getting into trouble around town."

"Trouble?"

Gavin nodded and continued to speak softly, "Between you and me, I hear he's been drinking."

"*Drinking*? Troy? Are you sure?"

"Afraid so. The clerk over at Murray's Liquor reported him buying a bottle of whiskey from a guy out back."

Delaney groaned. "Oh, no…"

Malcolm could hear the pain in her voice, a combination of disappointment and dread. Underage drinking was nothing new or earth shattering, but add Casey's addiction issues and it could be a ticking time bomb. "But you haven't connected him with Jeremiah's robbery, have you?" Malcolm asked.

"Not yet, but we're looking into his alibi. He said he was bowling that night, but I haven't found anyone who can vouch for him."

Delaney brought a hand to her forehead. Troy was a good friend of Felicity's. Malcolm was certain she was processing any possible connection between Troy and her daughter that could negatively impact Felicity.

"Gavin, you need to stop wasting your time and go and arrest Jeremiah this instant!" Lacy cried out.

Malcolm placed a hand to her forearm, silently urging her to keep quiet. There was no sense in letting the officer in on the fact they knew about Jeremiah's gambling debt. It might look as if they set him up. As it stood, neither he nor Nick had an alibi for the night of Jeremiah's beating—and both could be placed in the general whereabouts of Jeremiah's assault if the police asked the right people.

They'd told Delaney they had a conference call sched-
uled with a hotel of theirs in Australia, and due to the time
difference, had to do so at night. While that much was true,
the call lasted only thirty minutes. For the remainder of the
evening, they had followed Jeremiah. Nick wanted to know
who he was meeting, if the man from the forest trail was in-
deed the same man who had helped kidnap Delaney.

But following Jeremiah had supplied more questions
than answers. He had gone to a bar, and stayed at a bar. Inside. There was no way Nick or Malcolm could have gone in
after him without causing a scene. The man from the trail—
this Willie, just as Nick and Delaney had suspected—showed
up and stayed for about an hour before he left, agitated, but
alone. Numerous hoodlums and goons came and went, but
Jeremiah never exited the building. Not by the front door,
anyway. By three o'clock in the morning, he and Nick called
it off. The bar's lights went out. Jeremiah must have gone out
a back door.

Lacy shook Malcolm free. "You and I both know that
Gavin is wasting his time here. If he wants to know who
should be in jail, it's Jeremiah."

"And why would that be, Lacy?" Officer Shore peered at
her. "Is there something I should know?"

"Because," she snapped, but dutifully checked when
Malcolm tapped her foot with his. "Because," she said, "because he's a no good, two-timing scalawag who needs to be
in jail."

Malcolm smiled inwardly. *Good girl.*

Gavin grinned with a familiarity that came from a childhood spent growing up together. "Well, I can't arrest a man
for being dishonorable, Lacy."

"Well, you *should*," she huffed and crossed arms over
her chest.

Clearly she was not pleased Malcolm had reined her in,
but there was no way around it. At the clang of bells, Malcolm saw Felicity and Travis entering the diner. He hitched a

nod to Nick and Delaney, indicating they should look behind them.

They turned and Nick said, "If you'll excuse us, officer..."

"No problem. I need to get some coffee for the road." Officer Shore backed away, allowing them to pass. He waved to Felicity. She waved back, but her expression fell. Clearly she was not happy to see a police officer with her mother.

Malcolm and Lacy followed Nick and Delaney over to Felicity and Travis. Felicity brushed strawberry-blonde hair behind an ear, her freckled skin flushing pink. She seemed tense, nervous. Travis stood firm, giving a quick fling to the sweep of bangs hanging over his brow. Although the boy seemed calm and collected, Malcolm detected unease behind his façade of cool.

Felicity asked, "What did Officer Gavin want?"

"He was asking questions about Jeremiah," Delaney replied, subtly nudging her daughter and Travis away from overactive ears that might be lurking near. Gathering her daughter close, Delaney asked quietly, "Did you know Troy's been drinking?"

Malcolm noted she didn't mention the first word about Ernie.

Felicity sought Travis for support. "Do you want to tell her?"

"Tell me what?" Delaney demanded.

Travis stepped forward, Felicity hanging close by his side. "Troy is dropping out of college, Miss Delaney."

"Dropping out? Before he even got started?" Delaney's complexion went white, to the extent Malcolm thought she might pass out, her system over-taxed by bad news. Ernie, Jillian, Troy. It was proving to be an eventful morning.

Malcolm gauged Travis for signs of turmoil at home. His parents had to be upset. Were he and Troy still at odds?

"He wants to work with horses," Felicity said, defending her friend. "He says he doesn't want to go to college when it won't help him get the job he wants to pursue."

Malcolm could see the very notion angered Travis. Studious, polite and well-spoken, Travis screamed upper-classman, graduate degree. The boy oozed all the signs of success while Troy, on the other hand, was all bull and brunt force.

"Morton and Betty Ann must be out of their minds right now," Delaney murmured in reply.

"They're not happy," Travis confirmed.

"There's something else you should know," Felicity piped in, a mild tremor in her voice. "Troy has hooked up with Casey."

Despair trickled into Delaney's gaze. "I saw them together this morning..."

Malcolm understood her concern. Casey had dabbled in drugs. More than dabbled, from what Nick said. She had intentionally overdosed. Hooking her wagon to an under-aged boy messing around with alcohol had all the ingredients for a disaster in the making.

"Excuse me."

The group turned to discover Officer Shore standing behind them, Styrofoam coffee cup in hand. Malcolm swallowed hard. How long had he been standing there?

Nick spoke first. "Yes?"

Officer Shore's gaze sharpened on the lot of them, his focus coming to rest on Malcolm and Nick. "Where is Jeremiah?" he asked, his tone a tinge adversarial.

"Don't know," Nick responded placidly.

"He was here about an hour ago," Malcolm offered, exchanging a wary glance with his partner.

"Is there a problem?" Delaney asked him.

"The Police Chief just called. Seems there's a warrant out for Jeremiah's arrest."

"A warrant?" Lacy asked. "From Las Vegas?"

Officer Shore zeroed in her. "How did you know?"

She gulped and stammered, "Um, I know his girlfriend Loretta, remember?"

"And you didn't feel the need to share the information with me?"

Lacy looked to Malcolm. Officer Shore followed suit.

If only Lacy weren't an open book, reading the story aloud to the nice gentleman! But Malcolm remained mute. The less said, the better. As it stood, all the man had was supposition. If the officer was able to put him and Nick in the same vicinity as Jeremiah near the time of the mugging, it wouldn't look good.

A loaded tray crashed to the floor in the kitchen, snagging the officer's attention. The group followed his gaze, but no one said a word.

Officer Shore straightened. "Huh." His gaze teeming with suspicion, he muttered, "It seems I have a man to find. But don't go anywhere, you hear? I want to speak to you four again."

"Understood," Nick replied.

Officer Shore edged his way through the crowded entrance and Malcolm breathed a sigh of relief. Temporary relief. There was still the matter of assault and battery, the question of title, the question of paternity. Too many damn questions for him to keep track!

"Do you think he'll think we had something to do with Jeremiah's beating?" Delaney asked.

"We sure do look a lot guiltier," Malcolm acknowledged.

"Oh, *poo*—it's all my fault!" Lacy cried.

Malcolm slid an arm around her and pulled Lacy to his side, kissing the top of her head. "No it's not. Knowledge is not a crime."

"But the suspicion has been raised," Nick said.

"That it has," Malcolm agreed grimly.

"We better get going," Nick said.

The statement kicked Delaney back to the present. Ernie. She turned to Felicity and said, "Ernie's in the hospital."

Her daughter's brow puckered. "He is?" Travis put an arm around her narrow shoulders and stood staunchly by her side.

"Ashley called. We're going to see him now."

"Oh, no..." Felicity's eyes shone bright green.

Malcolm hated it for her. She was young, sensitive, the pain gouged deep. This was her great uncle they were talking about, a man who cared for her. Loved her. And now she might have to say goodbye.

"Travis, you'll take me, won't you?" she asked.

"Of course."

There was no question, no hesitation of any kind. The family would rally to Ernie's bedside.

Malcolm and Lacy walked out with them, and the couples head out to their respective vehicles. There was no need for Lacy to go. Ernie wasn't her family.

"I need to call Annie," Lacy said.

"Why?" Malcom asked.

She shrugged. "I need to tell her that Delaney is considering giving Casey half the property." Lacy turned her head up to him and cupped her eyes against the bright sunshine. "Is that okay?"

"Of course. You do what you feel you need to do."

Offering his elbow, he escorted Lacy down the sidewalk and listened as she called her sister. It was brief, excitement mixed with sadness, and when she ended the call, Lacy seemed pensive. Tugging her close, he asked, "What's the matter?"

"Nothing." She slipped the phone back into her purse and said, "It's weird how life works, isn't? Good news, bad news, they always seem to come tied together."

"How so?"

"Oh, you know..." Lacy carelessly dragged her boot heels against the cement, slowing their pace as she elaborated, "I learned about the gold and was able to tell Annie, which was good news, but then you and Delaney got mad at me for sharing." Malcolm chuckled, reveling in the feel of her body, the scent of her hair, her perfume. It was a little more than that, he thought, but okay. "I left Tennessee for a life of freedom in Atlanta only to find it wasn't anything like I imagined. Then I have the opportunity to come home and start over but I don't have anything to do," she said glumly, leaning into him as they walked. "It's not right."

Strolling together down the sidewalk, the feel of her arm looped through his reminded Malcolm of a different kind of stroll. "You have me."

"But you're not something to do," she said.

"I could be," he teased.

Lacy yanked on his arm. "Be serious."

He was—more serious than he'd ever been.

"I need something to look forward to, something to be excited about." She waved a hand ahead of them and whined, "What's there for me to do in this old place?"

"What about my job offer?"

"Well, sure, but that isn't something to do *today*."

Today. Yes, *today*. Malcolm took in the quaint street they paralleled, sidewalks lined with storefronts, pedestrians moving on idle, the green mountain ridge rising behind the town for an incredible vista. The sky was clear and blue, the temperature warm with a mild breeze. Her hometown was idyllic. This was beautiful country, a place you could settle down, even raise a family. Inhaling the view, Malcolm found he was looking forward to spending time here, building Serenity Springs, spending time with the woman beside him. It might be a town Lacy took for granted, but he did not.

Malcolm stopped. There was no doubt in his mind that Lacy would enjoy traveling the world, visiting new and exotic locales, but he bet she'd enjoy coming home again, too. Home. It was a word he was beginning to like the sound of, the feel. "Sweetheart, let's say we make it official."

"Make what official?"

He grasped both her hands. "Us. You and me."

Lacy looked at him as if in pure shock.

Malcolm chuckled, a rush of nerves barreling through him as he dropped to his knee.

"Are you serious?" Lacy asked.

"Never been more serious in my life. I know this sounds sudden, but you strike me as the spontaneous type—and *exactly* my kind of woman." Lacy blinked, her blue eyes glittering like a sheet of island water. "Is it possible to fall in love with a woman every day? To learn something new about her and want her even more?"

She gaped at him.

Growing serious, Malcolm caressed the slender hands folded within his and asked, "Lacy Louise Owens, will you marry me?" She stood speechless, those luscious lips of hers slightly parted. "I want to spend every waking hour with you. I want to hike with you, swim with you, make love to you until we lose ourselves and become one."

She remained silent. A jolt of angst fired hot in his chest. She wasn't going to decline, was she? "Lacy?"

She nodded—suddenly, eagerly—a smile seizing her face. "Yes, Malcolm." Lacy beamed and squealed, "Yes! Yes! Yes!"

Relief washed through him. "I don't have a ring," he confessed, rising to his feet, "but Vegas has some of the finest jewelry stores in the world. What do you say we head west? There's a flight leaving Atlanta this evening, and we can be married before midnight."

Lacy hopped up and down and flung her arms around his neck. "Yes! Yes! Yes!"

Malcolm hugged her tightly, luxuriating in her soft curves. Nuzzling close, he whispered, "You're going to make the cutest kids."

She pulled back abruptly. Concern doused her happiness. "But what about Ernie and Delaney?"

"We can be back by lunchtime tomorrow."

"We can?"

"If you want, we can."

A joyful pleasure shattered any and all reservation. "Oh, Malcolm, *call* them. Call them and tell them we're going but we'll be back the instant they need us!"

He laughed. "Will do, sweetheart, but in this particular instant, I need *you*." Malcolm ducked down and kissed her, kissed her deeply, thoroughly, emotions firing inside him like a Grand Opening Day. This was going to be some kind of *adventure*.

# # #

The End

Lacy's Favorite Fried Okra

1 lb. fresh okra (frozen, cut okra will do just fine)
2 cups yellow cornmeal
1 cup buttermilk
1 egg (optional)
1 tsp salt
1/2 tsp pepper
1 inch vegetable oil in pan (bacon fat for added flavor)

If using fresh okra, trim ends and cut into 1/2 inch pieces. In large bowl, whisk together buttermilk and egg. Toss okra in buttermilk ~ let marinate at room temperature for at least 15 minutes. Mix cornmeal, salt & pepper and set aside.

Heat oil in large cast iron skillet on medium heat. When hot, dredge okra in cornmeal mixture, coating well, then cook okra until golden brown, careful not to crowd okra in pan. Drain on paper towels and serve warm.

***Oil is ready when test piece bubbles immediately.

About the Author:

Dianne Venetta lives in Central Florida with her husband, two children and part-time Yellow Lab Cody-boy! An avid gardener, she spends her spare time growing organic vegetables, surprised by what she finds there every day. Who knew there were so many amazing similarities between men and plants? Women, life and love and her discoveries along the way provide for never-ending fun on her garden blog: BloominThyme.com.

You can also find her on twitter @DianneVenetta and facebook.com/DianneVenetta. Plus, learn how you can become a member of her street team, Bloomin' Warriors, where you'll be eligible for special discounts, advance excerpts, author swag and unique gift items throughout the year. For full details, be sure to check out her website, DianneVenetta.com.

Other novels by Dianne Venetta:
Romantic Women's Fiction
The Gables Trilogy:
JENNIFER'S GARDEN
LUST ON THE ROCKS
WHISPER PRIVILEGES

Women's Fiction
CONDEMN ME NOT

Mystery/Romance Fiction
Ladd Springs Series:
LADD SPRINGS #1
LADD FORTUNE #2
HOTEL LADD #3
LADD HAVEN #4
LOSING LADD #5

Read an excerpt from Hotel Ladd...

Chapter One

Annie Owens fiddled with the business card in hand, the matte finished paper growing worn from her constant handling. Colored green and tan with flecks of natural fiber, the earth-friendly tone of the company card was clearly communicated. *Eco-Domani*. Annie's gaze slid down to the name embossed in the lower right corner. Jillian Devane, President and CEO.

"What are you gonna do?" Candi Sweeney asked, a nervous edge creeping into her voice.

"I don't know," Annie murmured.

"She seemed real intent on talking to you."

Annie nodded, dropping her gaze to two half-eaten sub sandwiches on the coffee table before them, food Candi had graciously picked up on her way over after work. Her friend understood this was a significant development. Annie had to do *something*.

Six months ago Delaney Wilkins had signed over half of Ladd Springs to Annie's daughter, Casey. Ladd Springs, the mecca of rivers and streams, mountains and trails and springs—natural springs that were unique to the property—had been held by the Ladd family for generations. Delaney's uncle, Ernie Ladd, had recently passed away, willing the entire tract to Delaney's daughter, Felicity. Because she was blood kin.

Well, so was Casey. Ernie's son, Jeremiah Ladd, was Casey's father, making her equally entitled to the land. The logic was simple. It was Ladd land and she was a Ladd. Unfortunately, Annie had to prove the fact first, a process Jeremiah fought her every step of the way. But after battling him for years, she finally won when he showed up in town six months ago looking for his piece of the land. Ernie had re-

fused him outright. He was willing it to Felicity and no one
else. In the end, Jeremiah landed himself in jail for an unpaid
gambling debt, Ernie died and Felicity received title to the
property. Annie had secured her paternity test and proved
once and for all, Casey was Jeremiah's daughter making it
impossible for Delaney to ignore her rights. Eighteen long
years and a paternity test had proven it beyond a shadow of a
doubt. Annie's daughter was a Ladd. It was the reason
Delaney acquiesced and signed over half of the property to
Casey.

But the property consisted of hundreds of acres. If she
were to keep the property, Annie had to think, plan, strate-
gize—but it was the details regarding what to do that were
tripping her up. This was out of her league. She didn't do financial calculations. She did fingernails! A flurry of angst
peppered her chest. Flipping her gaze out through the back
windows of her apartment, Annie latched onto a range of
mountains. Saturated by a late afternoon sun, the Blue Ridge
Mountains were ablaze with orange, red and gold, clumps of
green tucked here and there in between. Beyond, the sky had
cooled to a bluish-lavender. Fall was upon them, dropping
temperatures into the upper thirties for the third day in a row.
There was even talk of snow.

Seated on the couch in the living room of the two-bedroom apartment she and her daughter called home, Annie
looked to Candi. Concern scored her dark brown eyes, her
heart-shaped face framed by stick-straight hair that fell in
flat-ironed points across her shoulders. Naturally brown,
highlighted by chunks of blonde, her hair was perfection.
Candi was a hairstylist, her best friend, the only one who understood what was at stake. "Annie? Are you listening?"

Caught by a sudden chill, a shiver raced through Annie.
What was she going to do? She knew what she *wanted* to do.
She wanted to call Ms. Devane. She wanted to speak with her
about the financial potential of her share of Ladd Springs.
Casey's share, Annie corrected. Over six hundred acres of
pristine forest snaked with rivers and streams and loaded with

springs she now owned. Trouble was, now that Casey retained title to half the property, Annie had to figure a way to afford it. That part wasn't as simple.

"Do you think this woman can help?" Candi pressed, hanging on the edge of her seat. She'd been Annie's closest ally throughout and truth be known, the reason Annie and Casey held title to the property. If Candi hadn't called Jeremiah back home from Atlanta, none of this would have happened. Casey would not have title to the property and Annie would not be in a position to earn money from it.

"Maybe."

"She seemed real eager to talk to you when she gave me that card." Upon receiving it, Candi had immediately rushed to Trendz, the salon where Annie worked as a nail tech and delivered both business card and message. *Please have Ms. Owens call me at her earliest convenience. I will make it financially worth her time.*

Seems Jillian Devane had a proposition for her.

Staring at the card in hand, Annie wasn't stupid. She'd heard the woman was in town to get revenge on Nick Harris, boyfriend to Delaney Wilkins and the owner of Harris Hotels. His company was currently transforming Ladd Springs—the other half of Ladd Springs that belonged to Delaney's daughter, Felicity—into an upscale hotel and spa resort for the very wealthy. Nick had signed a 99-year lease to use the land, land that old man Ernie Ladd had refused to sell, instead willing it to Felicity as a life estate. When Ernie died, the land became free and clear to be developed.

"Do you think Jillian Devane wants to build a hotel like Nick?"

Visions of an exclusive wooded retreat for elite guests swam through Annie's mind, guests who would pay top dollar to lose themselves in the mountains of Tennessee, the forests, the natural beauty of the Appalachians. Felicity was barely eighteen and stood to earn a fortune from her deal with Nick Harris while Annie and Casey had nothing but bills as a result of owning their share of the property.

"I don't know. Maybe," she hemmed. Annie knew full well Ms. Devane was interested in building a hotel. In fact, according to Annie's sister Lacy—her direct conduit to all things Ladd Springs—Ms. Devane had looked into purchasing land an hour north of here for that very reason. She wanted to ruin Nick's new hotel by building one of her own. Married to Nick's partner Malcolm Ward, Lacy had the inside scoop and dished it out readily to Annie—because Annie had forgiven the past problems between them.

Leaning forward, Candi grabbed a cheddar-coated chip from a shiny blue plastic bag. "Have you asked Cal about it?"

Annie looked at her friend, ignoring the loud crunching from her mouth. "I don't want to bother him with it."

"Why not? He helped you get the loan to pay the back taxes, didn't he?"

"He did," she acknowledged. Which was easy. His father, Gerald Foster, owned a bank in town and pulled the strings. Not that Cal didn't mean well, he did. Calvin Foster helped, because he was a decent man. As part of the Foster clan, he was a man of means, a man who'd been calling on her ever since his return from Arizona six months ago.

Annie grew up with the Foster brothers. They were four good-looking boys, wild and crazy and always out for a good time with the ladies, although Cal had been the most tame among them. His brother Jack married Delaney, and for a while, they seemed like the perfect couple. It wasn't until Delaney up and left him that everyone in town learned the truth. Jack was abusive. He was a drinker. A mean drunk, at that. After Delaney moved back home with Felicity, Jack left town and Annie hadn't heard a word about him since. Brothers Beau and Clint had remained in town, married, had children, held rank as respectable men in the community. Beau ran the Foster family ranch, acres upon acres of premiere pasture and mountains while Clint worked with his father at the bank, the biggest and most prestigious for miles around. Despite the rowdy reputation forged by the sons, the Fosters were a respectable bunch. They had looks, money, smarts...

Victoria Foster would accept nothing less. A socialite from Chattanooga, Cal's mother came from money and would not allow her move to the small town alter a single aspect of her lifestyle. The Foster estate was grand, the land was beautiful, the four sons were unruly—a fact Mrs. Foster refused to permit injure her standing in the community. It was one of the reasons Gerald Foster was so anti-drinking today. Zero tolerance was his motto, for his boys and his staff.

Although Annie had grown up with Cal, knew him from high school, knew his family through church, she had never thought of him romantically. He was nice-looking enough, but back then she'd only had eyes for Jeremiah. A year after she became pregnant with Casey, Cal had moved to Arizona and she hadn't seen or heard from him until her godmother's big Memorial Day party this past summer. When Ashley Fulmer through a party, everyone attended, giving Cal the perfect opportunity to reacclimate himself back into the community. Annie had definitely noticed him at the barbecue, the two dancing and chatting, erasing the passage of time between them as they began a new path forward together.

Candi pulled a sip from her coke, her cheeks hollowing. "I bet he could come up with an idea to help you earn some money with this woman. Cal is smart that way."

That's where Annie begged to differ. Yes, he was smart, but Cal had become friendly with Malcolm, a man equally invested in Nick's hotel development. If Cal let on to Malcolm or Nick that Annie was even considering a discussion with Ms. Devane, Annie had no doubt the men would be angry. Lacy had given Annie a blow by blow on the history between Nick and Jillian, how Harris Hotels and Eco-Domani were in constant competition and how six months ago Jillian Devane had paid a visit to Fran's Diner, putting Nick on notice she intended to build in Tennessee as well. If Annie worked with Ms. Devane in any way, it would be seen as crossing enemy lines, something you didn't do around here unless you packed two barrels and were prepared to fire them. "Why don't you ask him?" Candi asked.

"I think Lacy and Malcolm would have something to say about it," Annie replied. "Any involvement with this Devane woman will be seen as a betrayal."

"Well, Lacy and Malcolm don't have a say in what you do. They're not helping you make ends meet, are they?" Candi vehemently shook her head and said, "No, ma'am. It's your decision. Yours and Casey's, I mean."

Yes, Casey. Casey was the named owner, but Annie was the designated trustee. When Delaney had Felicity sign over half of the land, she'd stipulated Casey was not to receive control over the property until she turned thirty years of age, or she wouldn't receive the first acre. Because Casey was too young and not ready for that kind of responsibility. Because Casey had a history of instability.

But Annie was ready. Seemed responsibility was all she knew, like it was her whole life. Expelling a sigh, she smacked the business card onto the table. "I don't know what to do, Candi. I only know I wish it wasn't so damned hard."

Annie had finally won the battle—Ladd family recognition for her daughter and the procurement of her rightful inheritance—yet she had no way to keep it. Sure, Cal had helped her secure a loan to pay the back taxes but there would be a new tax bill this fall. In another month, she'd be facing the same dilemma all over again. Her eyes went quickly to the hills out the window. A panicky need to escape weaved through her soul. As it was, she was stretching her last dollar bill to pay the current loan for the taxes. How was she ever going to afford another payment?

Candi scooted close and wrapped an arm around Annie's shoulders. She hugged her close and Annie was grateful for the connection. It was warm, reassuring. Solid. "I know it's hard, honey, but you'll think of something. You always do," she added, eyes shining with encouragement. "You got that paternity test out of Jeremiah, didn't you?"

"I did."

"And the property out of Delaney."

"Yes."

"Well, you can get some money going, too." Candi hugged Annie to her side, a draft of her perfume rising between them. "I know you can."

Leave it to Candi to see the positive in her situation. It was her nature, always had been. Candi was the one who'd encouraged Annie in high school, convinced her to try out for the lead role in a school play, acted as cheerleader when Annie earned straight A's two semesters in a row, even encouraged her to chase after the boy she dreamed impossible to get. Her stomach tightened. Well, she couldn't hold *that* against her. Annie couldn't see past Jeremiah at the time and he was all she wanted. Now she wanted money. Income. As trustee, it was her job to not only pay the taxes but to ensure her daughter's future. She was entitled to a percentage of earnings for her time and trouble, but they were earnings Annie had to *earn* first. If she couldn't, all she'd be handing over to her thirty-year-old daughter would be a big fat tax bill.

"I'll talk to Cal," Annie said. "He's looking into some logging possibilities for me. We'll see what he's come up with."

"Logging? You mean to tell me you're going to cut down all the trees?"

Mildly amused by the look of horror pasted on Candi's face, Annie shook her head. "No, only a hundred acres or so. According to Cal, it might be all we need, until I can figure something else out, that is."

"Like how to rent the land to a hotel developer, same as Delaney?"

Annie suppressed a grin. Candi knew her better than anyone. Whether Lacy and Malcolm and Delaney and Nick cared or not, Annie was a survivor first, a group player second. She had to look out for Casey's future, same way Delaney had looked after Felicity's. Now in college, Felicity was set, her future carved in stone. *Gold* stone, Annie mused, a tinge of resentment curling her heart. Delaney included the section with the gold find in Felicity's half, enabling her daughter to not only earn income from Nick's hotel deal but from selling the gold discovered in a rock, deep in the forest.

Gold. On Ladd Springs. So far, the vein had yielded more than anyone expected and Nick and Delaney were taking full advantage. They were having a local jeweler design a pendant in the shape of a wishing well, a pendant they intended to sell in a hotel boutique store. It was supposed to represent the natural springs on the property, a symbol of eternal hope and spiritual fulfillment. To Annie it represented yet again how she and her daughter were left to fend for themselves.

Annie snatched the business card and glared at the telephone number. "I'm going to call her."

"You are?"

"Yes. There's no reason I shouldn't explore my options."

"That's right," Candi agreed, faithfully manning her imaginary pom-poms as she encouraged her friend. "No reason at all."

"Why can't I lease our property to Jillian? How would that hurt anything?"

"Exactly."

"I mean, if Nick and Malcolm are afraid of a little competition, how good can they be?"

"Now you're talking!" Candi bounced on the cushion beside her. "Why should they have all the profits from a hotel business and not you?"

While Annie couldn't quite share Candi's level of exuberance, a tinge of misgiving squiggling through her belly, she did share her viewpoint. Why shouldn't she be able to use her property any way she saw fit? Would they rather she destroy acres and acres of trees? After all, Nick's claim to fame was his sensitivity to the environment. Wouldn't that make him a hypocrite if he advised someone to log the land instead of build something in tune with Mother Nature?

Gaining steam, Annie decided it was the right thing to do. Casey was stuck in a dead-end job waiting tables at

Fran's Diner, and if Annie could give her daughter something better to look forward to, wasn't that what she should do? Her Aunt Fran was sweet to give Casey a job, but that didn't mean she had to keep it for the rest of her life.

"When are you going to call her?" Candi asked.

"Tomorrow." Annie twisted the card in hand. "I'm going to call her tomorrow."